Dear Reader,

I have always wanted to create a grittier version of a fairy tale similar to what the Grimm Brothers explored. I wanted to write a real-life fairy tale that had every possible wrenching emotion in it, but without any of that easy-way-out magic. So I set about creating a very twisted version of Cinderella. Only instead of making the heroine Cinderella, I wanted the hero to be Cinderella. I wanted the prince to be wildly romantic and kind and forever looking for his Princess Charming the way Cinderella had. So I gave him a big heart and introduced him to a stepmother who never liked him, and in turn, forced him to become a servant of a different sort. I then balanced his hardship by giving him a charming stepsister who absolutely adores him and who sought to protect him at every turn. Instead of a glass slipper, I thought a ruby ring would best unfold my fairy tale.

Now, as much as I adore England and its history, I have always wanted to set a story in beautiful Venice. So I started digging into its fascinating history and uncovered the cicisbeo (also known as Cavalier Servente). For those of you who don't know what a cicisbeo is, it was a practice in Italy amongst the nobility in the eighteenth and nineteenth century that allowed a married woman to keep a man, whom her husband agreed for her to have during their marriage, for a specified amount of time. It is said Lord Byron himself was a cicisbeo for a period of time to the married Contessa Teresa Gamba Guiccioli and that her husband was known to boast about it. Although scholars will argue as to whether a cicisbeo was also a lover to the married woman he served (some say yes, some say no), the lines blur enough for the story to swing either way. I'll leave you, dearest reader, to figure out on your own which way I'm swinging.

Much love,

Delilah Marvelle

Don't miss the rest of the Scandal series!

Prelude to a Scandal
Available Now!

The Perfect Scandal
Available March 2011

DELILAH MARVELLE

Once upon a Scandal

HQN™

Recycling programs
for this product may
not exist in your area.

ISBN-13: 978-0-373-77545-3

ONCE UPON A SCANDAL

For my mother, Urszula,
who planted sweeping romantic notions in my head
long before I really knew what a romantic notion
even was. I miss you and love you and I know that
I will see you again when I get to the other side.

Once upon a Scandal

PROLOGUE

A true gentleman will declare himself with a view
toward matrimony, whilst a true libertine will declare
himself with a view toward scandal. Although a lady
may think she can differentiate between who is the
gentleman and who is the libertine, at times, it may
prove to be impossible.

How To Avoid a Scandal, Author Unknown

Bath, England, August 21, 1824
Late afternoon
The Linford country estate

ALTHOUGH JONATHAN Pierce Thatcher, Viscount
Remington, was all but nineteen, and therefore in the
eyes of society very much a man, a part of his soul
had always secretly remained twelve years old. It was
the part of his soul that still believed in absurd notions
such as courtly love, magic and destiny. Though he
knew magic and destiny had no place in the head of
a real man as was defined by the real world, for him,
magic and destiny were but alternate words for hope,

and no one could ever convince him that hope did not exist. For it did.

And right now, in the setting of a sprawling garden in fading bloom and dwindling sunlight, hope ardently whispered to him that his time for love had finally come. It whispered that the young woman in the embroidered, flowing white gown and gathered blond curls who lingered in boredom beside her governess in the shade of her orchid parasol was going to change his life forever. If only he could convince her to change his life forever.

Jonathan refrained from mouthing Lady Victoria's name in reverence or staring at her through the demure crowd of chattering house guests dividing them. He had almost kissed Grayson's left boot for inviting him to the Linford house party. Almost.

Being in close quarters with Victoria over these next two weeks was going to ensure she was finally his in both name and heart. He simply needed to be mindful of the fact that the host was none other than her father, the ever brow-creased Earl of Linford, who was all too easily riled into shouting fits whenever anything displeased him. Fortunately, the gruff man liked Jonathan and often boasted that he was but another son.

Aside from his year-long acquaintance with Victoria, something far more unearthly drew him to her. There was an unspoken depth within those jade eyes that went beyond her seventeen years. Even as she spoke to him in that witty, self-assured manner that announced she needed no one and most certainly not him, never once had she duped him. He could tell that deep inside, she was an even greater romantic than him. She simply chose to deny it.

Veering toward his friend Grayson, Jonathan made sure his lips and his words were shielded from the men and women indulging in all the fruit, biscuits and cakes that had been lavishly piled onto silver trays and set upon tables around the garden.

"When should I declare myself?" he ventured. "Before I leave? Or upon my return from Venice?"

Grayson picked up the remaining sliver of Banbury cake from his porcelain plate and shoved it into his mouth. As he heartily chewed, he shook his dark blond head, his eyes darting across the length of the garden toward Victoria. "I would never condone rushing—" he said, in between several chews "—but given your predicament, don't wait. Based on my cousin's dowry alone, half of Europe is already lining up at my uncle's door."

Jonathan half nodded, his stomach clenching at the thought. "I only hope to God she feels the same."

Grayson sighed and set his empty plate on the corner of the linen-covered table beside them. "Whatever you do, Remington, don't be a sop and tell her that you love her."

Jonathan angled himself and lowered his voice. "And why wouldn't I? It happens to be what I feel."

"It doesn't matter what you feel. Victoria is a Linford of the worst sort. The moment you use the word *love,* she will call you out for being insincere."

"Insincere? By telling her—"

"Yes. By telling her. If you haven't already noticed, she is a lot like her father. Only without all the grumbling and shouting. And can you blame her, after all that has happened in her life? Stars cannot shine when clouds blacken the sky. It has nothing to do with you personally, it is simply the way it is. Which is why I suggest you be subtle over these next two weeks. Don't overwhelm her with your stupid goose antics or she will run. Regardless of what she does or does not feel."

Jonathan drew in a breath and let it out, reluctant to listen to anything but what his gut was telling him. And his gut was telling him subtle was not about to win the fair maiden. "Go distract her governess for me, will you? I need to talk to her."

"Now?" Grayson asked.

"Yes. Now. Go. Do it."

Grayson leaned toward him and hissed, "I didn't invite you here to watch you slit your own throat. You need to be subtle. Declaring yourself with my uncle and half of society thirty paces away is *not* subtle."

Jonathan rolled his eyes. "I don't plan on asking for

her hand here and now. All I want is a few moments alone without that damn woman at her elbow. You know what Mrs. Lambert thinks of me. I'm anything but honey on that old crone's lips."

"That is because you pose a threat to the commodity she hopes to sell to a duke. And I hate to point out your sad reality, Remington, but *you* are not a duke. Nor are you a marquis. Or an earl. Or—"

"Enough already." Jonathan glared at him. "Are you going to do this for me or not?"

"Forget it. I have already done more than enough to ensure each and every single one of your children bears my name. Boys. Girls. It doesn't matter. They will all be known as Grayson."

Jonathan stepped closer to emphasize that he was a full head taller and a few inches broader than Grayson. "Considering all the times I took a fist for you, you owe me this and more."

Grayson snorted. "What the hell do you expect me to do? Rope up Mrs. Lambert and shove her in a cupboard while everyone watches you play Romeo?"

"Yes. That is exactly what I expect you to do. I only have two weeks to extract a promise of matrimony from her. Two weeks. I need every moment I can get."

Grayson jabbed him beneath the cravat. "You have your whole life ahead of you. Your whole life. Why are you rushing into this, anyway? Hmm? From what

I hear, Venetian women send men into spasms that last all day and night. Enjoy a bit of that first, *then* come back to this."

Jonathan sighed. This wasn't about meeting a woman and having a few nights of passion. This was about meeting *the* woman and having a whole lifetime of passion. "Fifteen minutes."

Grayson shook his head from side to side. "Why must you always complicate not only your life, but mine? *Why?*"

"Oh, you think I complicate *your* life?" Jonathan lowered his voice. "I'm not the one stealing bank notes to pay for women who most likely will end up costing you vials of mercury."

Grayson puffed up his cheeks and deflated them with a single breath. "I don't need another father pointing out everything I do wrong."

Jonathan refrained from smacking him upside the head. "One father would never be enough to rein you in. Hell, six fathers wouldn't be enough. Just as you don't approve of *my* life, Grayson, I don't approve of *yours*. Which is why we must agree to disagree. Now, are you going to do this for me or not?"

Grayson sighed and scanned the garden around them. "I will ensure fifteen minutes if you promise not to tell my father about the bank notes."

Jonathan grinned and elbowed his arm. "Done."

Grayson elbowed him back. "Stay here. I'll send Victoria over and occupy Mrs. Lambert for you."

Jonathan pointed at him. "*You* are a good friend."

"A better friend than you will ever be." Grayson smirked, rounded him and the table, and strode across the lawn.

Jonathan adjusted the cuffs of his morning coat and stepped toward the nearest table laden with silver. Finding a tray that had been emptied of most of its biscuits, he leaned over it and used the polished reflection of the silver platter to see if his black hair was still decent. He brushed back a few unruly strands that had strayed in the wind from his forehead, straightened and stepped back, glancing toward where Grayson had gone.

Lady Somerville sauntered past with her elderly husband, heading toward the fountain beyond. Her dark eyes lifted and purposefully met Jonathan's across the distance. She offered a refined nod in passing as a slow smile touched her painted lips, then continued to watch him out of the corner of her eye in a heated, predatory manner that caused Jonathan's skin to crawl.

He ignored the blatant flirtation. Why was it that only married women found him attractive? Did he have the words *Play with me if you are over thirty* etched across his forehead? He was almost young enough to be their firstborn, for God's sake.

Jonathan paused as a slim figure dressed in embroidered white lace and India muslin appeared on the other side of the table he lingered by. His pulse drummed as Victoria angled her parasol against the puffed sleeve on her upper shoulder and quietly perused the silver trays of food.

God love you, Grayson, he thought to himself.

Jonathan drew a reassuring breath, grabbed one of the plates stacked for service and rounded the table toward her. He paused beside her and leaned in, offering up the plate. Though he wanted to convey everything that had ever been buried within him in that one pulsing moment, all he could do was hold out the plate and wait for her gloved hand to take it.

She turned, her full skirts brushing his trouser-clad legs, and lifted her pretty green eyes to his. Jonathan's stomach flipped as her full, soft-looking pink lips curved into a radiant smile. She edged back, setting a more respectable distance between them, but never once broke their gaze.

For a long moment, neither of them said a word.

He stupidly continued to hold out the plate, while she stood there as if he wasn't holding anything at all. Though she offered him no conversation aside from the playful glint in her eyes, he knew she was merely embracing the well-practiced role of a lady, with the eyes and ears of society gathered all but strides away.

"The Banbury cake deserves infinite praise," he offered conversationally, scooting the plate closer to her. "You might want to eat what little is left before I do."

She lowered her chin, adjusting the parasol on her shoulder, and glanced toward the sliced cakes. She lifted a blond brow. "Do you really intend to be a glutton and eat all four cakes?"

Jonathan let out an awkward laugh, realizing there really were still four Banbury cakes left on the trays. He cleared his throat, gesturing toward the plate he still held. "I was trying to make conversation, is all."

"Conversation about cake? I see." She promenaded the length of the table, offering him a taunting smile. "Whatever you do, my lord, don't comment on the weather next. In the past hour, six people have pointed out that there isn't a single cloud in the sky. I have been praying for rain ever since to ensure more cultivated conversation."

He chuckled and lowered his voice. "You needn't worry about uncultivated conversation here. In truth, I haven't even noticed the weather at all. Not with you dressed as you are. Might I point out how incredibly beautiful you look in that gown? An angel in her truest form. 'Tis a pity there aren't any clouds in that sky for you to sit on."

She let out a laugh and shook her head. "Why is it, my lord, that you had far more intelligent things to say when I last saw you?"

I wasn't leaving the country the last time I saw you. He pushed away the thought and focused on being subtle. Subtle, subtle, subtle. "How many more months before your coming out?" he asked, even though he already knew the answer.

She sighed. "Seven. Mrs. Lambert won't let me forget it. Nor will my father."

Seven months. He'd be gone all seven of those months, maybe even eight to ten of those months, depending on how long it took him to settle his stepsister into her new way of life. And then there was his stepmother. He hoped the woman not only stayed in Venice, but died there.

Jonathan met Victoria's gaze and knew if he waited to declare himself, he'd have to compete against a horde of richer, better titled men. He was only worth two thousand a year. And while that allowed for an excellent living most would envy, it only allowed for one estate. Unlike the five her father owned.

Victoria eyed him expectantly, silently prodding him to do more than just blatantly stare at her.

He wished to God he could just grab her and kiss

her and declare himself that way. "I'm leaving for Venice," he blurted, fingering the plate he still held.

She half nodded, causing her gathered blond curls to sway against her cheeks. "Yes, I know. After the house party. Grayson told me." A soft sigh escaped her lips. "I wish I could travel. Sadly, Papa is set against my doing any tours."

Was that delicious yearning in her voice meant for him? Or for the tours? "Might I write to you about my travels?"

Her green eyes brightened. "But of course. Who else will keep me from boredom but you?"

This really wasn't going anywhere. It was the same old, same old. Everything said, yet nothing said. Subtle simply was not going to win her over, regardless of what Grayson thought. In truth, Grayson's idea of courting a woman amounted to lifting her skirt and whistling.

Jonathan rounded the table and closed the remaining distance between them feeling as if his fifteen minutes had already dwindled to a mere one. He leaned in, offering her the plate once again, trying not to get too distracted by the alluring scent of soap and lavender drifting toward him.

"Victoria," he whispered, searching her face, memorizing the arch of those blond brows and how soft her porcelain skin appeared in the fading afternoon light. "Take the plate if you love me."

Her eyes widened. She edged back and glanced toward those in the distance. With the flick of her wrist, she shielded them from view with her parasol, then leaned in and tsked. "Being more amorous than usual, I see."

"Forgive me, but there are times when a man has to be."

"Oh? And what times are those? The end of days?"

"I want assurance of your devotion."

She giggled. "By offering me a plate?"

By offering you my life. He gestured toward the china still in his hand. "This plate is but a metaphor representing all that I am. Polished. Clean. Able to present, hold and endure whatever you place upon it, whilst allowing you to feast for both substance and pleasure, though surprisingly, it is also incredibly fragile. If dropped, it will shatter and become nothing but a worthless mess. I would say more, but we have an audience and this is about as forward as I can get without altogether grabbing you."

She stared up at him for an abashed moment and dropped her voice a whole octave. "So by taking the plate I would in fact be taking your heart? Is that what you are informing me of, my lord?"

He drew in a ragged breath. "Yes. Exactly."

"Ingenious." She smiled, leaned in and playfully tapped her gloved finger against the painted rim of the plate. "Have it polished and ready for my coming out. I'm certain I can find a place for you somewhere at the table. In the meantime, use *this* plate to enjoy however many Banbury cakes you can stomach. I should go, before Mrs. Lambert realizes Grayson is a decoy." She grinned, twirled her parasol once in a form of bravado and breezed past.

Hell. That was neither a yes nor a no.

Jonathan heaved out an exasperated breath and set the plate back onto the table. He turned to watch those delectable, curvy hips sway beneath her flowing, bright-white gown. She and that gown trailed across the length of the green lawn, past men and women wandering out toward the fountain in the distance.

He had two weeks to convince her that his heart beat solely for her. Two weeks. Because if he left England without extracting a promise of matrimony from those lips, he knew he'd return only to find her married to some lucky bastard and his heart would forever bleed in regret of what could have been.

SCANDAL ONE

A lady should never make promises to a gentleman without the consent of a guardian. It will only lead to a most compromising situation.

How To Avoid a Scandal, Author Unknown

Two weeks later, after midnight
The Linford country estate

THE SHARP crack of thunder startled Lady Victoria Jane Emerson from slumber. Her eyes fluttered open. Rain drummed against the large, latticed windows, echoing in the quiet darkness of a room she did not recognize.

She groaned. She was at the estate.

Oh, how she wished her father would let them stay in London. Although she had a genuine fondness for Bath itself, she loathed every inch of their one-hundred-and-thirty-year-old estate. It was a breathing cemetery—and more than enough Linfords had died in it throughout the decades to warrant that thought. In fact, the neighboring hillside beyond the main road was littered with gravestones and crypts of both the esteemed and the blackest of black Linfords. That same hill also harbored her mother, dead now four years past, and her twin brother, dead now almost two years past.

Lightning streaked the night sky, illuminating the massive hearth opposite her bed in a momentary flash of brilliant white. Victoria sank deeper into the warmth of the coverlet and scooted closer toward her dog, formerly her brother's. But instead of her fingers grazing soft, warm fur, there was nothing but cool linen.

She patted the empty space beside her.

"Flint?" She sat up and threw aside the coverlet. Thunder rumbled, punctuating the horrible realization that he was not amongst the linens.

"Flint?" She scrambled off the bed, noticing the door was slightly ajar. Faint candlelight peeked through the open crevice.

Not again. Whoever would have thought a short-legged terrier could get around so much? She hurried across the room, her nightdress flapping around her, and pulled the door farther open. She edged out into the passageway. The candles in the nearby candelabra were waning, spreading marred shadows across hanging portraits of relatives long gone.

Dread crept up her spine. It was so late, she doubted if any of the servants would be up to assist. Of course, if Flint started barking, everyone, including all twenty of their house guests, would be up in a blink. Then her father would deliver yet another stern lecture about the annoyance of keeping a mongrel who couldn't even be used for a fox hunt.

"Flint," she hissed out into the darkness. "Flint!"

There was no answer. Which meant he wasn't within hearing distance.

Drat him. She huffed out a breath, not wanting to leave her bedchamber, but knew a promise to her brother was a promise. During his last days, Victor had repeatedly insisted she watch over Flint and keep the blighter from harm. Mostly because Flint was a very stupid dog, notorious for chewing everything, and if not properly supervised, he would most likely die. The dim-witted creature was probably ripping something apart at this very moment. Perhaps even her great-grandmama's tablecloth in the blue drawing room. The one he'd been clamoring to—

She paused, her eyes widening. Oh, no. Her father would have him sent to the taxidermist within the week!

Victoria sprinted to her right and down the corridor, her wool stockings sliding several times against the smooth marble beneath her feet. Skidding, she caught herself against the nearest wall, rounded the dark corner and smacked straight into a massive body.

She screeched as large, bare hands steadied

her by grabbing hold of her shoulders. The earthy scent of allspice lulled her senses. She blinked and gawked straight at the expanse of a linen shirt hanging open, revealing a lean, muscled chest with curling black hairs. She scrambled out of his grasp, well aware who she'd find towering before her: Viscount Remington.

"Either I'm too tall for you, Victoria dearest, or you're too short for me. Which do you suppose it is?" He braced an arm against the wall beside them, preventing her passage, and leaned toward her, the tips of his slightly overgrown black hair sweeping into enchanting blue eyes.

The casual repositioning of his body caused his already unfastened shirt to gape open further, revealing not only his muscled chest, but also a portion of his lean stomach.

Victoria pressed her lips together, knowing she shouldn't judge him, considering she herself was in a state of undress, coiffed in a single braid and garbed in a ruffled nightdress without a robe. It wasn't the least bit respectable to remain in his presence, but the sparse light from the candles shifting across those handsome features whispered for her to stay.

She had always liked Remington. More than liked him, actually. He knew how to make her feel…happy. Even when she wasn't feeling particularly so.

He grinned, a dimple appearing on his shaven left

cheek. "I must still be sleeping. I was just thinking about you. And now here you are."

She refrained from snorting. "Considering how many female guests have been shamelessly fawning over you ever since you stepped into this house, I doubt you've really had time to think at all."

He chuckled. "Jealous, I see."

"Jealous? Oh, no. I was only jealous of the Parisian fashions they all wore."

He feigned a wince. "You belong in a garden with the rest of the statues made of stone."

She grinned. "Maybe I do. So. Did you enjoy your stay here with me and Papa?"

He sighed and eyed her. "No. Not really. I kept hoping for more time with you, but that annoying governess of yours was forever getting in the way. Do you know that I gave that woman a respectable missive to pass along to you this morn, and she up and ripped it in half, claiming you were already spoken for by some Lord Moreland? Grayson denies it, but I won't know peace until I hear it from you. Who is this Moreland and how long have you known him?"

She cringed and shook her head. "Lord Moreland is a family friend. Nothing more. Mrs. Lambert was merely being protective, as always. She has *very* lofty expectations for me. So lofty, in fact, that she claims I have no reason to settle for anything less than a duke.

Since every duke I've ever met is over fifty, I dare say I may never marry at all."

Amused blue eyes searched her face. "We most certainly cannot have that. Would you be willing to settle for a mere viscount instead? I am worth two thousand a year, have an estate in West Sussex and am available for matrimony whenever you are."

A more blatant display of flirtation she'd never endured. Whilst she secretly relished the banter they always shared, for he was dashing and divine, she knew the games men played. He wouldn't be the first man to flatter her for the sake of progressing his own interests. Nor the last.

She gestured toward his bared chest. "I confess I could never wed a man who wanders about my home with his shirt slung open like a pirate. I beg your forgiveness, Captain Blue Eyes, but we are not at sea, and I am not your mermaid."

He pushed away from the wall and straightened to his full height of six feet, towering impressively over her measly five. Pulling his shirt closed with one hand, he eyed her as if genuinely offended. "I happen to be the greatest gentleman you will ever have the pleasure of knowing."

Why did all men seem to think women were witless? She rolled her eyes. "If you will excuse me, I have far more important matters to tend to."

"Oh, is that so?" He scooted closer, the heat of his

skin scandalously drifting toward her. "I hope you weren't heading into the kitchen to swipe any of Mrs. Davidson's Banbury cakes, because I just came from there and I've already finished every last crumb."

She giggled. "What is it with you and Banbury cakes?"

He shrugged. "As you know, I leave for Venice on the morrow, and from what I am told, there won't be anything to eat but citrus, soup and macaroni. So I have been indulging more than usual." He quirked a dark brow. "Why are *you* wandering about? Hmm? Should I be concerned?"

Victoria stepped back and primly set her chin, trying to demonstrate that although she was in a night-dress, she was still very respectable. "I was merely looking for my dog. Flint."

"Ah. Your dog." His long fingers fastened the lone ivory button below his throat. "Well, Captain Blue Eyes is more than willing to assist in any manner you see fit."

"No, that won't be necessary. I—" Another crack of thunder made Victoria jump, causing her to scramble toward him. She inhaled a deep, steadying breath, and eyed the darkness around them. "It is unnervingly dark, my lord. And with you being the graybeard, I humbly ask you to lead the way."

"Graybeard?" He chortled. "Since when? Now

cease this *my lord* nonsense and call me Remington. We know each other well enough."

Mrs. Lambert had warned her about this. How men tried to lower all the barriers of civility before physically pouncing. Victoria shoved her blond braid over her shoulder, wishing she hadn't left her nightcap in the bedchamber. "I prefer to keep things civil and would appreciate it if you did, too."

"Civil?" He stared at her for a long, pulsing moment. "Are you informing me, Victoria, that there is absolutely nothing more between you and I aside from superficial civility?"

She was not going to play this game at the expense of her own reputation. Despite the fact that she liked him more than she'd ever liked any man, he was going to have to wait in line like the rest of them. "Nothing can exist between us, my lord, until my coming out. Surely, you—*being the greatest gentleman I will ever have the pleasure of knowing*—can understand."

He shifted his jaw, still observing her intently, and half nodded. Stepping back and away, he smoothed the front of his shirt, ensuring the open slit was not visible. "I should probably go find that dog of yours," he muttered. "It's not as if I'm going to get any sleep tonight." He turned and strode down the length of the corridor toward the great stairwell leading to the ground level of the home.

Victoria blinked, then glanced down the large

corridor. Lurking shadows shifted malevolently toward her, just beyond the reach of candlelight and tall, curtained windows. She swallowed, sensing something lingering, and refrained from shuddering.

She scrambled down the corridor toward the great stairwell, her breaths escaping in uneven pants. Her hand skimmed the length of the wood railing as she descended. She paused on the last stair. Upon hearing Remington's echoing steps, she rounded a darkened corner to her left and bustled after him.

Slowing, she shuffled closely behind his large frame, following him through the library, to the dome room, to the blue drawing room and then to the tapestry room. All the while, they repeatedly whistled and clapped, calling out Flint's name. For some reason, Flint still did not answer, which meant he couldn't be in the house. Stupid though he was, he *always* answered.

What if one of the servants had let him out and forgot to bring him back in? On a night such as this, he'd either drown or get eaten by a fox. A fox who hadn't feasted in days. Her stomach clenched. What a horrible guardian she was turning out to be. She couldn't even keep her own brother's dog out of harm's way.

Seized with worry, she rushed past Remington, stumbling around furniture, and dashed toward the north entrance hall. Unbolting the oversize oak doors, she flung them open and sprinted out into the night. She darted past the glass lanterns illuminating the vined entryway and past the limestone portico.

She stumbled on the gravel path and winced as rocks bit into her stockinged feet. The weather was unseasonably cold, and a lashing gust of freezing wind and heavy rain assaulted her as she squinted to see beyond the blinding darkness before her. She wandered farther out into the vast lawn beyond the carriage pathway, the rain drenching her nightdress, face and hair within moments.

"Flint!" she shouted above the whirling wind as a torrent of rain continued to whip at her, pricking her skin like the tips of needles. "Flint! Where—"

She froze, sucking in an astonished breath as her feet sank deep into thick, icy mud, suctioning her to the ground. Her night simply couldn't get any worse, could it?

"Victoria!" A reprimanding male voice caused her to jump. "What the devil are you doing?"

Then again, maybe it could.

Victoria jerked toward Remington, the lanterns beyond dimly outlining his tall, lean frame in the descending torrent of rain. His dark, wet hair was plastered to his forehead and neck, whilst that billowy linen shirt of his was no longer billowy. It had turned sheer and clung to his lean, muscled arms and wide chest.

Her own nightdress, which only boasted a chemise beneath, was also beginning to stick to the length of her body. Though she didn't have the sort of sizable breasts most females her age toted, she had more than enough to make her cheeks burn.

She crossed her arms over her chest. "You ought to go inside. You're getting wet."

"We are *both* getting wet." He gestured toward the open doors beneath the portico. "Come. The blighter is probably hiding somewhere in the house."

She squinted against the rain slathering her face. "No. He never hides and he always answers whenever I call. Which means he has to be somewhere outside."

Remington closed the distance between them. "I doubt he will even be able to hear us over all of this wind and rain. Now come. Come inside. I was hoping you and I could talk."

What a rum pot. Talk? At this time of night?

Victoria turned away, cupped the sides of her mouth and yelled out against the wind, "Flint! Where are you?"

"We are getting soaked to the bone."

"You really ought to cease pointing out what is already obvious." She paused, sucked in a large breath and then shouted as loudly as she possibly could, *"Flint!"* More rain and wind pummeled her as an agonizing chill overtook her limbs.

"Victoria, please. This is ridiculous. He's a dog. He has fur to protect him against the elements. You, on the other hand—"

"Flint! *Fliiiint!*" Panic edged into her strained voice and her limbs began to quake. Where was he? Why wasn't he responding? Flint never wandered far from the house. Not ever.

She spun in every direction, wondering which way she should go, but found that the night, wind and rain were blending together too much, making it impossible to see.

"Victoria." Remington grabbed her arm and pulled her back. "I promise to assist you in finding him in the morning. Now come."

She flung his arm away and stumbled forward, toward the direction of the open field. Her stockings were now sliding down her legs, being sucked in by the mud around her. "No. I cannot leave him out here all night. I cannot! He is anything but good at taking care of himself."

"Much like his lady." He stepped back toward her. "Please forgive this necessity." Large, warm hands grabbed her firmly by the waist, then yanked her straight up into the air, pulling her feet out of the mud and out of her stockings altogether, leaving them stuck in the ground.

Victoria gasped as she was effortlessly pitched up and over his hard shoulder like a sack of barley, her bare feet dangling out before him, her arms and long braid dangling behind him with her bum in the air. His grip dug into her hips and the night bounced with each large step he took back to the portico.

"What are you doing?!" she shouted, smacking his hard backside hidden beneath his soaked shirt. She froze, realizing she shouldn't even be touching any part of him, and certainly not his backside. She twisted against his shoulder. "My stockings! I... This isn't respectable! I am still in my nightdress!"

"So I have noticed," he drawled as he kept toting her back toward the house.

She collapsed against him, plotting her escape.

Stepping in through the doorway, Remington finally plopped her down onto the marble floor of the large foyer. She slipped and stumbled against the water pooling beneath her cold, bare feet.

He slammed the doors and bolted them with quick sweeps, flinging water everywhere. He turned and fell back against the doors. Blowing out a breath, he paused and glared down at her, his rugged face glistening from the water that continued to dribble down from his matted hair. "You do realize your father, not to mention your cousin, would have held me accountable for whatever happened to you out there?"

As if she cared. "I am *not* abandoning Flint on a night like this." She scrambled around him, trying to get to the doors, but he set his back against both knobs.

She pushed at his massive, wet body.

"I am not moving," he gruffly announced.

"Step aside."

"No."

"Step. Aside."

"*No.* You are not going back out into that rain."

She shoved at his body again, trying to get him to move away from the knobs, but her feet kept sliding against the smooth marble. Annoyed to no end, she gritted her teeth, fisted her hand and punched his shoulder.

He seized her upper arms, his hard grip pinching her skin beneath the sleeves of her nightdress, and fiercely spun her around, yanking her back against himself so she couldn't hit him again. He leaned over her, his broad chest and arms locking her against his chest. Icy water cascaded down onto her neck and arms from his drenched clothing. She stiffened, her eyes widening, realizing she was officially at his command.

He leaned farther down, bending her far forward and in turn, keeping her in place with his weight. "Cease being an impertinent child," he demanded, his warm breath heating the side of her chilled cheek. "He'll be fine. You, on the hand, won't be if you get any more drenched."

She trembled within his arms, the cold seeping deeper into her skin. "He is all I have left of Victor. And if that makes me a child, so be it. Now let me go. Let me go!"

Remington released her, allowing them both to straighten. Turning her toward him, he grasped her shoulders, pulling her close. The few waning candles in the sconces of the entrance hall dimly illuminated his rain-moistened face. He rubbed her shoulders. "Forgive me. Grayson has often told me how close you and your brother were."

She looked away, refusing to give in to emotions that were pointless to feel. It wouldn't change the fact that her brother was gone, having succumbed to small-pox after a servant had exposed him to it. Sometimes she wondered why it hadn't been her.

Remington's fingers pressed into her shoulder blades, silently assuring her that she was not alone. Not wanting or needing his pity, she pushed away his heavy arms and swiped away droplets of water running down the sides of her face and chin.

"Victoria."

She glanced toward him. "What is it now?"

"I...leave for Venice tomorrow."

She sighed, unable to hide her own disappointment knowing she wouldn't see him until her coming out. "Yes. I know."

"I may not return in time for your debut. Which is why I was hoping you could…" He winced.

She stared up at him, dreading whatever he had in mind. "You were hoping I could what?"

He shrugged and glanced away. "I…wanted to give you something, is all. Something that would—"

"You had better not be asking me for a kiss, Remington. Because you won't get it."

He cleared his throat and shook his head before setting his broad shoulders. "No. I…in truth, I wanted to give you something that will help bring Flint back."

She sighed. "A whistle won't be of any use. That dog hates whistles."

"It's not a whistle." He drew closer, his wet hair glistening as black as night, and dug into his soaked trouser pocket. He held up a dainty, gold-and-ruby ring by the tips of his fingers. "Here. Take this."

Sometimes, men were utterly useless, weren't they? "I do believe my intelligence is being insulted. How is a ring supposed to bring my dog back?"

He let out a gruff laugh and grabbed up her chilled hand, forcing it open. Holding the ring up between them, he set it against her palm and pressed her hand tightly closed. Water from the sleeve of his shirt dribbled onto her hand, raising more gooseflesh on her already cold skin.

He lowered his voice. "My mother gave this to me shortly before she passed eight years ago. She and I were very close. From what I am told, a Gypsy gifted it to her. All you need know is that the worth of this ring will prove itself to you in time. Believe in its magic, and I assure you, all will come to pass. I am giving it to you so you can wish for anything you might ever want or need whilst I am away."

Victoria opened her hand and blinked down at the ring. She glanced up at him. "Surely, you jest."

"I do not."

"You are a man of nineteen. You don't actually believe in real magic, do you?"

"Age should never exempt one from hope. Which is what defines true magic." He tapped at her hand, still holding her gaze. "Place the ring on your finger, whisper to the stone whatever it is you most desire and it will come to pass. I promise."

She snorted. "Are you trying to melt butter in a wig? There are no magic rings in this world."

He lowered his chin and drew closer. His hand reached out and brushed her cheek, his warmth making her cool skin tingle. "How do you know there aren't?" he murmured, staring at her lips. "Have you whispered your most intimate desires to every single ring that exists in this world?"

"Well, no, I…" She froze, fully aware that he was inching in closer. His dark head lowered as he tilted his face toward her own.

She gasped, scrambling out of his reach, and

stumbled, her bare feet sliding across the cold marble floor. She didn't want or need her father to catch her being irresponsible. Not when her coming out was only seven months away.

She bustled toward the dim, sweeping stairwell, and chanted to herself that she needed to leave. Her hand, which still held his ring, trembled, though not from the cold.

"Victoria. Please. Don't leave. Not yet. I need this moment between us to last. It may be as many as ten months before I see you again." There was a tender huskiness in his voice that made her melt with yearning. It was a yearning she didn't think she'd ever feel for anyone. Or want to feel for anyone. Not after the losses she'd endured.

Though she did pause, her pride insisted she not turn, lest she give in to the pathetic yearning she felt by flinging herself at him like a squirrel into a pile of nuts.

He cleared his throat. "I don't go about seducing women, if that is what you think I am doing. Ask Grayson. My father was a true gentleman to his very last breath, and since his passing, I have honored his legacy. So much so, in fact, that I haven't even allowed myself to kiss anyone."

She spun back toward him and met his gaze across the short distance between them. "You've *never* kissed a woman? At your age?"

"Don't tell me you've already kissed some lucky bastard, or I will hang myself for admitting what I just did."

She bit back a laugh, realizing how serious he was. She shook her head, her wet braid clinging to her shoulder. "Of course I haven't kissed anyone."

"Good. Because I am not one to share with others."

Her fingers tightened around the ring he'd given her, the sides of the stone digging into her palm. "I wouldn't worry about others. I'm not even allowed to be alone in the presence of a man who isn't a relative. You know that. Even this would be considered very…"

He closed the distance between them. "Very what?"

"Improper."

His dark brows came together. "Genuine intentions could never be improper. I swear upon my honor that I have never once pursued a woman the way I am pursuing you. But *this…you…us…*it is meant to be. I can feel it."

"You can feel it?" she drawled. "Oh, dear. That cannot be good. You may require leeches."

He glared at her. "I am being quite serious."

She giggled. "Yes. A bit too serious, I see."

"Victoria." He lowered his voice, leaning toward her. "I am not being insincere. I am merely conveying what I feel. What I have always felt. Destiny has been whispering your name to me ever since our eyes met. I cannot let this go. I cannot let *you* go. To do so would be to walk away from everything I feel."

Victoria gawked up at him. It was as if he really did believe in all the silly things that existed in story-books. Silly things like magic rings and destined courtly love meant to conquer all. Why, she hadn't believed in such nonsense since she was…*thirteen,* when her mother died and shattered not only her father's life, but her own. And when Victor had died… the last of whatever true happiness she'd known had died, too. Love could conquer quite a bit, that she knew, but it couldn't conquer death. Which was why she wasn't about to let it conquer her.

"How can destiny be whispering anything to you?" she challenged. "You don't even know anything about me, aside from all of our superficial banter."

"I know quite a bit about you."

"You do not."

"My dear, I have exhausted myself with all the inquiries I've made about you. I believe I know more about you than I know about myself."

"Oh, is that so?"

"That is exactly so."

"Then tell me. When and where was I born?"

He tilted his head and pushed away her wet braid

from her shoulder. Her heart fluttered from the touch and she felt herself leaning toward him.

"I need more of a challenge than that, Victoria."

"So you don't know."

"I do know."

She jabbed his wet chest. "Then answer it."

He caught her hand with his, keeping it from poking him. He smiled and lifted it to his mouth.

Full, warm lips brushed against her chilled skin, sending tingles of heat darting through her entire body. Wild tingles that made her breath and her pulse catch.

Meeting her gaze, he rubbed his fingers against her hand and indulgently replied, "Both you and Victor were born on the ninth of April in the year eighteen hundred and seven in the east wing of this house. You came first and your brother second. Whilst you thrived at birth, Victor was very frail. Though physicians did not expect him to live, he did, and as a result, your parents were always very protective of him. In time, however, you became far more protective and mothered Victor to annoyance."

She blinked and yanked her hand out of his. This was far too intimate to be respectful. "Who told you that?"

"Grayson. I had him tell me everything about you. And I do mean everything."

"Everything?" she echoed.

"Everything."

"You can't know *everything*."

"Oh, but I can. Ask me another question."

"I will." She rolled his ring against the palm of her hand and eyed the end of the wood banister beside them, trying to come up with a question. "Who is my favorite author?"

"Daniel Defoe. *The History and Remarkable Life of the Truly Honourable Colonel Jacque* is your favorite. And though you've tried numerous times to get Grayson to unearth a copy of *The Fortunes and Misfortunes of the Famous Moll Flanders,* Grayson knows you are far too young to be exposed to such devious content."

Her eyes widened. Oh, she most certainly was going to gibbet Grayson for this. "What else did my cousin tell you about me?"

"Things you would probably deny. But things I cannot help but find extremely endearing." His eyes flicked down toward her lips. He leaned in, hovering close. His breath heated the air between them, the scent of rain and allspice drifting all around her. "I want you to kiss me. I *need* you to kiss me. Because right now, destiny is telling me that if we do this, our lives will never be the same."

She drew in a breath.

In her heart, she wanted to believe this romantic sop. She wanted to believe that if she kissed him and allowed herself to submit to whatever he was offering, her entire life would be transformed and all of her doubts about relationships, people, life and death would dissipate into a pile of rose petals she could toss into a fountain. Could a kiss change her entire life like the tip of a fairy wand changing one apple into a whole pie? There was only one way to find out.

"Don't move," she warned.

"I won't," he whispered.

Victoria eyed the quiet darkness of the foyer around them. Knowing she was probably going to regret it in one way or another, she raised herself onto the tips of her bare toes, hooked a hand behind his strong neck and yanked him down toward her. She pressed her lips against his surprisingly warm and soft mouth.

Lean, muscled arms slid around her and molded her closer against the length of his rain-soaked body. Everything swayed and spun. It was incredible.

Ever so slowly, their pressed lips parted in unison. After a moment of awkward hesitation, their tongues touched. Her pulse leapt. The faint taste of sweet, spiced cake made her realize Remington *had* in fact been in the kitchen eating Mrs. Davidson's Banbury cakes.

His hot, wet tongue slid against her own as he deepened their kiss. All of her melted into a tingling disarray as she pressed herself against him, wanting and needing to be near him. Remington groaned against her mouth, his large hands drifting toward the back of her waist and skimming her entire backside through her wet nightdress.

She gasped, realizing she was allowing too much, and broke their kiss, pushing herself out of his arms. That was *not* what she had expected. It had only made her realize she was capable of feeling so much more than she'd ever imagined, and in turn, losing so much more. "There." She tried to sound indifferent, even though her heart pounded and her throat tightened. "Is destiny well pleased?"

His hands dropped heavily to his sides, but his eyes remained closed. "Destiny wants you to do it again."

She let out a nervous laugh and stepped back. "I think not. My father would send me away to Scotland if he caught us doing this. And then what? We would never see each other again."

He opened his eyes and stared at her, his chest rising and falling heavily, emphasizing how wet his shirt was and how incredibly attractive both he and his chest were. "So you want to see me again? Why?"

Her cheeks burned. "Well…I…like you. I have always liked you. You know that."

"Like?" His voice was gruff. "I like Banbury cakes, but I'm not going to take them to the altar and give them my name and my children. I want to know. What do you really feel for me, Victoria? Tell

me. Aside from *like?* That kiss told me you are well beyond like."

She blinked up at him, realizing she had placed herself in a very awkward situation. He was trying to extract promises. Mrs. Lambert was going to have a fit. "You cannot expect a lady to divulge what she feels."

"If you and Mrs. Lambert think my intentions are villainous, then neither of you know a thing about me." He searched her face in the shadows, the silence of the house interrupted by the steady rush of rain outside. "Are you going to place my mother's ring on your finger? Or are you going to deny what it is I *know* you feel?"

Kissing him had been a horrid mistake, because now he seemed to think she was in love with him. Young though she was, she understood how attachments caused one's fingers to slide off the ledge of reality. Her own father's grip had slipped years ago. "I will keep your ring on my finger this one night, to assure you of my fondness, and will return it to you in the morning before you leave. But that is all I am willing to offer."

"No. I am asking you to keep it on your finger until I return from Venice."

"Keeping it would insinuate far too much and I am not in a position to be granting you or any man favors.

Now, please. Don't tell anyone about this. Not even Grayson."

He raised a forefinger and tapped it gently against his lips. "I will tell no one. I am and will forever be your protector from this night forth." He lowered his finger, never once breaking their gaze. It was as if he were silently announcing to her that she was now his. All his.

She swallowed. "If you really seek to pursue this, Remington—"

"I do. Believe me, I do. By God, I have been—"

"Then I suggest you prove your worth in seven months. Not a day sooner. Good night." Feeling her damp skin tingle beneath the continued heat of his gaze, she quickly turned and scampered up the stairs.

Odd though it was, she couldn't even remember how she got back to her room. With trembling hands, she bolted her bedchamber door, stripped off her damp clothing and put on a dry chemise and nightdress. Burying herself within the linens and coverlet of her bed, she turned on her side and fingered the ring in her hand.

She drew in a shaky breath and let it out, praying that if Flint was indeed outside, he had found shelter for the night. Heaven forbid that whilst she had been indulging in an incredible kiss with an incredible man, Flint had drowned.

Bringing the ring to her lips, she whispered against the polished ruby, "I beg of you to prove yourself by returning Flint to my side."

She held her breath and blinked, expecting something to happen. When nothing did—and why would it?—she slid the ring onto her finger, wanting and needing to believe in real pixie magic. The way she used to before loss had destroyed whatever was left of her family, her happiness and her heart.

Late morning, the library

VICTORIA SAT, staring vacantly at her hand which lay across the unopened book resting upon her lap. Remington's ruby ring shimmered as she tilted her hand back and forth. Although her father had abandoned the last of his remaining house guests to assist Remington in finding Flint out in the surrounding fields, they had been gone all morning. It did not bode well.

"You are supposed to be reading," Mrs. Lambert ordered with artificial patience from where she sat in a cane chair opposite Victoria. "Regardless of Flint's absence, you have responsibilities that cannot be swept aside. One must exude staid refinement even during the most trying of times."

"Yes, Mrs. Lambert." Exude staid refinement, indeed. There was far more to life than putting on superficial airs. Her dog was missing, possibly dead, and she wasn't even supposed to care?

Victoria huffed out a breath and grudgingly paged open the red leather-bound book, *How To Avoid A Scandal*.

"Ladies do not huff out breaths." Mrs. Lambert's brown eyes pinned her with an agitated stare.

"Yes, Mrs. Lambert." Setting her chin, Victoria held her open book up with the refined poise expected of her. She didn't understand why she was being forced to tolerate the teachings of an etiquette book in preparation for her coming out, which was still a whole seven months away. Not seven days away.

She read the very first page:

Whether or not a lady possesses excellent character, astounding wealth, esteemed rank, or is simply a mere Miss with nothing more than a face and a figure to recommend her to the world, society will still demand the same of each and every woman: perfection. If this appears too daunting, this author can assure you it most certainly is. Society is a ruthless creature expecting perfection in everything a woman does, yet it rarely applies those same expectations toward men. This manipulated form of prejudice creates an unfortunate imbalance that allows men to deviate in ways that put women at a disadvantage. This disadvantage is what ultimately compelled me to offer an array of words in an attempt to rescue and retain a sensibility in a woman. There is only one reason as to why a lady should read this book, and that is to prevent her from becoming a flapping fish upon a hook.

Victoria wrinkled her nose. Why did she suddenly feel intimidated by the very idea of being a woman?

Several male voices floated down the corridor, followed by heavy booted steps thudding in her direction.

A high-pitched bark echoed within the house.

Victoria's heart leapt. She slapped her book shut, setting it on the arm of her chair, and jumped to her feet in disbelief. "Flint?"

Mrs. Lambert closed her own book and sighed.

Standing in the doorway of the library, wearing a wool greatcoat, was Remington. His silken black hair was windblown and scattered and his boots well muddied as he gripped a very wide-eyed, mud-matted and exasperated Flint. Flint barked again, excitedly squirming his tiny, tawny furred body in an effort to be released.

Remington's bright-blue eyes met hers. "I found him in an overturned barrel on the other side of the field. Do you still want him? Or shall I toss him back outside?"

Victoria grinned, but otherwise couldn't move. She

was simply too mesmerized by Remington to even think. He really was divine. In so many ways.

Her father, somewhat out of breath, staggered in behind Remington, his lopsided cravat unraveling. He shook his unkempt blond-gray head, stern dark green eyes flicking toward her. "You need to ensure the servants don't let that dog out again without a leash. I'm tired of tending to your responsibilities at every turn. If you can't oversee the needs of one goddamn dog, then you can't keep him."

Her grin faded. Since the passing of her mother, there were times she barely recognized him anymore.

"There is no need for such harsh words, my lord. She is undeserving of them." Remington quickly bent and set Flint onto the floor.

Flint sprinted toward her, his nails clicking against the wood floors as he dripped and flung mud. Mrs. Lambert squeaked in protest and scrambled back toward the chair she'd risen from, gathering her morning skirts to keep them away.

Victoria dropped to her knees and didn't care that Flint's muddy paws climbed up onto the folds of her new lilac gown. She reveled in the cold, muddy kisses that drenched her entire face. "Flint," she breathed down at him, ruffling the damp, dirty fur around his head. "You aren't nearly as witless as you lead everyone to believe. You survived a storm all on your own, didn't you? Yes. Yes, you did. You even found a barrel to hide in. I am so proud of you. And Victor would be, too."

She squeezed Flint tightly against herself, causing him to yelp. He ducked and scampered back out of the room, no doubt in search of a meal from the kitchen.

Her father sighed and met her gaze pleadingly. "It appears Remington is more of a gentleman than I. I should have never spoken to you with such vile impatience. 'Tis unforgivable."

Victoria smiled, feeling at peace with her father once again. "There is no need to apologize, Papa. Flint is my responsibility. Not yours."

"Good. I am pleased to hear we understand each other. Now go. Carry on with your lessons. I will visit with you once the rest of our guests depart. Perhaps a bit of chess?" Her father smiled, turned and disappeared from the library.

Victoria glanced toward Remington, who continued to linger in the entryway, and rose to her feet, smoothing her skirts. "Thank you." He always had an amazing way of making everything right.

A grin ruffled his lips, causing his shaven cheek to dimple. "I told you the ring was of merit."

How could she not adore this man when all he continued to do was try to get her to adore him? Aside from valiantly coming to her defense, he'd also tramped through muddy fields all morning. Not even Grayson, drat him, had been willing to look for Flint, and her father had only gone out into the fields because Remington did.

She glanced over at Mrs. Lambert, who had turned away to gather a set of books for their upcoming lessons. She needed to return the ring. She had kept it on her finger long enough.

Victoria darted across the length of the room, toward Remington. Halting before him, she slid the ring from her finger and held it out with a mud-crusted hand. "I believe the magic lies not in this ring, but in its master. I bid you a glorious journey and promise to write if you promise to return in time for my debut." She smirked. "I will need someone to vie for me. You may be the only one."

His grin faded. He observed her for a solemn moment. Glancing toward Mrs. Lambert, he whispered hoarsely, "Put it back on your finger. Please. We are done playing games. I will see you upon my return."

She blinked up at him. He wasn't…was he?

He jerked a mud-streaked thumb toward the corridor behind them. "I leave for Portsmouth in an hour and from there to Venice. Grayson knows where I'll be staying. Retrieve the address from him." He lowered his voice, his lean face flushing as he now seemed to almost mouth the words, "I will compete for your hand upon my return, let there be no doubt. I only hope you won't already be spoken for because after last night, I..." He glanced toward Mrs. Lambert and winced. "I should go." He offered a quick bow of his head, turned and disappeared.

Her eyes widened as she glanced at the ring still pinched between her fingers. He really did intend to vie for her hand. Heavens above. This wasn't a mere wayside fancy, was it? He really did harbor an affection for her. One she had sensed all along and yet one she had refused to acknowledge for fear it would be a farce and lead to something beyond her control as a respectable lady.

But it had already fallen beyond her control, hadn't it? She had kissed him. Willingly. She had taken his ring and whispered to it because he told her to. Willingly. Although she had fought her adoration for him since their very first exchange of words, deep inside she knew she couldn't fight it anymore. She had to assure him that she felt the same. Before he—

She frantically shoved the ring onto her finger and rushed out of the library. Her gown rustled around her slippered feet as she dashed after him down the corridor. "Remington?"

He paused and swung back toward her, his blue eyes capturing hers. "Yes?"

She came to an abrupt halt before him. Lingering, she wrung her hands. "I—"

"Lady Victoria!" Mrs. Lambert shrilled from the library. "Wherever have you gone to now?"

Victoria cringed, knowing she didn't have much time. "I will write the first letter. I will also ensure Mrs. Davidson sends a few of her Banbury cakes to you in Venice. Would you like that?"

"You honor me." Grabbing her hand with cool fingers, he brought it to his lips and kissed the ruby she had placed on her fourth finger. "Never part with this ring. It is worth far more than I could ever put into words."

Her bare hand trembled within his larger one. "It belonged to your mother. Why would you entrust it to me?"

He stared down at her. "If you don't know why I am entrusting it to you by now, Victoria, I have failed not only as a man, but as a human being."

Her lips parted. "Are you asking me to—"

"Yes." He leaned in closer, his hold tightening. "Will you have me? I have been waiting weeks to ask. Weeks. Long before the house party. Please say yes so I might speak to your father at once."

She stared wordlessly up at him. This was madness. They had only known each other a year and yet…she felt as if she'd *always* known him.

Mrs. Lambert whisked into the entryway and came to an abrupt halt, causing her pinned gray hair to quiver. She gasped. "Lady Victoria. I demand you step away from Lord Remington at once."

Victoria defied the command by tightening her grasp on Remington's large hand. It wasn't every day a lady was asked to become a wife. But would he return? And if he did, would he still want her once he had seen what the world had to offer? She refused to taint this wondrous moment. As her mother had once said, "One cannot embark upon an adventure without stepping onto a path. And there is no greater adventure than love." *Love.* Is that what this was? The sort of love her parents had once shared?

Leaning toward Remington on the tips of her slippered toes, she whispered quickly, "Let our letters determine what will become of us before we tell my father anything more. Agreed?"

"Agreed." Remington bowed his head and rested his warm forehead against hers. "My stepsister is engaged to a British nobleman in Venice, which is why I am even—"

"Lord Remington!" Mrs. Lambert's slippered heels click, click, clicked against the marble floor as she marched toward them, closing the vast distance between them. "I am without words. Does my presence mean nothing to either of you?"

"Forgive me, Mrs. Lambert." Remington lifted his forehead from Victoria's and ever so slowly slid his fingers from hers, as though he were trying to memorize every inch of her hand against his own. He stepped back and offered Victoria a quick bow, setting his hand against the brass buttons of his waistcoat. "I reluctantly depart."

She smiled. "I reluctantly allow you to depart."

He smiled, turned and strode away, his greatcoat shifting around his muddy boots and tall frame. When he reached the end of the vast corridor, he paused. Glancing back, he gave her a huge, saucy grin bursting with pride.

Her heart squeezed as she held up a hand in parting, wishing he didn't have to go to Venice.

Ever so slowly he rounded the corner, his large hand playfully dragging against the length of the wall, as if he were forcing himself to leave. Then he, and his reluctant hand, disappeared.

Victoria let out a breathy sigh and refrained from whirling about the entire corridor like a top.

"Lady Victoria," Mrs. Lambert chided, coming into full view. "I do believe your current reading is coming at an opportune time. I will expect you to have the entire book read within the week. I will also expect you to memorize and recite twenty different passages. Is that understood?"

"Yes, Mrs. Lambert."

"You will now follow me."

"Yes, Mrs. Lambert." Not caring if the woman noticed, Victoria lifted her hand and admired the mud-streaked ruby ring on her finger as she dutifully breezed back into the library. Was there a connection between Flint's return and the ring? Not likely. But Remington was a fantastic magician of a different sort. The sort who made a wary soul such as hers give away not only a kiss, but her heart.

SCANDAL TWO

A lady should never engage in secret correspondences. For who is going to supervise all the words being scribed? Rest assured, much can and will go wrong, and much to a lady's chagrin, there will even be documented proof.

How To Avoid a Scandal, Author Unknown

September 15, 1824

MY DEAR *Remington,*
Grayson is completely beside himself with grief now that you are gone, and has become rather annoying as a result of it. He is forever demanding I play chess with him whenever he visits, and claims I am the only one who can play as well as you. I never realized how close you and he were. It pleases me to no end knowing how fond Grayson is of you and only confirms everything I already know. Though I constantly ask him questions about you, and Grayson pesters me to disclose what it is I feel, I haven't confessed

to anything. Not yet. I am convinced everyone will only dismiss it as calf love if we present this prior to my coming out. And while I have yet to fully understand what it is we share and what it is I am submitting to, I do know I cannot brush this or you aside. As for that adorable little fool you rescued, he is still getting into trouble. During my French lesson, Flint managed to yank down my great-grandmama's tablecloth in the blue drawing room and shattered what used to be Mama's favorite antique vase. Papa was livid and threatened to make sausages out of him, even though I know he never would, since Flint is all we have left of Victor. I miss my brother, and think of him often, for he was my dearest friend and the only person I was able to confide everything to. Unlike before, however, I don't feel quite so haunted. Perhaps it is because I now have new memories to replace the old. I find myself lingering by the staircase where you and I kissed, and do it more often than I should. Even Mrs. Lambert noticed my lingering and asked why I was always loitering about the staircase. It was embarrassing. Please write and tell me everything about Venice.

Ardently awaiting your return,

Victoria

16th October, 1824

> *My darling Victoria,*
> *I would like to begin my first correspondence by finally confessing how in love with you I really am. I have been in love with you for quite some time. I carry your letter with me in the inner pocket of my coat and pull it out whenever I think about you. Which is often. My stepmother insists I am daft for submitting to you so blindly. Of course, she thinks everything about me is daft. She claims I am terribly naïve when it comes to women, and at nineteen, I suppose I am. But I would rather be naïve than a superficial ingrate like the rest of the men around me. I often wonder why my father remarried at all. My stepmother is so prickly, quick to judge and prefers harsh words over any patience or kindness. Surprisingly, my stepsister, Cornelia, is nothing like her. She is very dedicated to being a good person and loved my father very much, which will forever merit my respect. Indeed, Cornelia is the only reason I continue to strive to please my stepmother at all.*
> *Venice is incredible. I now understand why this city is so celebrated. The air is incredibly lush, with scents constantly changing depending upon the winds, and because the city is surrounded by both sea and sky, not a single*

day appears to be alike. To my disappointment, Venetians do not share the same passion for hunting that we do in England, not even in the plains or the hills, which are considered country. But they do excel in the art of catching birds, which isn't all that surprising, considering there are more birds in this city than people. In the Laguna around Venice, men crawl into submerged tubs with weapons in hand and shoot everything in sight. The shooting of birds appears to be as popular as keeping them for pets. Whilst many are confined, I visited one palazzo in which all the birds flew about quite freely. Imagine hosting a ball in London whilst birds flap, chirp and deposit droppings on the furniture and guests at every turn. The ton would have a fit. Thus far, I have ridden countless gondolas. Indeed, what a carriage is to London, a gondola is to Venice, and surprising though it may be, there are those who claim to have actually never seen a horse at all. Each day, as I glide along water pathways and watch buildings float by, I think to myself how unfair it is that I am unable to share this city with you. After we marry—and we will—I insist we come to Venice, so that we can fulfill the potential of what seems to be a very romantic city.

At night, it is quiet, and decrepit buildings

shine like new in the moonlight. The stars above shimmer, whilst the lit lanterns on the gondolas sway over rustling waters. I wish to share this and more with you. By the by, there is much more to eat here than merely citrus, soup and macaroni. There are melons, chocolate, cod, mussels, and the chefs in every noble home I have visited thus far are all, surprisingly, French. I am beginning to believe that Napoleon, damn him, invaded every country's kitchen. Despite the food being exceptionally good, I do hope you will still send along those promised Banbury cakes. I miss them. Though not nearly as much as I miss you. I don't wish to be forward, but every night I stare up at the ceiling of my room and think about you, and wonder what it would be like to have you in my arms and in my bed. This need to be near you is overwhelming.
I am and will forever be yours,
Remington

November 15, 1824

MY DEAR Remington,
I had Mrs. Davidson bake six Banbury cakes for you. You should be receiving them shortly, although I cannot promise they will arrive intact. Let us hope they do. Venice, as you describe

it, sounds so divine. You will be happy to hear that Grayson intends on visiting you there in the next few months. I am livid, knowing I am unable to join him. Why is it he can go anywhere he pleases with whomever he pleases, whilst I remain confined in the library with Mrs. Lambert until my coming out? I prefer experiencing the world as opposed to learning about it through texts. What is worse, while I wait for my coming out, I am being forced to read and re-read a certain etiquette book, How To Avoid a Scandal. *Although there is a vast amount of valuable advice to be found within its pages, the art of being a true lady, as is defined by this book and, I suppose, society, is rather horrifying to behold. I do believe I shall find myself ostracized for breathing the wrong way.*

Now with regard to your bed… Though no one knows of our correspondences, except for Grayson and my lady's maid, who both sneak your letters in and then sneak my letters out, I was compelled to ask Mrs. Lambert a few questions—questions that came about after I had read what little is stated about matrimonial duties in my etiquette book. Mrs. Lambert refused to answer, and instead forced me to write the words "I am a respectable lady" four hundred and fifty times. As I do not wish to be

*forced to write "I am a respectable lady" four
hundred and fifty more times, I demand you
elaborate as to what truly does go on between
a man and a woman.
Yours faithfully,
Victoria*

December 5, 1824

*MY DARLING Victoria,
Where is a gentleman to begin? I should never
have mentioned my bed at all. Being a gentleman, I shan't go into too much detail, just
enough to ease your curiosity and save you
from further punishment. When I mentioned
my bed, I was referring to the art of love. It
involves no pretenses and consists of breath,
passion and pleasure that in time will lead to
the creation of precious life within your womb.
There is far, far more than this, I assure you, but
I am unwilling to scorch the tip of my quill or
this parchment. Simply know that I am looking
forward to our wedding night and think about
it more often than a gentleman should. As a
result of this restlessness within me, I have been
distracting myself in many new ways. I travel to
the plains often and carve every tree I pass with
your name, so even though you are not here,
everyone will still know of you. Fortunately,*

*by overseeing the last arrangements for Corne-
lia's wedding I have been fairly occupied. She
is thrilled, as it is a good match. I now know
I shall be returning to England in a little less
than two months, shortly after the wedding. I
cannot wait to see you and sweep you up into
my arms and scandalize everyone. By the by,
many thanks. I received all six Banbury cakes.
To my distress, all six had become one enormous crumb. After eating what I could salvage,
I took the rest to the Piazza San Marco and
shared my crumbs with all the birds. They were
all rather appreciative, and now, every time I
visit the piazza, the birds seem to remember
me and ardently flock to me expecting more. I
am therefore asking you to send more Banbury
cakes for my new Venetian friends. Christmas
will be here soon. How odd to know I will not
be celebrating it in England.
I am and will forever be yours,
Remington*

December 25, 1824

*MY DEAR Remington,
A Merry Christmas to you and your family. I
confess Christmas is never as merry for me
or Papa as it should be. Our Victor died on
Christmas morn, now two years past, and so*

our celebration today was shadowed by his empty chair and untouched setting at the table, which Papa insists we set for Victor the way we always have done for Mama. I could hardly eat having to stare at those two empty settings. I found Papa lingering in the doorway of Mama's empty bedchamber. It saddened me so, and achingly reminded me of how much he truly loved her. Though I tried to comfort him, he waved me away and preferred not to speak of it. It made me realize how much I have become like him, always waving others away. You would have adored Mama and Victor, and I know they would have adored you. They were very good at giving advice and forever voicing the brighter aspect of everything. Much like you.

Now as for this naughty business involving your bed, I cannot help but believe anything involving you will be divine. Even if it is naughty. Mrs. Davidson will be sending along another six Banbury cakes for your Venetian friends. You should receive them shortly after this letter. I would write more, but I confess I am exhausted after having spent the entire evening crying over Victor. I promise to write much more next time. I also promise to be more cheerful.

Yours faithfully,
Victoria

February 28, 1825

> *MY DEAR Remington,*
> *I did not write because I have been waiting to hear from you. I realize you are probably very busy with your new life. I can only fathom how tedious it must be to orchestrate a traditional British wedding set in the heart of Venice. I imagine it would be like trying to eat crumpets with macaroni. I confess, though, I am disappointed you did not write even to wish me a merry Christmas. Grayson has informed me you haven't written anything to him in two months, either. He worries. As do I. Please write and assure us both that you are well.*
> *Yours faithfully,*
> *Victoria*

March 2, 1825

> *MY DARLING Victoria,*
> *Please forgive my lengthy silence. I did not know how to go about writing this letter. In an effort to increase my funds and offer you a better prospect upon my return, I invested far more than I should have into a Venetian venture that has closed its doors due to corruption. As a result of my stupidity, I am ruined. My*

secretary and bookkeepers are trying to make sense of whatever finances I have. Though they all assisted in placing this investment, one cannot predict where greed hides and festers within seemingly respectable establishments. Although the men responsible for the corruption have been found and named, the money they swindled from me and others is all gone. I hope they hang every last one of them, as I was not the only one affected by their greed. I have been advised to sell my estate and furnishings in West Sussex as well as everything I have here in Venice, lest whatever meager finances I do have disappear. I am overwhelmed by this imposing weight. Cornelia does not blame me, but she does nothing but cry. What is worse, plans for her wedding were terminated after it was made known how ruined we truly are. Aristocracy is so heartless and superficial in its affections. The dowry that was supposed to be allotted to Cornelia has been put toward our debts, though little good it has done. My stepmother is in complete denial. She still goes out and purchases extravagant things we cannot afford and refuses to return them despite my pleas. Creditors have been demanding payments for weeks. Payments I do not have. There is one measure of hope left, which I am considering. I was offered a

*rare opportunity to financially redeem myself,
though it is far beneath my position in life. I
would be nothing more than a servant, but it
would eliminate my debts and ensure that my
stepmother and Cornelia will live comfortably
again. This position, however, would require
a contract and obligation to stay in Venice for
another five years. The thought of not seeing
you for a year, yet alone five, is unsettling and
agonizing. But what am I to do? Allow my duties
toward my family to fall away? I was the one to
place this hardship upon them and I must be the
one to right it. Their well-being and happiness
depends upon it. I wish you were here to advise
me, as my thoughts are pulling me in directions
I do not wish to go.*
Ever yours,
Remington

April 6, 1825

MY DEAR Remington,
*Out of desperation, I presented your letter to
Papa and begged him to let us marry before
my coming out. I regret ever turning to him
at all. I have never seen him so unwilling to
listen to reason. He overturned every piece of
furniture in my room and despite my pleas, retrieved and destroyed all of your letters. It was*

like watching my own soul burn in the flames of hell. Though he insists I cannot associate with a ruined man, I assure you that nothing, not even my father, will keep us apart. I informed Grayson of everything and begged him to travel to Venice in my stead. He is very grieved and will be leaving within a week. My uncle, kind soul that he is, has graciously gifted a very generous sum for you, which we hope will eliminate all debts. Wait for him to arrive and do not bind yourself to anything that will keep you from returning to England. Until I receive word from you or Grayson, I whisper for your good fortune into your mother's ring and patiently bide my time.
Yours faithfully,
Victoria

May 15, 1825

My darling Victoria,
Your devotion to me is humbling and beyond anything I deserve. I could never separate you from your father. Never. The man has already lost a wife and a son; do not bring him more pain by forcing him to lose a daughter. I understand your father's concerns and, like him, refuse to bind you to a ruined man. You will have nothing if you marry me, and you deserve

far, far more. You deserve a man who will be able to oversee your happiness in a way I no longer can. Though my own hand trembles at scribing this, I must release you of your affections. I cannot be selfish in this, even though I desperately want to be. You are eighteen now and have most likely begun your first Season. I beg of you to submit to finding a husband worthy of you. If you love me, Victoria, which I know you do, all I ask is that you honor me for the rest of my days by keeping my mother's ring on your finger. That way, you and I will forever be wed in spirit. I hope you will understand and forgive me for having already taken the position long before Grayson arrived. My financial circumstances were simply too dire. I hope that you will continue to write as it is all I will have left of you. For although I am releasing you of your affections, I assure you I am not releasing myself of mine.
Ever yours,
Remington

June 28, 1825

REMINGTON,
Despite a successful Season that resulted in eight offers of marriage, I have refused them all. My father threatens to send me to a convent

at every turn, but, devoted fool that I am, I keep informing him that no other man will ever love me as much as you. Am I a fool to think that? I am beginning to think I am. Grayson has at long last sent word from Venice and has informed me that you are doing quite well on your own and that you actually had no need for my uncle's money at all. I am confused as to what position you have taken that would have enabled such a miraculous financial recovery. Was there ever a position? Were you ever in need of funds? Or was it an excuse to rid yourself of your obligations toward me after a better prospect had presented itself? Grayson refuses to elaborate, but I fear you have placed a pretty mask upon the ugly face of deceit. If this position *you refer to has caused you to abandon your noble intentions and wed another, I beg of you to inform me of it. If there is no other, and you are merely living beyond your means, live with what is only necessary, and marry me. I do love you, Remington, and ask that you love me by being faithful and truthful. To admit to the love I feel for you in ink whilst offering to abandon my father to be at your side in Venice is the sacrifice I am willing to make for you. What will be your sacrifice?*
Victoria

August 1, 1825

VICTORIA,

　　Your words of love overwhelmed me and filled me with a new hope I had not felt in months. Wretched though it is, I am committed to five years here in Venice. Neither you nor Grayson could ever truly understand the difficulties of poverty and narrow circumstance. Neither you nor Grayson could ever understand how it forces even the best of men to poison everything they believe in merely to ensure the well-being of those they love most. You are a greater fool than I if you think I could ever betray you by wedding or loving another. My soul will forever be yours. No matter what path I take in this life, I will remember all that we have shared and vow, in your honor, never to marry, regardless of what does and does not happen. Though I want to tell you what has become of me and what it is I have committed myself to, I cannot and will not, lest you judge me. I prefer death itself, Victoria, over having you judge me. Due to recent events beyond anything I can control, we cannot associate. Do not even breathe my name. If you oppose me in this, rest assured, I will not reply and will burn every correspondence you send upon its arrival. Understand that I only do this because I love you

and seek to protect you and your good name.
Live well and without regret and remember you
will always be loved by me. Always.
Yours ever,
Remington

September 26, 1825

REMINGTON,
Grayson refuses to inform me of your where-
abouts or what has become of you. He claims
he has been sworn to secrecy. I worry to no
end and despise you and him for betraying me
in so cruel a manner. With the Season over,
I do nothing but stare at books whose words
hold no meaning. At night, I cry, feeling that
I have buried yet another person I love. Why
would you condemn me to a life without you?
Why would you condemn me to never knowing
what has become of you? Does pride truly mean
more to you than I do? I only wish to understand
you, not judge you. Within my soul, I knew this
would happen. I knew from the moment I gave
in to this stupid passion I felt for you that you
would only disappoint me and shred what little
remained of my heart. I simply thought that
after having endured all the losses I have, I
would have been more prepared for the pain
you are forcing me to swallow. And yet I am

*not. This is beyond anything I ever wanted to
feel again. At the very least, write and assure
me you have not been harmed. I fear for you
and the life you have fallen into.
Ever faithfully and always yours,
Victoria*

DESPITE THIS and fifty-two other letters Victoria sent
over the next two years, Remington was true to his
word and never replied. Not once. And with each un-
answered letter, the love she had once dared to feel
for him faded with her disappointment—till soon, she
was sure there was no love left at all.

SCANDAL THREE

April 4, 1829
London, England

A MUFFLED groan startled Victoria out of a dreamless sleep. Flint jumped down from her lap onto the floor, scampering toward her father's bed, and whimpered. Victoria stumbled up out of the upholstered chair. Gathering her full skirts, she bustled toward the bed, thankful for the few candles still flickering in their sconces.

She lowered herself onto the edge of the feather mattress and slid a trembling hand up the length of her father's arm, hidden beneath the sleeve of his nightshirt. His arm was bound with linen that had been soaked in narcissus water to assist in healing his lesions.

Victoria swallowed and eyed the linen strips covering his face. "Maladie de Bayle," the physicians had grimly announced, upon her father's insistence that she finally know the truth about his illness. Syphilis. It was a secret her father had kept in unspoken shame for years after he had contracted it from a less than reputable establishment.

No amount of arsenic, mercury, guaiac, or jars or tins with salves and powders concocted by quacks could save him now. All she could do was make life bearable for him over these next few months until his body could no longer fight the inevitable.

The earl's roughened hand grabbed hers, causing her heart to skitter. His bandaged face jerked toward her. "Where is he?"

"Who?" she whispered.

Dark green eyes squinted up at her from beneath the layers of bandages covering everything but his eyes and lips. "Victor. Where is he? I must speak to him. Bring him to me, so I may tell him I am dying."

Tears burned her eyes as she shakily clasped his hand with both of hers. The physicians had warned her of this. Delusions were but the beginning of what she could expect over these next few months.

She swallowed, trying not to envision her brother's playful, bright jade eyes. "Victor isn't here. He…died. But I am here and will continue to be. I vow."

"No. No, no, no. My son is not dead." The earl shoved her hands away and fumbled with the linens around him. "Where is he? Why is he not at my side? And who are you? What do you want?"

Victoria bit back a sob and shook her head. "I am your daughter. Papa, 'tis me. Victoria. Surely you recognize me?"

He squinted up at her, his chest heaving. His brows creased. He shook his head and rasped, "No. Leave."

Tears stung her eyes and tumbled forth, trickling down her cheeks. She tried to keep her body from trembling as she lowered her lips to her father's hands and kissed them. "Do not send me away," she begged. "Please." She clung to his hand, wishing they could both somehow return to the way things used to be. When she, Mama, Victor and he had all been a family.

Hesitant fingers touched her pinned hair and fingered it. "Victor has your hair," he murmured in awe. "Flaxen. How very odd. Why do you have his hair?"

"Victor and I were twins," she whispered. "Surely you remember me, Papa. I am your Victoria."

He shook his head against the pillows. "No. No, your hair is too long. You are not my Victor. Tell him I will not see anyone but him. Tell him. Now go. Be of use and find him." He pushed her hands away and shifted against the pillows.

Victoria released another quiet sob and blindly

smoothed out the linens around him. Once he died, there would be nothing left of her or her heart. Fortunately, the physicians had assured her he still had at least another six to eight months within him.

The ruby-and-gold ring on her finger glinted within the candlelight. She lifted it to her lips and whispered against the polished ruby the same words she had whispered to it these past many weeks: "Cure him. Please. He does not deserve this. He doesn't."

Though she had long since lost faith in the ring's ability to grant wishes, what else did she have left to believe in? Nothing. Absolutely nothing.

All grew quiet and her father's sleepy, heavy breaths filled the room. Flint, who had been loitering beside the bed, veered back toward the chair by the hearth and hopped onto it. After turning a few times, he settled himself against the cushion and laid his furry head against his paws. He huffed out an exhausted breath through his nostrils and blinked several times, his brown eyes observing her with a sadness that seemed to reflect her own.

Even Flint knew her father was dying.

"Such is life," she whispered to Flint. "We live, we love, we suffer because we love, we suffer some more because we want to believe there is more to life than suffering, and then we die."

Flint shifted, closed his eyes and gave way to sleep.

Though Victoria fought to stay awake and watch over her father, her eyes grew heavy and her body weak. She scooted onto the edge of the bed and draped herself beside him, trying not to touch him lest he wake. Closing her eyes, she drifted.

What seemed like a heartbeat later, she squinted against morning sunlight peering in through the open curtains of the window. The chambermaid had forgotten to pull them shut for the night.

Victoria blinked and carefully slid down and out of her father's bed. She turned back to her father and tilted her head to one side to better observe him. Dust particles floated in the bright rays of light streaming in, illuminating his bandaged face. His exposed lips were parted and his eyes were still closed as his chest peacefully rose up, then down, up then down.

If only she could give him equal peace when his eyes were open. Dearest God. He no longer knew who she was.

Victoria shakily swiped away a long, blond lock that had fallen out from her pinned hair to the side of her face. It would appear the time had indeed come to submit to her father's last dying wish. That she, Lady Victoria Jane Emerson, be wed before he was unable to attend her wedding.

Her uncle and Grayson had been scrambling to procure her father's choices in suitors for weeks and would be officially introducing her to all three soon.

Though it was not by any means appropriate, considering her father still had months left to live, she knew the sooner she married, the sooner she could become the sort of daughter he deserved. The sort of daughter she'd never been during her debutante years. It was time to admit that the husband she had always wanted and needed no longer existed. And sometimes, though only sometimes, she actually wondered if he had ever existed at all.

SCANDAL FOUR

An old Swiss proverb distinctly cites, "God has a plan for every man." I confess the Swiss have a tendency to mislead. Because God's plan is meant for every woman, too.

How To Avoid a Scandal, Author Unknown

Five days later
The onset of evening

WHEN A lady celebrated being two and twenty, and came to the realization that all of her debutante friends had been wed and were now beginning to welcome children, her own birthday became a reminder of all the things she had done wrong. Fortunately, her years of being a spinster were at an end and she could now hold her head up high and join the rest of respectable society.

Victoria shifted in her chair, eyeing her father, who kept fussing with his cravat at the dining table. How she wished upon all that was ever sacred that her father had respected himself more these past nine years. His refusal to remarry after the death of her mother, which in turn had resulted in loneliness laced with unmet needs, had all come at a very high price.

Gathering her fork and knife, Victoria glanced toward her cousin, Grayson. He sat in silence at the farthest end of the table, which stretched the length of the dining hall. Grayson, odd soul that he was, always sat there. No matter how many people were dining. He was like an eagle perching itself upon the highest branch—he always wanted a view of the world. It had also once been her mother's seat at the table, though she doubted Grayson even remembered.

In honor of Grayson's weekly Thursday night visit, she had decorated the entire dining hall with bluebells, hoping to make everything more festive. Of course, Grayson didn't appear to notice or care. He'd been wordlessly staring her down ever since she'd taken him aside and discreetly explained that she now went by the name of *Camille*. Though she had no idea who *Camille* was, her father kept insisting that was her name. So Camille she was.

Grayson's brown eyes met hers from across the dining table. "You shouldn't be feeding into his delusions. 'Tis wrong. 'Tis morbid and wrong."

Of course it was morbid and wrong, but who was she to argue with a man whose mind was as fragile as his health? In all but five days, she had gone from being nameless to adored. She preferred being *Camille* as opposed to not being anyone at all.

"As long as he is happy, Grayson, I am happy." She offered her cousin an amiable smile, refusing to acknowledge that the situation was in the least bit bizarre. She gestured toward his untouched supper. "I hope the peacock is to your liking. One of the physicians recommended it as a weekly regimen. He claims they have documented proof of its ability to cure."

Grayson leaned forward and lifted a brow. "Peacocks would be extinct if that were true."

She blinked. She hadn't even thought of that.

Grayson leaned back against his chair and waved toward his plate. "I am not eating this. And you shouldn't make him eat it, either. It has a stench."

"Everything in life has a stench," the earl interjected with clear agitation. "Even you have a stench. Now eat it. Food is food. And if *I* have to eat it, then *you* have to eat it. Rude, I say. Coming into my home and telling me my food has a stench."

Victoria glared at her cousin, silently reminding him that he shouldn't rile her father. "This isn't about you, Grayson, or what you find appetizing. This is about ensuring Papa's health and comfort."

Grayson's mouth thinned. "He wasn't like this when I last saw him. He has become delusional. This cannot be good."

She pinched her lips together, refusing to admit to him or herself that her father was fading.

"Delusional?" The earl dragged his chair closer to the table, his gaze flickering toward Grayson. "I do beg your pardon, but I am not delusional. I remember quite a bit. Especially about you, Grayson. Why, you just returned from Venice all but two days ago, did you not?"

"No. It was four months ago, Uncle."

"Ah. But I remember you being there. Yes. Once I am well again, you and I will charter a ship and visit those fops. There is someone there I have been meaning to call upon." The earl nodded. He paused, his silvery brows coming together. "Though I cannot remember who. Who is it, Grayson? I think you know him. Was he not your friend? A good friend, at that?"

Grayson winced and occupied himself by staring at the contents of his plate.

Victoria drew in a shaky breath and let it out. Even after five years, Grayson was still ridden with guilt, as well he should be. Because she knew full well who it was he'd been visiting in Venice all these years, although he'd never once had the decency to admit it.

The earl turned his squinting gaze to her and patted the edge of the table with a bandaged hand.

"My dearest Camille—perhaps you can travel to Venice with us."

Grayson, who'd been nudging his peacock with a fork the whole time, sighed and threw down his silver with a tinkering clatter. Bracing his hands against the table, he slowly rose. "Uncle, she is not *Camille*. She is your *daughter. Victoria*."

"Grayson!" Victoria exclaimed, her heart pounding.

"You cannot hide reality from him. 'Tis wrong." Grayson returned his gaze to the earl and said softly, "Uncle. Surely you remember your daughter. How is it you remember me, Venice and my friend, yet not your daughter?"

Victoria gasped and jumped to her feet, whipping the napkin onto the table. "How dare you? Do you not understand that he panics when his version of reality is challenged? I have been dealing with it all week. *All week!*"

Her father slammed a hard fist onto the dining table, shaking every plate, glass and piece of silver set on it. His graying blond hair tumbled down onto his forehead. "I would bloody remember if I had a daughter. 'Tis *you* who is delusional, Grayson. *You!*"

Victoria drew in a ragged breath, desperately willing herself not to cry. It was unbearable to see her father like this. He truly was lost in his head.

Grayson fell back into his chair, eyeing her. He

shifted and glanced toward her father, offering in a soft tone, "Forgive me, Uncle. I have had too much sherry. We should all eat. I hear peacock is excellent for one's health."

Victoria swallowed and seated herself again. At least her dear cousin still had a heart.

Grayson lowered his gaze to his meal. Grabbing his fork, he pierced the peacock on his plate and placed a piece of its white meat into his mouth. He chewed and then paused, his features twisting. Leaning toward his plate, he spit it out and glared at her. "Gut me. Have you tried this? It tastes like burnt piss."

Her entire family was about as refined as gnomes. It didn't help she was the only female left in the family to oversee this deranged chaos. "I understand peacock isn't the most savory of meats, Grayson, but there are physicians who insist it may prolong his life." She leaned toward the table. "And who knows, it may prolong yours. Now set an example and eat it." Victoria eyed her father, who had yet to unfold his napkin. She reached out and patted his side of the table. "You really must eat. Eat."

Grayson blew out a breath and eyed her from across the table. "So. *Camille.* Assure me, despite all of this, you still intend to meet your suitors and wed. My father has been extremely worried, and rightfully so, about whether or not you will oversee your obligations. Your inheritance depends on it."

Victoria kept her hand from jumping to a plate and throwing it at his head. As if she wanted to think about men and marriage! "I have repeatedly assured you and your father of my compliance. There is no need to be crass. We will discuss this at a later time."

The earl blinked and fully turned toward her, shifting in his seat. "Are you getting married, my dear?"

She swallowed. "Yes."

He grinned and clapped in approval. "I will have to send a missive to your mother in France at once. She will be quite pleased to hear it. She was convinced you would forever be a devoted spinster."

She winced, not even wanting to know who her mother in France was, and pushed herself away from the table. How was she to rationally explain anything to him anymore? It was an involved game she wasn't mentally prepared to play. She didn't want to argue over what was real and what wasn't. Because it didn't matter. Not to her.

Grayson rose from his seat, as well. "I think it best he be placed into better care at once. My father would be more than willing to—"

"Damn you, Grayson!" The earl hit the table with his fist again, causing everything on the table to chime and rattle. "Cease discussing me as if I were not even here."

Grayson stared at Victoria in exasperation before pleadingly whispering, "You cannot continue to live like this. I will not allow it. Nor will my father once I inform him of how much my uncle has deteriorated within a short week."

Victoria blinked back tears. "I have the best physicians calling upon him daily and every servant at my disposal. Surely you do not mean to separate us."

Grayson's expression stilled. "No amount of love is going to save him. You have upcoming duties. He won't be able to remain at your side after you marry."

Tears blinded her, but she refused to give in to them. She was trying so desperately to be a good daughter by submitting to the familial duty that her father had asked of her before he lost the last of his rational mind. Although she was being forced to marry a man she knew she would never love, she certainly wouldn't be the first woman to do so. Nor the last. It was the least she could do to honor her father. But despite what Grayson thought, she was not abandoning her father, either.

She fisted her hands in an effort to prevent them from shaking. "I know I cannot save him, Grayson. But I *can* make whatever time I have left with him memorable. And I will. Whatever husband I take, I will expect him to open his life and his home to me *and* my father. Otherwise, I will not marry. For I cannot and will not abandon him."

Grayson swiped his face with a hand. "No man

will agree, given his illness. Vile whispers about his state are already flitting across London."

She narrowed her gaze. "London has never been known for mercy, has it? And if there is no man willing to take mercy upon what I hold dear, then I will not marry at all."

"Enough, enough of this nonsense!" The earl slammed his bandaged hand against the table. "You will marry whoever will have you, Camille. Your mother wants it so."

Her cousin groaned and fell back against the chair, raking a hand through his hair. "I need brandy. Lots of it."

Victoria couldn't help but share Grayson's sentiment.

The earl smoothed his wine-stained cravat against his throat and, with pursed lips, marched over toward her side of the table, his gait faltering. He paused beside her, intently looking her in the eye.

She sucked in a breath and braced herself for whatever outrageous thing he was going to say next.

Her father leaned in and patted her cheek assuredly. "I will return by morning." He nodded, turned away and as he slowly made his way toward the entryway, yelling out to no one in particular, "I am ready to depart, sir! Thank you for being so patient and allowing an old man to eat."

Quick footsteps echoed in the distance, drawing

steadily closer and closer. Victoria's brows rose as a large, bearded man, dressed in wool riding clothes, veered into the dining hall from the servant's corridor.

Oh, dear God. Who was this?

She scrambled back.

Grayson's chair screeched across the floor as he jumped to his feet. "What the hell is this? Uncle, who is this man?"

The earl turned and gestured obligingly. "I am most fortunate to have fine, devoted servants. They assisted me in securing a very special service few can afford. This gentleman here will be escorting me to my own virgin. 'Tis my hope that by the end of this night, I will at long last be cured."

Victoria gasped. The servants had assisted her father in securing this man, thinking that such vile, superstitious rubbish about lying with a virgin might cure him? Though she supposed her own insistence on serving her father peacock had most likely encouraged the servants to think outside of traditional means.

Grayson jogged toward them and jumped between her and the advancing tough, who was eyeing her appreciatively. Pushing her farther back with his own body, Grayson announced curtly over his shoulder, "Victoria, you will retire. Now. Go. I will oversee this."

She sighed. "I am not leaving. And there is only one

way to oversee this." She leaned around her cousin, peering at the man. "Sir? I will *triple* whatever his lordship is offering in return for your departure. Understand that he is very ill and unaware of what he is doing."

The earl snorted. "I am attempting to prolong my life is what I am doing. Now *you*." He pointed at the large tough and then pointed at Grayson. "Give this nephew of mine a good fist for interfering with my business and I will ensure you get an additional ten pounds. Fifty if you do it right."

"Yes, milord!" The man jumped forward and swung a large, gloved fist at Grayson.

Victoria gasped as she and her cousin dodged and darted off to the side. Grayson snatched up a chair, swinging it up high above his shoulder, ready to let it fly. "Victoria, get the bloody servants! *Now!*"

Victoria dashed past, knowing the situation had indeed gotten out of hand.

"Camille!" her father shouted pleadingly after her. "I vow upon my honor I would never have let him harm you!"

She wasn't worried about herself. She was worried about Grayson, whose head was now officially worth fifty pounds, thanks to her father. Flint suddenly dashed past her and into the dining hall, barking viciously, adding to the chaos as more shouts echoed down the corridor. She skidded out into the hallway, knowing that if there was anyone who could take on a tough until all the servants arrived, it was Grayson who spent most of his time boxing at Jackson's.

The crash of porcelain shattering against the floor exploded in the distance like thunder. She winced as she snapped toward the direction of the servants' quarters. "Assistance is required in the dining hall!" she screamed, her voice echoing all around her. "In the dining hall! At once! Hurry!"

Within moments, a group of male servants dashed past her and down the corridor, sprinting out of sight into the dining hall. Victoria gathered her skirts, turned and dashed after them.

Flint's barking grew steadily louder, as if he were insisting she move faster. She slid to a halt on her slippered heels, her breath escaping in uneven gasps, and paused, realizing everything had grown eerily quiet, aside from Flint's barking.

All the chairs lay toppled on their sides, and the linen on the table hung lopsided, barely clinging. Food, wine, crystal, china and porcelain lay scattered everywhere while—

Her eyes widened as she caught sight of Grayson. He rigidly held a carving knife against the throat of the large man, pinning the man against the wall with his own body. Her father and the servants merely gawked.

"Grayson!" Victoria rushed toward her cousin,

reached out and grabbed hold of his wrist. She yanked back his arm, ignoring his resistance. She gritted her teeth and jerked the knife back and away from the man's throat. "Grayson, don't. Don't do this. Please. Please, don't."

Grayson's chest rose and fell in visible heaves as he glanced toward her. His brown eyes sharpened with a blazing intent she'd never seen in all her two and twenty years.

"Grayson," she pleaded, digging her fingers into his wrist and edging his rigid arm farther back. Though her arm ached from the effort, she feared that if she let go, even for a moment, his arm would jump and slice that throat in a single sweep.

Grayson's resistance softened as he slowly lowered his arm and the blade. He stepped back, his gaze veering to the bearded man, who sagged against the wall with a breath.

Grayson extended the knife toward her, tilting the edge of the steel toward himself. "Take it. Take it, before I use it and hang."

Oh, God.

She scrambled toward him and pried the blade out of his hand. Turning, she tossed the carving knife toward the farthest corner of the room, away from them, where it clattered out of sight. She drew in several calming breaths and swiped her hands against her embroidered skirts, thankful it was out of his hand.

"Now leave," Grayson growled. "Leave before I slit more than your throat."

The man nodded, pushing away from the wall, and darted out of the dining hall, clearly relieved to have escaped.

Victoria let out a breath, the pounding of her heart dulling. "Grayson…"

Grayson jerked toward her and pointed at her, missing her nose by an inch. "Enough. Your father will be permanently moved out of this house and into my father's care within the hour. Before you or he end up dead. You may call upon your father as often as you please, for however long you please, but therein ends your rule. If you oppose me in this, in any form, I will ensure he ends up in the Lock with the rest of the syphilitics and you *never* see him again. This isn't a goddamn game! This is your life and whatever is left of his. Do you understand me?"

Victoria fought to keep from sobbing. Grayson was right. He was right. She wasn't capable of caring for her father, with his delusions progressing so rapidly. Though she didn't want to admit it, his mind had disintegrated far too much, and no amount of love she had to give was going to change that. She was never going to have her father back. Not ever. Not the one she loved and not the one she wanted. "I understand."

SCANDAL FIVE

We are forever warned never to bargain with the devil. But the devil is far too busy gathering souls to have any time to barter with mere mortals. 'Tis mortal men a lady should in fact beware. Especially those men who ardently claim to be gentlemen. In truth, the only thing gentle about these men are the deceiving little words they coo.

How To Avoid a Scandal, Author Unknown

Three days later, evening
On the far east side of London

JONATHAN PIERCE Thatcher, Viscount Remington, slammed the door of the quarters he was letting for the month and leaned heavily against it after his brisk walk through the city. He'd forgotten how dirty, dreary, cold and wet London could be. Five years cocooned in Venice had certainly warped his once-genuine appreciation for London.

A lone candle flickered its greeting within the sconce hanging on the stained plaster walls of the corridor. Reveling in the silence, he pushed away from the door. Removing his leather gloves and top hat, Jonathan stripped away the damp cloak from his shoulders and tossed everything into the crate at his booted feet. He paused, noticing a set of muddy prints that were not his own.

A pulsing knot seized his stomach. Was someone stupid enough to try to rob him? Reaching beneath the back of his damp evening coat, he yanked his dagger from the scabbard attached to his waist. Tossing it into his right hand, he gripped it and pointed the blade out to the side.

He edged into the adjoining room, his muscles tightening. The burning coals in the hearth sent dim light and fuzzy shadows shifting across barren walls and the dilapidated brass bed in the corner. The broad back of a tall, blond-haired gentleman in an expensive greatcoat lingered before the fire. Black leather-gloved fingers tapped the rim of his top hat.

"Grayson." Jonathan lowered his blade and blew out a breath, his body relaxing. "I wasn't expecting you until morning." He grinned, striding toward him. "How have you been, *vecchio?*"

Grayson swung toward him, the glow of the fire illuminating the edges of his greatcoat. He shoved his top hat beneath an arm, his disheveled dark blond hair falling onto his forehead. "I've been better. And I do beg your pardon, but I am not old."

Reaching beneath the back of his gray wool coat,

Jonathan slid the blade into his scabbard. Still grinning, he struck out a bare hand. "'Tis damn good to see you."

"And you." Grayson's gloved hand grabbed his and gave it a solid shake before releasing it. He glanced around the small room. "If you insist on staying in this piss of a flat instead of taking residence with me, at the very least have the decency to bolt your door. This isn't Venice."

Jonathan shrugged. "A roof is a roof and I have my blade. I'm only staying long enough to settle unfinished business. Speaking of unfinished business…" He grinned, glorying in the moment he thought would never come. "So. How is she? Does she know I'm here to see her? Have you told her? What did she say? Was she at all receptive? Livid? Thrilled? What? Tell me."

Grayson snorted. "You are prattling like an actress on gin."

Jonathan gritted his teeth and hit his shoulder. "Cease being an ass. Out with it. When do I get to see her?"

"Uh…"

"Tomorrow?"

"No. Not tomorrow."

"The day after?"

"Remington."

Jonathan lowered his chin. "No. I am *not* waiting

to see her. Do you understand me? I have waited long enough. Five bloody years, to be exact."

Grayson cleared his throat, his brows coming together. "Believe me, Remington, I understand. But you see—"

"No. None of that." Jonathan pointed at him rigidly. "Her father assured me that once my contract was over, I could return to London and vie for her. And I will. That is the only reason I'm even here. To vie for her. I have it all in writing. You know I do."

"Yes, yes. I know. And you will vie for her as was promised. Understand, however, that when my uncle made those promises, he omitted *how* you were going to be vying for her."

Jonathan dropped his hands to his sides, the frantic beat of his heart drumming against his chest. "What the devil did he omit?"

"Others."

"Others?" he echoed.

"You won't be the only one vying for Victoria's hand. There will be two others set to vie alongside you. But only two."

Jonathan drew in a sharp breath and angled his body toward Grayson. "The earl didn't tell me that. He said—"

"I know. I know what has been scribed by him." Grayson drummed his fingers against the top of his hat and sighed. "I can only apologize for my uncle.

He has never been a man to make things easy for anyone. And now, with his health being what it is, that is more true than ever. There are things he simply didn't disclose during your correspondences. Things he should have disclosed, considering it involves his estate and testament."

Jonathan leaned in closer, his brows coming together. "His testament? Is he…dying?"

Grayson turned and made his way back toward the hearth, half nodding. "Yes. Over a year ago, shortly before you and he started corresponding after he received the letter the *marchesa* wrote on your behalf, his physician informed him that the syphilis he'd contracted from a prostitute years ago had progressed beyond any known cure."

Dear God. No. "Syphilis? Are they certain of it?"

Grayson nodded. "Yes. Quite certain of it. He has actually had it and known of it for years. Only it is finally beginning to ravage the last of him. According to all eight physicians involved in his diagnosis and care, he has about eight to ten months left."

Jonathan swallowed. He couldn't even imagine what Victoria was living through. She and her father had been inseparable.

Grayson swiveled toward him. "According to the solicitor, I have to be formal in my delivery of what was set forth. So tolerate it." He cleared his throat.

"On behalf of my uncle, the sixth Earl of Linford, who regrets that he cannot personally deliver this message, I am here to announce that you, Viscount Remington, are being summoned to vie for Lady Victoria Jane Emerson's hand, so that she may be wed before his passing. Do you accept being one of three, knowing that you may or may not become her husband depending on her choice in men?"

Jonathan's lips parted. "I'll be expected to compete for her hand? Alongside a bunch of roosters?"

"Yes. Two roosters."

"Jesus Christ. I… If I have to vie for Victoria against two others, what chance have I? None. I already planned on crawling on my knees for the rest of my life in an effort to prove my worth to her, but with two others involved, how am I to—"

Grayson reached out and adjusted the lapels on Jonathan's evening coat. "You can do this. I know you can."

Jonathan stepped back and swiped his face. "How am I… The moment I disclose why I disappeared, she will run straight into the arms of whoever is standing next to me. I know she will."

"You are overcomplicating this. Victoria doesn't need to know. The less you tell her, the better off you will both be. And if, after you and she are married, the truth happens to fall out of your hat, so be it. Face it then. Not now. Get her to marry you first. After you two are married, what will it matter?"

Jonathan glared at him. "She would hate me. You may not see the value in a wife loving her husband, but I will not do that to her. I've already tormented her enough."

Grayson shrugged. "Do whatever you think is best. Simply know that she will look for reasons to run and if you give them to her, she will." Grayson paused, his brows coming together. Cocking his head, he reached out and fluffed the ends of Jonathan's green lace cravat. "What the hell is this? *Lace?* Forgive me, but we cannot have you prancing about London in such foppery. One look at your cravat and she most certainly will run."

Jonathan gritted his teeth and shoved Grayson's hands away. "If she intends to judge me based upon my cravat, which happens to be high fashion in Venice, mind you, then I cannot readily expect her to accept *anything* about me, can I?" He hissed out an exasperated breath. "Why is the earl doing this to me? He knows I have yet to redeem myself. How am I to do it with two other noses in my face?"

Grayson stepped back toward the hearth. "Did you really think he was going to up and hand Victoria over without allowing her to decide her own fate? This is about her happiness, Remington. Not yours."

Jonathan half nodded, respecting that sentiment.

Sad though it was, with two others vying for her, it was going to take more than him crawling on his hands and knees. It was going to take pixies. *Which did not exist.*

Aside from whatever misgivings Victoria already had toward him due to his abandonment, he knew the moment he shared the sins lining his soul, she would do more than run. She would hate him for the rest of his life. And in truth, he preferred she remember him for what he once was. Not what he'd become.

Jonathan sighed. "What chance have I against two others? None. I would only be tormenting her and myself. Perhaps it is best I return to Venice and leave this be."

Grayson rolled his eyes. "My God, shall I fetch the whip for you so you can finish lashing yourself with it? You are being given an opportunity to compete for her. *Take it!*" Grayson yanked out the top hat from beneath his arm and whirled it once between his gloved fingers before setting it atop his head. He angled it. "I've known you for eleven years, Remington. That is a good amount of time to get to know a man, wouldn't you say?"

Jonathan glared at him, sensing a parade of manipulation ahead. "What does that have to do with anything?"

Grayson's brows rose as he glanced toward the ceiling, seemingly searching the heavens for the patience to speak to a simpleton. "Remember Eton? Hot coppers, I do. It was the worst of all my social experiences. Indeed, everyone there assumed that because I had my nose in a book I deserved to have that same nose pummeled. Do you remember?"

Jonathan bit back a smile, recalling all the times he'd put up a pair of fists for Grayson, who only ever covered his head and never fought back. "We destroyed many a hall together. Many."

"No. *You did*. I was always half-crippled before you ever got to me. My point is, even then, you were forever setting aside yourself for others. 'Tis a noble quality, to be sure, but a quality that will force you to cradle everyone's happiness but your own. I wish to God you would cease blaming yourself for the situation you fell into. It is done. You are free and if it weren't for your *marchesa* digging up whatever grace she had left within her, you would not even be here. After enduring hell and counting down the days and hours toward reclaiming Victoria, you intend to walk away? Because of competition? The Jonathan I once knew would have put up two fists and started swinging."

"I am not particularly fight-worthy," he groused. "I would be but a pauper amongst princes."

Grayson sighed. "What are you worth, anyway? Hmm? Out with it. You never told me."

Jonathan seethed out a breath, not wanting to think

about it. He was worth less than a fourth of what he'd once had. "If I were to convert everything from Venetian lire? Approximately three hundred pounds a year. More than enough to ensure Victoria an excellent living in Venice."

"Three hundred pounds a year?" Grayson let out a long whistle. He shook his head and kept right on shaking it. "Bleed me, you will have no choice but to live in Venice...*but*—" Grayson pointed at him, a slow grin overtaking his lips "—if Victoria marries *you,* all of your financial woes will be at an end and you can live wherever the hell you want. As her husband, you would inherit my uncle's entire estate upon his death. Almost a hundred thousand pounds."

Jonathan choked. "Hell. That is a disturbing amount of money. No man should be worth that much."

Grayson eyed him. "I know you don't want the money, Remington, but consider it another dividend worth fighting for, attached to everything else you ever wanted."

"I could care less about the money. I have more than enough to live with. I just..." Jonathan shifted toward him and lowered his voice. "Be honest in this. Do you think Victoria would even give me a chance against two others?"

Grayson snorted. "The moment my cousin discovers you are one of the three, she may throw a fit and smack you around a couple times, but trust me when

I say she'll still be waiting at St. Paul's. Do you have any idea what my life was like when you ceased responding to her letters? Do you? Allow me to compose a delightful sonnet which I shall appropriately dub, *'Grayson, how I despise thee.'*"

Grayson cleared his throat and lifted his voice into an unbecoming female octave. "*'Grayson, do you see Remington whenever you go to Venice? You do, don't you? I know you do. Why else would you travel there so often? And why do you refuse to tell me what has become of him? You had best tell me something, Grayson. Tell me or I will slice all of your extremities off with a carving knife, starting with the one you love most.'*"

Jonathan rolled his eyes. "You exaggerate. She would never threaten a soul."

"The woman has gone savage since you've last seen her. I genuinely fear for whatever poor bastard ends up with her." He let out a laugh. "You being that poor bastard. Now, are you going to vie for her or not? I have to give Mr. Parker an answer by tomorrow afternoon."

Jonathan eyed him. "Mr. Parker?"

"The solicitor for my uncle's estate."

Jonathan blew out a long breath. What a mess. Her father was dying and Victoria was expected to partake in some matrimonial charade that would end up affecting her for the rest of her life? As for redeeming himself? It was one thing to become her husband and prove his worth to her then, but quite another to set himself against the wall alongside two others and let her weigh who was best. For best, he most certainly was not.

"Here." Grayson reached into the inner pocket of his greatcoat and pulled out a round, gilt frame bearing a miniature portrait. He held it up, stepping toward him. "It was painted last year."

Jonathan's jaw tightened as those achingly familiar dreamy green eyes met his. Thick, curling, long blond hair softly framed Victoria's beautiful oval face. Her full pink lips were set into a playful yet demure smile. One he remembered all too well.

The playful innocence that still lingered in those eyes and that face silently called out to him. God, how he wished he could go back to that night. That night when she had kissed him and held him and made him believe that his mother's ring actually bore real magic.

Jonathan reached out and gently slipped the miniature from Grayson's fingers, compelled to hold it. He grazed his forefinger across her womanly face, the rough paint shattering the illusion of soft skin.

Grayson tapped the outer frame. "She needs you, Remington. And with her father's death imminent, more so than ever. She will have no one but the husband she takes. Do you really want to lose the best thing you ever had because of your stupid pride and fear of getting rejected?"

Jonathan swallowed at the thought. Although he had been unable to let Victoria go, he knew he had destroyed the man she once knew and loved. Hell, he didn't even know who he was anymore. His tastes, his needs, his wants had all been erased and replaced with the tastes, needs and wants of Bernadetta di Sangro, *Marchesa* Casacalenda and her savage of a husband. Such was the life of a Cavalier Servente. And though his contract had reached an end, his resentment toward the life he'd been forced into had not. Jonathan fingered the portrait. He had lost five years of his life. Five years that should have all been spent with Victoria.

Grayson nudged his arm. "Keep it."

"Thank you. I will." Jonathan tucked the miniature into the inner pocket of his own coat. "Allow me to see her before the others do. I need time to reconnect with her."

Grayson leaned back. "Oh, no, no. I am afraid I cannot play favorites. Not in this. There are legalities as to how things are to be conducted, or everything, including the inheritance, will be void. Do you really want to play games with that large a fortune? Do you?"

"No, of course not. I simply…" He sighed.

Grayson leaned in close, lowering his voice.

"Though I am not permitted to disclose what is planned, if you need me to disclose the details as a means of providing you a measure of assurance, I can do that. But that is about all I am able to offer in this. The rest will be up to you."

Jonathan shifted his jaw and nodded. "I appreciate your assistance in this."

"And?"

"I wish to take it."

"Good. This remains between you, me and the walls. Do you understand?"

"Yes."

Grayson angled toward him. "Here it is. All three suitors will remain nameless to each other and to Victoria until the night of introductions. It allows everyone a fair chance to compete. Over the course of one evening, each man will be escorted into a private room with Victoria and expected to answer a designated set of questions. After all questions have been answered, Victoria must decide between you and the others. That is all."

Jonathan stepped back and raked his hands through his hair before dropping them to his sides. "What sort of questions will I be asked?"

"Hell if I know. But it doesn't matter. All you have to do is enter the room and the competition is over."

Jonathan threw back his head and laughed. "You have far too much faith in me."

"And that is what makes me a good friend." Grayson drew his brows together and glanced about. "You are not staying in this heathenish abode. You are coming home with me. Tonight. I also intend to drag you over to my tailor. I cannot stand looking at you. You look like Casanova in the flesh. And that is no compliment, I assure you."

Jonathan gestured grandly toward the length of his dove-gray attire, the embroidered celadon waistcoat and his green lace cravat. "I happened to pay a sizable amount to look this damn good."

Grayson snorted. "I don't care what you paid. It's hideous. If I were you, I would get your money back."

Jonathan snickered. "I am not buying new clothes merely because *you* cannot appreciate Venetian fashion."

"Forget I even care. Now, are you doing this or not? I'm exhausted and need some goddamn brandy. I've been doing this all week. You aren't the only man on the list."

Though doubts still plagued him, he simply had to hope to whatever God there was that enough remained between him and Victoria to ignite what had once been. "I will vie."

Grayson smacked his hands together and grinned. "Splendid. I will inform Mr. Parker of it at once." He gestured toward the side of Jonathan's waist. "Now hand over that blade."

"Whatever for?"

"Have faith. I don't plan on gutting you. I will leave that for Victoria." Grayson wagged his upturned fingers, waiting.

Faith. Now there was a word he'd long since lost sight of. Jonathan reached back and yanked it loose from its scabbard. He presented the small blade.

Grayson grasped the handle, playing with its weight. He paced away, turning on his booted heel and then whipped the blade hard across the room.

A loud thud echoed within the room as Jonathan jerked toward its direction. Jonathan gestured in complete exasperation toward the handle now sticking out the wall. "Are you on opium?"

Swiveling back toward him, Grayson pointed at him. "It stays in the wall. I cannot have you wearing blades like some tribesman. People are more civilized here and are likely to get nervous. If you feel the need to tote a weapon in public, I'll buy you a cane. Now gather up whatever you came with and meet me outside."

Grayson paused. "Oh." His brows came together as he patted his outside pockets. "I almost forgot." He yanked out a small red-leather-bound book with edges that had been frayed white, approached Jonathan and smacked the book against his chest.

Jonathan scrambled for it with his hands, catching it before it slipped and fell to the floor.

"My uncle wanted you to have it. There is an inscription inside. Read it, count your blessings and meet me out in the coach." Grayson patted him on the back, swept past and disappeared out into the corridor. The entrance door creaked open and slammed shut.

Jonathan turned the worn book right side up and blinked down at the fading gold-lettered words: *How To Avoid a Scandal.* His brows rose in astonishment. Victoria had once mentioned this book—it was the book she'd been reading during their correspondence.

He smoothed its front with a hand, then opened it, revealing an overly slanted inscription within, written across the full length of the very front page in black ink.

Lord Remington,
I am pleased to hear about your unprecedented success in Venetian society. Your determination to make a better life for yourself will suit what I believe my daughter needs. What you hold was once Victoria's mandated reading. Though she tried to toss it, I pilfered it and discovered your name scribed throughout its pages. It astonished me. My own dear wife,

Josephine, used to scribe my name in a similar manner on the pages of her books, claiming great books deserved to bear the name of a great man within their pages. I never realized that before my wife's death, she had shared this unusual tradition with Victoria. Since my wife's passing, I have not been the sort of father I should have been, and I now firmly believe my Josephine has spoken to me from beyond and is insisting I ensure our daughter's happiness before I pass from this world myself. In honor of what this book represents, I hope you will treat my daughter with the dignity and worth of a debutante embarking upon her first Season. May God bless you both. It is my hope she will choose you out of the three.

Linford

Jonathan swallowed, eerily reminded of his own father, who despite carrying a stern male façade, always knew when to yield. He'd always held a respect for the earl. After all, the man had only ever wanted what was best for his daughter. But was he, Jonathan Pierce Thatcher, Viscount Remington, truly what was best anymore? He had to believe he was. If only for Victoria's sake. For although he had sold every part of his soul over the years, the dream of what he and

Victoria had once shared remained the same. Sweet and pure.

Jonathan slowly paged through the entire book. He bit back a smile as his name appeared throughout, sometimes on the side, sometimes at the top, sometimes at the bottom. It reminded him of the way he'd carved an entire row of mulberry trees on the outskirts of Venice with Victoria's name. He paused on one of the pages with his name and read:

Husbands are like flowers. Tedious though it may be, they must be tended to daily. If there is not enough sunlight beaming within your smile or you forget to water his soul with the right words, patience and attention, his stem will wilt and his head will sag. Unlike a real flower, however, your husband cannot be ripped from the ground, tossed and replaced by another. Which is why you must tend to the garden that is yours. His very existence relies upon you.

Jonathan slapped the book shut. He most certainly had not expected to find his name next to *that*.

SCANDAL SIX

Many women dress preposterously in the name of being fashionable and unique. I dare say, God did not intend for us to wear clothes, and so one can easily forgive eccentricity from time to time. But there is an enormous difference between wanting to look one's best and failing and dressing for the sake of being vulgar and creating an unnecessary scandal.

How To Avoid a Scandal, Author Unknown

April 16, 6:53 p.m.
The night of introductions

GRAYSON'S TIGHT features rhythmically appeared and disappeared into the shadows as light from passing gas lampposts filtered in through the carriage windows. "That gown is revealing far more cleavage than I, as your cousin, ever want to see. Cover yourself up with that shawl, will you?"

Victoria rolled her eyes. The décolletage on her verdant lace and silk gown wasn't *that* low. "Lest you forget, Grayson, I am no longer a debutante and therefore I can wear whatever I like." She shifted toward him. "Will I be able to visit with my father after introductions?"

"No. Not tonight. I need you to stay focused. You can visit with him tomorrow for however long you like."

She sighed. "How is he whenever I am not about?"

"In good spirits. We always ensure someone is with him when we are not at his side." He grabbed his silver-headed walking stick from the seat beside him, and rolled it back and forth in his gloved hands.

Victoria eyed him. Grayson only ever fidgeted when something bothered him. "What is it?"

His hands stilled, his gaze lifting to hers. "Hmm?"

She gestured toward him. "You appear anxious. Are you?"

Grayson stared at her before glancing away and shrugged. "I keep thinking about the evening ahead and only hope all goes well for you, is all."

She sighed, already exhausted at the prospect. "Who are these men anyway? And why do you refuse to tell me anything about them? I would think—"

"We've already discussed this, Victoria. I am not allowed to answer questions pertaining to this night or these men. That is for your father's solicitor to do. Not I."

One would think she was about to be introduced to the king himself.

The horses whinnied and the carriage rolled to a stop. The small glass window at her elbow revealed the looming, three-story home of her uncle, its glass windows brightly lit from inside.

Her stomach squeezed as she realized that all of her dreams of what matrimony should have been and could have been had dwindled down to this. Some man she would never love would be touching her and kissing her and bedding her. For the rest of her life.

The carriage door swung open, revealing a dimly lit pavement. The footman unfolded the steps.

Grayson lowered his head to keep his top hat from hitting the door of the carriage, and jumped down onto the pathway beneath the portico without using the steps. He turned back, extending his gloved hand.

Victoria stood and took Grayson's hand and swept down onto the pavement.

Grayson offered her his arm and together, they entered through the open doors of her uncle's home. She drew in a steady breath, ready for whatever her father had planned. Slowly, she walked across the black-and-white marble tile of the large foyer, already feeling as if she were a pawn being played on a huge chess board.

The lanky butler stoically closed the entrance door.

Grayson gestured toward his left. "This is Mr.

Parker, the solicitor to your father's estate. He will be ensuring everything is conducted accordingly."

Victoria's eyes darted over to the bald man bearing three sealed parchments in his gloved hand. He was dressed in a formal, brass-buttoned evening coat, an overly starched and knotted cravat that indicated his valet was of no use at all and a pair of well-pressed trousers.

Mr. Parker smiled assuredly.

She smiled in turn and swept toward him. "Good evening, Mr. Parker. I was informed by my cousin that you will be answering my questions. So my first question is this: Why are *you,* a solicitor to my father's estate, involved in the introduction of my suitors? I think it very odd."

"I will answer your questions in due time," the man awkwardly provided.

Well, that was informative.

Grayson removed his top hat, smoothing the sides of his blond hair, and approached. "Forgive my inability to provide a proper introduction." Grayson swept a gloved hand back toward her. "Lady Emerson, this is Mr. Parker. Mr. Parker, this is Lady Emerson."

Mr. Parker bowed, lowering his bulbous chin against his knotted cravat. He straightened and cleared his throat. "Shall we commence, Mr. Thorbert?"

"Yes. In a moment." Grayson stripped his cloak and turned to the butler, holding it out along with his top hat. The lanky butler gathered everything with quiet civility.

Grayson turned back toward them and sighed. "There we have it. I am ready."

Mr. Parker gestured past the foyer to the corridor beyond. "If you please. Everyone is already gathered upstairs."

Her throat tightened. The idea of meeting suitors in the presence of a man representing her father's estate was unnerving. She dared not fathom what it meant. Did her father think she was going to deny her duty or his choice in men?

Lifting the hem of her gowns lightly above her slippered ankle, she quietly followed Mr. Parker and Grayson past elegant round alcoves displaying a series of bronze and marble busts of dignified men propped on Roman columns. It had been months since she'd last visited her uncle's home. Of course, nothing had changed since she'd last seen it; it was still very pristine and very boring. Her eyes followed the wood railing toward an oversize landing that led to various doors and the receiving room upstairs.

Grayson gestured for her to mount the stairs after Mr. Parker. She quickly followed the solicitor as Grayson trailed behind. Once she alighted on the landing, both Grayson and Mr. Parker hurried down one of the corridors. Two male servants in dark livery made their way toward them with silver platters, settled themselves against the walls and stoically remained there until she, Mr. Parker and Grayson had passed.

Low male voices drifted toward her.

Victoria followed Grayson through a large, rounded entryway. The dignified drawing room looked the same, its arched ceilings still bearing elegant ribbon plasterwork, the long row of windows on the other end of the room draped with heavy, brocaded curtains.

Although the large room wasn't brightly lit, there was a coziness reflected not only in the burning hearth, but also in the soft glow of candles in sconces set outside of gilded mirrors gracing the powder-blue walls. Four men of varying sizes and coloring were seated on the far side of the room in wingback chairs, quietly conversing. The oldest of the four, with thick, graying brown hair and a curling mustache, was not a suitor—*thank goodness*—but her uncle, Sir Thorbert.

She paused and eyed the rest of the men who had yet to note her arrival.

Grayson leaned toward her and whispered, "Settle yourself in. I will return in a moment."

She spun toward him, her eyes widening. "You don't intend to leave me unchaperoned, do you?" she whispered back. "I don't know any of these men."

He patted her cheek. "My father is here to serve as chaperone. And rest assured, you know two of the three. I'll be right back." He winked, turned and disappeared.

Two of the three? She didn't even know that many men. She spun back toward the room. Dread drummed through her as moisture pricked the back of her neck beneath her gathered and pinned curls.

Mr. Parker sighed, reminding her of his presence, and strode past, heading to the other side of the vast room.

She awkwardly edged forward, scanning the faces of the seated men. One of them was none other than the ever serious Lord Moreland, the son of her father's deceased childhood friend. Heaven help her. Who else had her father wrangled into vying for her? It was a pity fest.

Victoria bit her lip, her gaze falling on the dark-haired gentleman who was angled almost completely away. The one closest to the window. She lowered her chin, eyeing his waistcoat and high collar, which were shockingly snowy-white against not only his sun-bronzed skin but also the ruby-red cravat knotted around his neck. He was the only one wearing any color.

He sat with the others in a studded leather chair, his gloved fingers rubbing his shaven chin as he intently listened to whatever her uncle was saying. He shifted, lowering his hand down toward his muscled thigh, which was accentuated by well-fitted trousers.

She knew a lady wasn't supposed to gawk at a man's hands, thighs or anything else, and yet…Victoria edged closer, as if being pulled in by some invisible rigging held between herself and this man.

Mr. Parker paused before the group and said something in a muted voice that faded across the expanse of the cavernous room. Drawing steadily closer, Victoria continued to eye the dark-haired gentleman. She knew him. Didn't she?

His shaven jaw tightened as he leaned far forward to listen to Mr. Parker's muted words. He glanced toward her, then paused. He shifted his entire body in her direction.

Victoria's heart skittered as vibrant blue eyes met hers. No. No, it couldn't be. It…*couldn't.*

His dark brows rose, as if genuinely surprised by what he saw, too. His eyes swept the length of her gown as he stood, smoothly unfolding his well-muscled limbs to an impressive height that had to be well over the six feet she remembered him to be.

Dearest God.

It was Remington.

It was none other than the man she'd once loved and whose ring she still wore. The man who had never answered a single one of her letters for reasons she had always feared to even question.

Lord Moreland and the others beside him leaned

forward in their chairs, glancing past Mr. Parker. All of them stood to acknowledge her presence.

Panic cut off her breath as she took step after step back, her eyes never once leaving Remington's. Though she was by no means a coward, the last thing she wanted to do was say things no one needed to hear.

Remington strode toward her, heatedly holding her gaze the entire time, his chin lowering slightly as she, in turn, stumbled farther and farther back. That rugged face was as handsome as ever, bronzed from years under the Venetian sun, while his broad frame had alluringly filled itself out, giving him the well-muscled appearance of a grown man.

Anguish seized her as he headed straight for her. Spinning on her slippered heel, she gathered her skirts and whisked out of the room and into the corridor. She drew in several steadying breaths, feeling as though her chest was about to collapse.

Her vision momentarily faded at the edges. Her gloved hand shot out and she balanced herself against the nearest wall. As she held herself in place she felt as if she was going to heave up everything she'd eaten. Ever so slowly, she leaned in and set the side of her cheek against the cool, hard surface of the silk lampas wall, the blaze of her face unbearable.

Remington. Remington was among the three. Her

father had somehow unearthed the man she'd thought was dead.

Her uncle's stout frame appeared in the doorway. His booted steps echoed into the corridor as he quickly approached.

He darted toward her. "Victoria?" Rounding her, he leaned toward her, touching her sleeved arm. Her uncle's full face, along with his curling, graying mustache, appeared in her view. "Victoria, look at me."

She lifted her cheek from against the wall and turned toward her uncle, leaning her entire back against the wall in an effort to keep steady.

His brown eyes searched her face. "Do you require anything? Salts? Wine?"

Victoria fought the heat in her cheeks and shook her head, unable to say or do much more. She drew in softer, calmer breaths, but her body still felt… *numb.*

Hurried steps echoed out into the corridor toward them and eventually paused. She froze as a tall, muscled figure filled her sight, now lingering close beside her. The crisp scent of mint surrounded her.

It was Remington.

Her eyes swept toward him and crept past the brass buttons of an ivory-and-silver-threaded waistcoat, which emphasized his solid, broad chest. She forced her gaze to creep farther up, past that ruby silk cravat, up to his full lips.

The moment she met those striking blue eyes, which still held so much wrenching unspoken romance, all of the blood drained from her head as if an invisible cork had been pulled. It was indeed Remington. Only older. And like a fine wine, he had improved with age.

He searched her face in equal disbelief and leaned closer, tilting his head toward her. "Victoria. I… Are you unwell?" His deep voice was low and lush with concern. And though his diction was still quite British, there was a soft hint of something more exotic and romantic. It was as if Venice had not only deepened the color of his skin but had also painted his tongue.

All of these years she'd endlessly plotted what she would say and do if she ever had the opportunity to see him again. She had counted out the many ways she would smack him, punch him, yell at him and, yes, even curse at him for making her suffer and worry day after day after day. Yet for some reason…all she could do was gape like a fish that had been pulled out of the depths of murky waters.

His black brows came together as he glanced at her uncle, who still lingered beside them. "Sir Thorbert. Must everything be conducted tonight? Clearly, she is unwell."

Victoria blinked as the crisp scent of mint drifted toward her again from Remington's evening coat.

He no longer smelled of allspice. He smelled like a...man.

She swallowed and dug the tips of her gloved fingers into the wall. At least she'd worn her finest. At least she looked like a ravishing woman he'd forever regret wounding.

Her uncle sighed and patted Remington on the back. "I appreciate your concern, but we simply cannot postpone this. The sooner we do this, the better. You know that."

Remington nodded and shifted toward her, his large frame blocking her against the wall. Lowering his head toward hers, he peered at her face and searched her eyes. "I realize this is awkward, but have you nothing to say to me? At all? Be it good or bad, Victoria, I wish to hear it. I really do."

She shifted away from his body. She wanted to run and escape the intensity of his gaze, but that would reveal to him—and to herself—that he mattered. And he didn't. Not anymore.

Remington lowered his chin against his red cravat. "Is it your intention to perpetuate my suffering with this silence? Is that it?"

Her cheeks stung. Perpetuate *his* suffering? *His* suffering? It was *he* who had left *her* to suffer all these years with *his* silence.

She clenched her jaw and refrained from smacking him. No. She was going to save all the smacking for

Grayson. Her cousin had known all along, and for it, she was going to maim him. She was going to maim him, then bury him, so he might suffocate beneath the earth, and just as he was about to take his last breath, she'd dig him back up and maim him again. And then maybe, just maybe, it would make her feel better.

Regardless…she couldn't stay here. Not with Remington still probing her face and her body with his eyes and a blatant disregard for the fact that nothing remained between them. She pushed off the wall and edged away, trying to maintain a sense of dignity given the situation.

Remington stepped toward her and reached out a gloved hand to help her. She jumped away, not wanting to be touched, and quickly rounded his towering frame.

He dropped his hand back to his side. "Victoria."

Though she could hear the aching hurt in that pleading tone, how else was she to treat him? With reverence? With joy? After what he had done to her?

"Victoria," he repeated, following close behind, "at least acknowledge me. Please."

Dear God, she couldn't stand it. She couldn't stand hearing that tone and those words, which made her feel as if *she* were the one who had inflicted all the pain.

How dare he?

How dare he?!

Swinging back toward him, she pointed rigidly up at him. "I gave you fifty-three chances to prove yourself, Remington. *Fifty-three.* All of them came to you in the guise of letters, and you didn't have the decency to respond to a single one. I will forever hate you for what you did to me. You will *never* be able to redeem yourself. *Ever.* Go back to Venice or wherever the hell you were frolicking all of these years, you—you...*bastard!*"

His eyes widened as he stepped back.

She swung away and bustled down the vast corridor toward...*Grayson.* Oooooh. Her eyes narrowed as she marched toward her cousin. Her heels clicked hard against the marble beneath her feet, and she wished it was his head she was pounding into.

Grayson hurried toward her, glancing over at Remington and her uncle and then at her. "Wait, wait. What is this? Where are you going?"

"Where do you think I am going?" she flung back, closing the remaining distance between them. "I am going home. Where I belong."

"Oh, no, no. You have an obligation toward this family and toward your father."

Oh, no, she didn't. Not at this price.

Halting before Grayson, she glared at him, then lifted her hand and smacked him hard across the face, stinging her own palm through her satin glove.

Grayson's flushed face jerked back toward her. He nodded, but refused to look at her. "Fine. Good. Yes. I suppose I deserve that."

"I'm pleased to hear you think so." She leaned toward him, too angry to think about what was happening. "First you tell me nothing and allow him to disappear from my life. And now you tell me nothing and allow him to reappear? Whilst you decide whatever it is you do or do not want for me, I am going home. Once I have regained a sensible amount of composure, I will return on the morrow to visit with my father and pretend none of this ever happened." She swiveled away toward the stairwell leading to the entrance below.

Grayson grabbed hold of her arm and yanked her back.

She stumbled toward her cousin in disbelief. "Unhand me! How dare you—"

"You are not leaving," Grayson growled, jerking her toward him until their noses were practically touching. "Smack me all you want, if it will better serve you, but your father orchestrated this all for you. *You*. At the very least be gracious."

"*Gracious?*" she echoed into his face. "And to whom am I to be gracious? To the man I no longer know or wish to know? To the man who actually has the gall to show up after five years and think I would consider him fit to even spit upon, let alone marry?"

She feigned a laugh. "Someone keep me from castrating you and every man in this building!" She yanked her arm away from his pinching grasp. "Why didn't you tell me what my father had planned? *Why?*"

Her cousin huffed out a breath and eyed her. "Because of how you are responding right now. Your father knows you and your damn pride better than you know yourself."

"I see. And how long did you know about Remington being one of the three? Hmm? How long?"

Grayson cleared his throat and shifted from boot to boot. "About a year. Give or take a few weeks."

Her eyes widened. "A whole year? *And you said nothing?!*" She sucked in a savage breath, stepped toward him and smacked his shoulder. She lifted her hand again, gritted her teeth and then smacked his shoulder again, harder, in case the first one hadn't hurt.

Grayson shoved her hands away from himself and stepped back, glaring at her. "Are you done? There is no need to make everyone think you are irrational *and* daft."

"I hope they think that and more!" she boomed, her voice echoing all around them, waving her hands about for a more lunatic effect. "How dare you do this

to me? How dare my father do this to me after I have devoted every breathing moment of my life to him? I was willing to fulfill my duty as a daughter without questioning whatever worth I had left. But to bring Remington back into my life when I have buried him is the last thing I will *ever* submit to. *Ever.* My life is not a game to be played with."

A figure loomed behind her cousin.

She stiffened.

With gloved hands locked behind his back, Remington rounded on them. He eyed her and paused directly beside them, hovering well over not only her head but also Grayson's.

That crisp scent of mint lingered, annoyingly making her even more aware of his presence.

In a low tone, Remington finally announced, "I wish to be removed from consideration. I will not permit the loss of her inheritance due to my involvement."

Victoria drew her brows together and snapped her gaze to her cousin. "The loss of my...inheritance?"

Grayson seethed out a breath. "As always, there you go being a bloody Jack Adams, Remington. I told you, she doesn't know anything. It was supposed to be formally and graciously announced by Mr. Parker."

Remington leaned toward her cousin and growled, "Yes, well, now she knows. Remove me from the goddamn list. I have my pride, too. Let her marry one of the other two and retain the estate that way."

Her heart pounded as her brain pieced together the horrifying reality of Remington's words. Her father was forcing her to decide between a complete stranger whose name she had yet to learn; Lord Moreland, whom she'd always considered more of a brother; and Remington, whom she had known once upon a dream.

She stared at Grayson. "Are you informing me that if I do not marry one of these three men, my father will disinherit me?"

"Yes." Grayson's tone was hard but patient. "I realize this is going to be very difficult for you to accept, but with your father's mental capabilities progressively dwindling, we have decided to accelerate all plans, lest your father be unable to attend your wedding at all. Which is why you only have until midnight tonight to decide which of these three men you will marry."

She gasped. *"What?!"*

"Based upon your decision—" Grayson coolly went on as if they were discussing daisies "—you will then be joined by special license within the week. If you choose not to marry, that is your right. But if your father dies, and you are unwed in the manner as was set by him when he was still of sound mind, the entire estate will pass on to a list of charities. You will have nothing. If poverty is what you desire, I will graciously extend my own home to you."

Victoria closed her eyes and could actually feel her soul shriveling. Though money had never mattered to her, she still needed a bed, clothes and food, and had no intention of living with Grayson like some orphaned child he had to take pity upon.

She opened her eyes and asked in an overly calm tone that rang strange in her ears, "Has my father not arranged even the smallest of annuities for me?"

Grayson breathed out through his nostrils. "No. Nothing. There is no negotiating what has been set, considering his mental state. The solicitor will not allow it. Which means you receive all or nothing. You will be expected to marry one of the three or lose everything."

She swallowed. In some way, she deserved this. She deserved this for rising against her born duty as a daughter. Her father had pleaded with her throughout the years, again and again, that she accept an offer for her hand. Any offer. She, in turn, had denied him, wishing to only stay at his side, all because she knew no one would ever measure up to Remington. So now, her father was laying out the final command with his last challenge of, "You want Remington? You can have him. Secrets, lies and all."

It was obvious what needed to be done. She needed to rise to the challenge of her duty like the grown woman she was, and take the inheritance that was rightfully hers. But that didn't mean marrying Remington. "Out of respect for my father and my duty, I will abide by whatever rules have been set and will choose a husband knowing I will be disinherited if I do not. Lord Remington may choose to stay or leave. It matters not to me."

Annoyed with her evening shawl, which kept sliding from her shoulders, she removed it and whipped it toward Grayson.

Grayson fumbled to catch it. "Assure me you don't intend on removing anything else."

She rolled her eyes. "Once a libertine, always a libertine, I suppose. Even toward his own cousin. Let us be done with this. I am not waiting until midnight to collect what is rightfully mine." She smoothed her hair away from her face with a gloved hand, set her chin and swept past everyone, hoping to demonstrate that despite the situation, she was still very much in control of what was and wasn't going to happen.

Upon entering the vast adjoining room, she slowed and eyed Mr. Parker and the other two men, who stood on the far side of the room.

The more dashing of the two had kind, soulful dark eyes, chestnut hair and defined cheekbones—Lord Moreland. She had never realized he wanted to marry at all. He rarely associated with people and led a very quiet life.

The other man, whom she did not know at all, had sharp, blue eyes and blond hair that was almost shockingly white. His pale features were a bit too regal and eerily reminded her of a porcelain doll. She had never liked dolls, even as a girl. She had always stuffed them into trunks because she hated the way they looked at her. Especially at night.

Victoria knew by the tension in their stances that they were both nervous. Which she could readily understand. It was every man's aspiration to marry into a fortune of a hundred thousand pounds. Her father, in fact, had acquired his fortune by marrying her mother.

But what was Remington's reasoning in all this? Why would he reappear after five years of silence and openly vie for her hand? Was it money he sought? Money he still did not have? Or was it *her* he sought?

Whichever it was, it didn't matter anymore. She would rather marry Lord Moreland, a longstanding, honorable family friend, than attach herself to a man she would never trust and certainly never love again.

SCANDAL SEVEN

'Tis best to avoid any man with a tainted past. For such men carry tainted hearts not meant to last.
How To Avoid a Scandal, Author Unknown

JONATHAN'S PULSE thundered as he beheld the stunning and alluring curve of Victoria's body as she whisked away, her verdant evening gown accentuating her poised, self-assured movements. All of those soft, blond curls that were gathered and pinned atop her head swayed, each sway exposing the erotic pale length of her neck beneath. By God, she had grown so beautifully into that body. She had also grown into full womanly pride.

"Romeo," Grayson drawled, leaning in from behind, "Your Juliet is waiting to be serenaded."

Still watching the sway of Victoria's corseted hips as she moved farther into the room before him, Jonathan reached out and slid her shawl from Grayson's shoulder, bringing the silk up to his nose and mouth. The soft scent of soap and lavender caused his grip on the silk to tighten as he momentarily pressed its softness against his lips. She still smelled the same.

It was achingly bittersweet to vividly remember so much about her, and to physically want her all the more because of it.

Even the lavender scent that clung to her shawl was enough to make his body stir. Though his pride told him to walk away from this and her, considering all that she'd just said, his body, mind and heart chanted for him to fight. This was his Victoria, for God's sake. Of course she wasn't going to submit easily. She had never been one for submitting easily to anything. He owed it to her to fight for them. To fight for what they'd once had. Damn whatever was left of his pride.

He folded and refolded the long strip of silk and tucked it into his coat pocket to keep as a memento. He strode into the room after her, and after several long strides, settled in beside her. He slowed when they both reached Mr. Parker and the other suitors.

Victoria rounded him, setting a notable distance between them, and set her chin. Other than the rigid squaring of those slim shoulders and the setting of that stubborn chin, she didn't even look at him, let alone acknowledge him.

Mr. Parker cleared his throat and held up a gloved hand. "On behalf of Lord Linford, I extend appreciation for your attendance, gentlemen. I ask that you all arrange yourselves side by side, so that

I may commence the evening with a simple set of instructions."

Jonathan stepped toward the other two men and settled himself between them. He paused, glancing toward each man, and realized that both were notably shorter than he was. A whole head shorter.

Mr. Parker settled before them and held up three sealed parchments in his gloved hand. He wagged them. "Each parchment bears a name and contains questions the earl felt would best represent each suitor. They are questions Lady Victoria will read aloud and questions you, as gentlemen, will individually answer during a private, one-hour session. We all recognize that these are very unusual circumstances. But we must also recognize this is a man's last will and testament, and, as such, we are humbly appointed to abide by what was set almost a year ago."

As Jonathan half listened to Mr. Parker's words, he stared intently at Victoria, hoping she would look at him at least once. She didn't. She merely lingered between Sir Thorbert and Grayson, her eyes fixed somewhere in the distance. She hated him. She really—

Her jade eyes suddenly met his, causing his stomach to flip. The last time he'd felt his stomach flip in response to a mere glance, he'd been nineteen. He never thought he'd feel that again.

He smiled.

Victoria looked away and reset her chin.

Jonathan's smile faded as he flexed his gloved hands and continued to study her profile. Her face had thinned, but that seventeen-year-old was still there in those arched blond brows, that sharp little nose and the pale, soft skin his hand had once intimately grazed.

The visible tops of her pale breasts appeared fuller than he'd remembered, and she wore her hair in looser, larger curls, as opposed to the tighter ones that had once framed her face. It was torture to be standing only a few paces away and realize he had lost five years of his life with her.

"Allow me to present your designated set of questions." Mr. Parker stepped toward them and handed out the parchments. "Each seal remains intact until your appointed hour with Lady Emerson."

Jonathan slipped the parchment from Mr. Parker's gloved hand and turned it over to reveal *TO THE RIGHT HONOURABLE VISCOUNT REMINGTON* scribed in black ink.

Mr. Parker briefly met each of their gazes. "Lord Stanford, Lord Remington and Lord Moreland, at midnight, Lady Emerson will tell me the name of the man she intends to wed, which I will formally submit and announce. That man must then wed her by special license within the week. For those men not chosen, a thousand pounds will be gifted in appreciation of their participation. Now that you have all been informed of the earl's intent, is everyone still willing to vie? Rest assured, your name can be removed from the list at any time."

Jonathan fingered the parchment in his hand, wondering if he was doing the right thing. Though it appeared Victoria did not want him and would prefer to marry her own uncle over him, he'd be damned if he was going to allow misfortune to continue to rule his life. He was going to prove his worth to her. He was.

Lord Stanford stepped forward and ripped his parchment in half. He tossed it to the floor with a sigh. "Forgive me, but I am not in the least bit comfortable with these rules. As such, I prefer to leave. May God bring peace to the earl." He offered everyone a curt nod and strode past, his heavy steps thudding out of the room and fading.

Jonathan drew in a breath and let it out, tucking the parchment into his pocket alongside Victoria's folded shawl. This was good. This was *very* good. With only one man left to compete against, he actually stood half of a chance.

Although…

Jonathan eyed the regal profile of the gentleman on his left. Lord Moreland. Christ. It was the same damn Lord Moreland whom Victoria's governess had tried to intimidate him with years ago. All of this was really too eerie, and a bit too metaphorical to swallow. It was as if his entire life was rounding backward.

Mr. Parker huffed out a ragged breath and rubbed the back of his bald head, eyeing the torn parchment left behind. Dropping his gloved hand back to his side, he continued, "Judging by your silence, gentlemen, you are agreeing to vie. I will be allotting an additional thirty minutes to each of you, seeing as Lord Stanford has renounced his involvement.

"Let us formally commence by deciding who will be first." He drew his bushy brows together, dug into his pocket and withdrew a coin. He held it up. "Lord Remington. Which will it be? The laureate head of the sixpence? Or the shield and crown?"

Jonathan eyed the coin. He didn't know if he could wait another hour and half to be alone with Victoria. He'd already been forced to spend well over eighty-seven thousand hours apart from her. Hours he had pathetically counted out throughout the years like a child who sought to count all the stars in the sky.

When he was younger, he'd always picked the shield of a sixpence and had always won his luck that way. So, in honor of his younger self, the man he used to be, he would pick the shield. "I request the shield and crown."

Mr. Parker nodded. "The shield and crown it is. Lord Moreland, you have been designated the laureate. Let chance decide." Mr. Parker hesitated, then tossed the coin up and toward them.

Jonathan watched the coin as it rolled past him, tilted and settled flat onto the floor. As small as it was, he couldn't make it out. He stepped toward it, leaned forward and drew in a breath. It was the shield and crown.

He glanced up, his eyes darting over to Victoria. "'Tis the shield and crown."

Victoria pinched her lips together, her gloved hand grabbing hold of her uncle's upper arm. Sir Thorbert leaned toward her, patting her hand.

It was obvious Victoria was nervous about being alone with him. As well she should be. There wasn't going to be a single word left unsaid.

Mr. Parker hurried over, leaned toward the coin and plucked it up, holding it for all to see. "It is indeed the shield and crown. Lady Victoria? Lord Remington? Please follow me into the Painted Room."

Jonathan cleared his throat and followed Mr. Parker, trying to regain control over the erratic beat of his heart. Victoria dutifully trailed behind. Jonathan slowed his steps and momentarily considered turning and extending his arm to her, but squelched the thought. He doubted she'd accept it.

As he followed Mr. Parker down the corridor, his head pounded, and he felt as if his journey would never end. Every now and then, he glanced back at Victoria to ensure she was following. She was always a few steps behind, her gaze firmly fixed on his boots.

He couldn't help but wonder what she was thinking. He doubted that she was admiring the shine and worth of his leather footwear.

Mr. Parker paused before an oak door at the end of the passageway. When Jonathan and Victoria both quietly settled before him, Mr. Parker spoke. "No physical contact. Is that understood?"

As if he would abide by some stupid rule that would prevent him from touching his Victoria. Only she could keep him from doing that. Fortunately, he wasn't being forced to promise anything. He was simply being asked if he understood the request. "Yes. I completely understand."

Mr. Parker offered a curt nod. "All questions must be answered. Whatever time remains afterwards may be used as you see fit. Lord Remington, do you have your sealed parchment?"

Jonathan patted his pocket. "I do."

"Present it to Lady Emerson the moment the door closes." Mr. Parker yanked the door open, drew his shaggy brows together and slid his gold chain from his pocket, withdrawing a watch. He glanced at it. "I will return at exactly fifteen minutes past the hour of nine. There is a clock on the mantel should you need to be reminded of the time." Mr. Parker sniffed, returned his watch to his pocket and gestured toward the open door.

Jonathan eased back, sweeping a gloved hand toward the dimly lit room beyond, and eyed Victoria expectantly.

A pink flush overtook her pale cheeks. She hesitated, as if sensing that more than her virtue was at risk, but breezed into the room all the same, her full skirts rustling.

Jonathan offered a curt nod to Mr. Parker, adjusted his evening coat and strode in after Victoria, yet again admiring the sway of those corseted hips and her admirable backside.

A soft thud echoed, announcing that the door was closed.

Jonathan paused, his brows coming together, as the pungent aroma of freshly cut roses pierced his nostrils. He tensed as he skimmed past Victoria's silhouette, standing before the burning hearth, and glanced toward his dim surroundings, half expecting the *marchesa* to be waiting in the shadows along with her husband.

All Jonathan could make out, however, was a small empty room, whose paneled walls had been intricately painted from floor to ceiling with tranquil scenes of grassy hills, skies and valleys. Hence the appropriate name.

A lone silver candelabrum lit the entire room with

twelve candles. Jonathan eyed the unusual amount of yellow and white roses set in countless porcelain vases placed strategically on every table in the room. It reminded him of all the roses the *marchesa* had always had him arrange throughout her home. He had come to hate roses.

Victoria turned away from the marble hearth. She seated herself on the embroidered, pale blue sofa set directly before it and arranged her skirts.

Jonathan rounded the room and paused before her, trying not to notice the exposed curve of her beautiful neck, extending down to the tops of full, round breasts that were emphasized not only by her corset beneath, but also by the white stitched ribbon edging her décolletage. He'd never believed, not even after the earl had contacted him to announce he could vie for Victoria, that he'd actually see her again.

She continued to stare aloofly past where he stood, gazing toward the coals in the hearth, setting her small gloved hands primly onto the lap of her gown.

He knew he deserved her disdain, but he did not think he deserved to be treated as if they had never met. Jonathan stripped his evening gloves from his hands and tossed them at her feet, announcing to her that all pretenses were gone.

He lowered himself onto the cushioned sofa beside her, purposefully ensuring that the side of his hip and trouser-clad thigh grazed against her.

She stiffened and drew in a breath.

Jonathan draped his left arm around the back of the sofa and leaned toward her, his body trapping hers against the corner. His gaze drifted to the curved expanse of her pale throat. Though he wanted to submit to the yearning that burned within him by touching the curve of that throat with the tip of his bare finger, he had no intention of rushing their involvement, despite his desperate need to erase the years they had spent apart.

He dipped his head and leaned in toward her. The soft scent of soap and lavender clung to her heated skin.

He resisted fingering her blond curls, which looked so soft. "Though you may not believe me, I think about you as often as I breathe."

She hesitated, then turned her face toward him, her full lips only a tantalizing breath away. Her green eyes solemnly searched his face. "Ever the romantic sop, aren't you?"

His jaw tightened, along with his grip on the rounded wooden edge of the sofa behind her. "I had nothing. Your life would have been miserable."

"My life certainly didn't turn out any better without you. If you haven't already heard, my father has less than a year to live. I don't need any more grief in my life." She looked away and leaned toward the arm of the sofa, away from him. "Please do not sit so needlessly close."

If only she could understand everything he'd been through since she'd last seen him, and how much this moment meant to him. "I will not touch you. But I will not move, either. I've waited years. I need to be near you."

She lowered her gaze and watched her own gloved finger as it trailed back and forth along the carved wooden arm of the sofa.

He ached as he watched her hand, wishing that hand would touch him instead. "Victoria. There were so many times I wanted to write. So many."

She glanced toward him tartly. "So why didn't you?"

"I couldn't."

"That doesn't answer my question."

"I know. But I promise over this next hour—"

"Did you even bother to read any of the letters I sent? Any of them? At all?"

He swallowed and lowered his gaze. "No. I…didn't live at the address you were sending all of your letters to. But my stepsister was there to receive them all. Despite my request that she burn your letters upon arrival, Cornelia defied me and pocketed all fifty-three. My stepmother informed me of it a little over a year ago. When I confronted her and demanded she relinquish them, she refused, stating unless I answered them, they were hers, not mine. Though I wanted to read them, I knew what awaited me in those letters. Your hate. Your anger. I still haven't been able to force myself to read them. In the end, I never wrote, Victoria, not because I didn't want to, but because it was best for your safety."

She jerked toward him, her knee bumping his thigh. "For my safety?" Her blond brows came together. "Whatever do you mean?"

Damn his own infernal tongue. He was saying far too much, far too soon. There was so much to explain to her. Too much. Jonathan slid his arm from around her and shifted away from her, struggling not to think about the life he'd been forced to lead all these years. A life he'd been unable to crawl out of due to his own stupidity.

He eventually confessed in a quiet, apologetic tone, "I was a *cicisbeo,* Victoria. And the husband whose wife I served was a bastard. I didn't want him or anyone else knowing anything about you, lest you or your reputation be harmed as a result of our connection."

Victoria stared at him for an abashed moment, then glanced away, back toward the hearth. She drew away, leaning toward the arm of the sofa. "So you were a paid lover to another man's wife?"

"Yes."

"You slept with a married woman—after all your talk about the sanctity of love?"

"There is far more to my story than you think."

She rolled her eyes and held out her hand. "Now that we have a complete understanding of one another, might I have the sealed parchment that was provided to you?"

"No. I am not done speaking."

She continued to coolly hold out her hand. "Lest you forget, there are rules we must abide by and I will not permit my inheritance to be put at risk. Now give me the parchment. Or I will leave this room. Don't think I won't."

Damn her and this entire situation. He yanked out the parchment from his coat pocket and paused when her shawl cascaded out and unraveled onto the cushioned space between them.

She eyed her shawl. Then him. "A thief, too, I see."

He snatched it up and dangled it before her. "Frankly, dearest, I was hoping for a silk stocking."

She snatched it out of his hand, draped it around her neck and set her shoulders. "I'll have one of my servants deliver it for you on the morrow. I most certainly cannot have you being displeased. Not after all that you have done for me."

He lowered his gaze. "You really despise me."

She sighed. "No. But I don't like you, either."

"It is all the same to me." He leaned toward her, closing the space he'd earlier created, and held out the sealed parchment, hoping to God that this indifferent and bitter façade of hers wasn't real. He prayed it was a mask of pride she had placed over the endearing woman he once knew and loved.

She snatched the parchment from his hand. Cracking the red wax seal, she unfolded the paper. She scanned what was written, reading through it line by line, and paused. Her eyes widened as she fumbled to fold the parchment back together. She seemed unable to.

Jonathan reached out and stilled her gloved hands against his own. Tightening his bare hand against her small gloved ones, he slid closer, setting his thigh and hip against her, bundling her gown. He tried to cast aside the intimacy of his touch. God, how he tried. "What does it say?"

She shook her head.

Keeping one hand firmly against hers, he used his other hand to slip out the parchment. As he tried to tug it away, her fingers tightened. "Victoria. It is important we abide by the rules. Now, what does it say?"

She squeezed her eyes shut tighter and allowed her fingers to loosen. "After you read it, burn it."

Burn it? He slid the parchment loose and quickly unfolded it. It read:

My dear Victoria,
I know this comes many a year too late, and
that I have not been as understanding during
the times that you needed me to be, but I ask
you to set aside the past, look toward the future,
and be happy in the way your mother and I once
were. You will need someone to look after you
once I am gone, and according to Grayson,
Lord Remington can do that and more.
Your Papa, always

No questions. Not a single one. Only a simple, heartfelt wish for their happiness, along with the firm belief that he could deliver that and more to Victoria. Jonathan swallowed, feeling his heart and head pounding in unison. It wasn't by any means relevant if Victoria thought the words deserved to be burned.

Jonathan shifted against the cushion of the sofa and willed himself to remain indifferent and calm, even though he wanted to grab her and shake her and demand she give him an opportunity to redeem himself.

He gestured toward the parchment. "Do you really want me to burn this?"

She stared at the hearth. "Yes. It means nothing."

Jonathan nodded and watched his own hands fold the parchment. It was nothing more than words on paper. It did not mean it would end things between them the moment he burned it. Even though for some reason he felt like he was about to burn everything they had ever shared.

He rose and with a flick of his wrist tossed the letter onto the burning coals. He blankly watched the parchment as it blackened and curled. The red wax of the seal bubbled and hissed in protest as it dribbled and disappeared into the coals.

He turned to Victoria, who'd been watching the parchment burn along with him, and announced, "I still love you. Nothing will ever change that. Not even your wicked disdain."

She pinched her lips together, tears glistening in her eyes. She glanced up at him, her features twisting. "Do not speak to me of love. Love could never be so cruel."

"I never meant to be cruel. I swear it. I swear it upon everything I am and ever was and ever wish to be." He kneeled before her, her skirts pushing against his chest and gathered her gloved hands, promising himself he would keep his touch brief. He paused as his bare skin grazed something. Something he hadn't noticed before.

He glanced down, and fingered her gloved left hand, just above her knuckle. She was wearing a ring.

His ring? He glanced up at her in astonishment,

his breath almost jagged. "Are you still wearing my ring?"

She dragged her hands from his. "Don't be ridiculous. I tossed it the moment you ceased writing."

He narrowed his gaze at the thought that she would maliciously toss the only thing he had left of his mother. "Why would you do that? Knowing what it meant to me? Knowing it belonged to my mother?"

"I suppose anger can make one cruel."

"Obviously. So what ring do you now wear in its stead? Remove your glove. I wish to see your hand and, in turn, your vanity."

She cupped her gloved hands together against her chest, burying her left hand beneath the right. "You have no need to see my hand."

"I say I do. Show me your hand."

"Last I knew it was my hand, not yours."

"What are you hiding?"

"I am not hiding anything."

"Good. Then you will not mind if I impose." Jonathan grabbed her left hand, jerking it away from her chest and held her wrist fiercely between them, so she wouldn't be able to wrench it away.

Victoria gasped and struggled against him, her other hand pushing and punching at his shoulder. "Don't touch me! How dare you—" She hit his shoulder.

Despite the repeated blows against his arm and

shoulder, he dug his fingertips into the wrist of her satin glove. In one swift motion, he forcefully stripped it from her hand, flinging it aside.

Victoria stilled. Her eyes widened as her exposed, pale hand dangled between both of their faces, revealing a glinting ruby-and-gold ring on her fourth finger.

Jonathan's breath hitched. His mother's ring. The one he had asked her to keep on her finger in memory of their love. He had hoped. He had prayed. But he never truly thought—

"Victoria," he breathed, his chest tightening.

He savagely brought her hand to his mouth and buried his lips and nose against her soft skin, refusing to let go for fear that this moment would disappear. A moment that achingly whispered to him that not all had been lost between them after all, and that she was merely tormenting him in the name of her own pride.

"Release my hand," she choked out, wiggling her hand against his hold.

Jonathan's grip tightened. "No. I will not."

He turned her palm upward and gently trailed his lips across the soft, curved surface, then trailed them toward her wrist until they met the ruffled sleeve of her gown.

He lifted his eyes to hers. "You have honored me all these years. I am without words."

She tried yanking her hand from his grasp again. "I always thought it was pretty. The fact that I wear it means nothing."

Jonathan gritted his teeth at her resistance, leaning against her legs and in turn trapping her against the sofa with his body. "Look at me and tell me you feel nothing. Tell me you do not even feel the merest whisper of what we once shared, and I will gladly walk out of this room and out of your life. Do it. Say it. Save us both the misery of living with memories that apparently no longer mean anything."

Her full lips parted. Yet not a single word tumbled forth. She simply stared at him, her breath coming in uneven, visible gasps. The rapid rise and fall of her chest brought his attention to the full breasts displayed by her gown.

Jonathan trailed a bare finger toward her other hand, the one set on her lap that remained gloved. He slowly stripped that white satin evening glove from her wrist, palm and fingers, receiving no resistance. He tossed it beyond the sofa and rubbed her pale, soft hands, watching his large fingers rubbing against her much smaller ones. He could feel himself physically and emotionally coming alive again. It was amazing.

"It is so strange to be touching you again," he murmured, still watching the movement of his fingers against hers. "You are the same, and yet in many ways you are not."

He lifted her right hand to his lips and, unable to refrain, slid the tip of his tongue across her skin, savoring every inch of its salty sweetness.

Her hand trembled. "Remington. Please."

He withdrew his tongue. "I do not wish to hear meaningless words brought on by pride. Victoria. We are being given an incredible opportunity to return to what we once shared. Do we take it? Or do we abandon it once and for all?"

She shook her head. "Cease. Cease this. My mind is too muddled to—"

"Shh. Give yourself time. Simply know that I do not need time. I still want this. I still want you. That has never changed." He released her hand. Unable to resist, he slid his bare hands up the length of her thighs, hidden beneath the fullness of her gown. Incredible thighs that were firm beneath his palms.

His muscles tightened. "You have grown into your curves beautifully. Do you know that?"

She drew in a shaky breath, but otherwise did not resist the movement of his hands against her gown and thighs. "You are making it difficult for me to even think."

"I do not want you to think. Thoughts are not always reliable once tainted by pride and prejudice." His hands veered toward Victoria's corseted waist and rounded in, pausing just beneath the curve of her breasts hidden within her bodice. Jonathan swallowed tightly, refraining from touching them, and fingered the silk of her bodice instead. "Tell me what it is you feel instead. The truth. For that is all I wish to know."

She closed her eyes, her chest rising and falling in uneven takes that matched his own. "I feel as though I have lost the last of my mind by allowing you this much freedom."

He leaned in closer. "So why are you letting me touch you? Why are you not pushing me away? Is it because you still want this? Is it because you still want me?"

Her eyes fluttered open and met his gaze, confusion illuminating them.

To have her this close after all these years was maddening. And despite her obvious confusion, he'd be a fool not to live in this moment. He could feel himself growing unbearably hard, but forced himself to suck in a harsh breath in order to maintain control. He gently placed his hands on her hips and leaned toward her, eyeing the fullness of her moist lips. Those beautiful, soft lips that he'd dreamed about since he was nineteen. "Kiss me."

"Remington." Victoria grabbed his shoulders, her fingertips savagely digging into his evening coat. Though she did not push him away, she did not allow him to lean any closer, either. She continued to rigidly hold him in place, her arms visibly trembling. "No. Enough. I cannot submit to this. I intend to marry someone else. Anyone else. Anyone but you."

"You do not mean it."

"Yes. I do."

"No. You cannot." He pushed away her arms and savagely reached up and held her face in both hands, forcing her to look at him. Those beautiful jade eyes he'd thought he'd never see again met his. He focused on nothing else but those hauntingly sad eyes, and tried to keep himself from claiming her mouth and her body, whether he had the right to or not.

It wasn't mere lust and desire that raged within him and demanded he do so. No. It was the last of his soul, that wanted to be saved. A soul that desperately needed to erase all memories of the *marchesa* from his skin, from his body and from his mind. He wanted to replace all of it with what he had always needed. His Victoria.

"Tell me you want to return to what we once had," he demanded, his thumbs repeatedly tracing the soft curve behind her ears as he continued to fiercely cup her face against his hands. "Tell me, *bella*. I need to hear it."

Her eyes widened as her breath came in more frantic takes. "Whether or not you choose to accept it, I am changed. I have moved on. And so should you. We cannot return to what we once had."

Jonathan released her and leaned back, his arms dropping heavily to his sides. She was going to let this opportunity drift by without even giving them a chance. And here he thought *his* soul was going to cast shadows. Hers appeared to drift in a fog.

He stumbled to his feet, away from the sofa. Adjusting his evening coat to hide his arousal, he strode toward the other side of the darkened room, trying to put as much distance between them as possible.

The clock on the mantel chimed. Fifteen minutes were all that remained. What could he possibly say in fifteen minutes that would enable her to understand that although he was not the same man, he had kept a sliver of the old Jonathan meant for her and her alone?

Common sense and his own goddamn pride demanded he leave her and London and return to Venice to what little family he had left, but how could he abandon the only true sweetness he'd ever known in his life? Her. Them. Happiness could have been theirs had he not been so irresponsible. He had to fight for her. He had to.

He strode back toward her and rounded the sofa. He swept up his gloves, which still lay at her slippered feet and pulled each one on, adjusting his fingers against the leather. "I want you to know everything.

Where I went. What I did. Who I associated with all these years and why. All I ask is that you try to forgive me for what I submitted to. For that, I am not proud. But everything I did, I did for Cornelia and my stepmother. And that I hope you can respect."

She blinked rapidly, fighting tears, and rose to her feet, shaking her head. Bringing her hands together, she frantically fumbled with them. After a few solid tugs, she removed the ruby ring from her finger and held it out. "I have suffered enough at your hands and wish to suffer no more. Please. Take it. We are done."

He drew in a ragged breath and let it out, willing himself to remain calm. Willing himself not be angry with her. "You wound me, *bella*."

"I do not mean to wound you."

"And yet you do. Why? Why do you refuse to listen to the words I have to say? It is because you fear that in the end, you will submit to me and wound that stupid pride?"

"No. If you haven't noticed, Remington, I have grown into a woman. A woman who has no need to reattach herself to a past created by her own naïve understanding of relationships. Which is why I intend to give my hand to Lord Moreland, not you. I have known him since the age of ten and can trust him in a way I cannot trust you. I think it best for everyone. I really do."

And he thought letting her go the first time had been suicide against his soul. This was far worse. For at least then, he hadn't lost her to another man. He stepped back, fisting his hands. "It may be best for you, but it is not best for me."

She lowered her hand with the ring and turned away. "Suffering has a way of sharpening one's understanding of the real world."

"It also has a way of sharpening your tongue."

She glared at him. "I have suffered far too much in your absence to stand here and listen to this."

He shifted his jaw. "Have you considered that perhaps you are not alone in your suffering? Do you have any idea what I have been through since you last saw me? *Any?* Neither you nor I are the same, but that doesn't mean—"

A loud knock and the creaking of hinges caused them both to swing around.

Mr. Parker stepped into the doorway. "Lady Victoria. Lord Moreland will be joining you shortly. Lord Remington? Your time is done." Mr. Parker swept his hand out toward the corridor.

Jonathan swung toward Victoria one last time and stared her down. "Though I have yet to redeem myself in countless ways, and I am more than prepared to crawl for you and set aside my pride, I cannot mend what has come to pass if you do not give me the opportunity to mend it. We can be happy if you wish it.

But only if you wish it." He offered her a curt bow,
formally announcing that he was done speaking, then
left the room, dreading the stroke of midnight and the
news it would bring.

SCANDAL EIGHT

A lady must always uphold the promises she makes.
Which is why it is imperative she never make the
wrong sort of promises.
How To Avoid a Scandal, Author Unknown

WHEN REMINGTON had disappeared out into the corridor along with Mr. Parker, Victoria drifted back toward the sofa and sat, feeling as though she had no pulse and no breath left. She stared at the burning coals before her, mindlessly fingering Remington's ring.

Despite everything, she had managed to remain true to herself. She had managed to remind herself that emotional attachments always brought pain and loss. Always. She'd known that since she was thirteen.

Victoria fingered the ring one last time, then raised the ruby stone to her lips and whispered, "Release us of each other. Tonight." She tucked the ring into a small pocket on her bodice. Even though the stupid ring never did anything she asked, she had fallen into the embarrassing custom of still asking it for things.

In many ways, it had been her only friend. Always there.

Steps approached, announcing another game was about to begin. She drew in a breath and let it out.

Mr. Parker gestured for Lord Moreland to enter. Moreland nodded to Mr. Parker amiably and stepped into the room. The door closed.

Moreland's dark eyes captured hers.

Despite his chiseled, handsome face, there was no flutter in her stomach to be had. Not that she wanted there to be any fluttering. She was done complicating her life with fluttering. As she'd learned, it only led to a pathetic form of misery. She wanted simple and reliable. And Lord Moreland was simple and reliable. She had known that since she was ten.

Moreland adjusted his evening coat around his solid frame and made his way across the room, his booted steps and the movement of his long legs smooth and refined. He paused before her, withdrew the sealed parchment from within his inner coat pocket and presented it with a gloved hand.

She slipped the parchment from his fingers and brought it onto her lap. "Thank you."

He gestured toward the space beside her. "Might I?"

"Of course." She smiled. "I certainly wouldn't ask you to stand for the next hour and a half."

"I appreciate that." He smirked and seated himself

on the other end of the sofa, as far from her as possible, against the carved wooden arm.

She blinked, wondering why he was putting almost a rude amount of distance between them. It wasn't as if they didn't know each other. They had spoken repeatedly on the many occasions he had visited her father over the years.

He awkwardly smoothed his gloved hand against the side of his chestnut hair, as if he was rehearsing something in his head. He paused and glanced toward her, shifting against the cushion. "I should probably admit that I had no idea what I was getting involved with when your cousin arrived at my door."

She sighed. "I can only apologize."

"I wouldn't be here if I didn't think you were of any worth, Victoria."

"Let us hope that is a compliment."

"It is."

"Thank you." She cracked the seal on the parchment. "I never realized you held any interest in matrimony. You've always led a quiet, solitary life, haven't you?" She lifted a brow. "Might I ask why you are vying for my hand? Or am I being too forward?"

He leaned toward her. "You were always overly forward in nature, Victoria. Which, I will admit, I have always found charming. Why am I vying for you? Let us say I am challenging myself to step outside my usual way of life." He cleared his throat and gestured toward the parchment in her hand. "Shall we proceed?"

"Yes." Victoria unfolded the parchment, revealing twenty questions written in black ink, all of them in her father's slanted, sloppy hand. The effort her father had put into this was astonishing. Especially considering he didn't even know who she was anymore.

She missed her father, gruff though he had been at times. She missed the way he used to nudge her when he was trying to convince her to agree with him on something he knew she never would. She missed the way he used to say her name whenever he took it into his silly head to taunt her about something. That man was gone now. But at least she could say she'd known him and that he had been her father.

Victoria swallowed, drew her brows together and read the first question. She sighed, forcing herself to say the words. "How many children do you want?"

Moreland's brows rose a fraction, his shaven face actually flushing. He shrugged. "I never considered an actual number. Though I will admit to being drawn to larger families."

"And what is your definition of a large family?"

He shrugged again. "Seven or eight. Ten, at the very most."

Victoria's eyes widened as she bit her tongue to prevent her from saying anything she oughtn't. Heaven forbid her poor body have to endure *that* many pregnancies and *that* many births. Furthermore, to produce *that* many children, she imagined the man would have to be in her bed every night!

She cleared her throat at the thought and quickly moved on to the next question. She blinked down at the words and inwardly cringed, her fingers crinkling the edges of the parchment. Her father appeared intent on making her suffer through this. "Do you believe you are capable of being a good husband?"

"I wouldn't be a horrible husband, that I know. Although I most certainly would pose more than the unusual set of challenges. The real question is, are you capable of being a good wife?" He shifted toward her and sighed. "If you and I were to marry, Victoria, is it your intention to take Lord Remington on as your lover? Or is he already your lover?"

Her cheeks burned, displaying just how mortified she really was. "You have no right to lay such accusations upon me."

"Do not chide me. I see the way he looks at you and the way you look at him. And that earlier escapade of him dashing out into the corridor after you, followed by shouts, was rather revealing."

She cringed.

He caught her gaze. "I've always liked you. Which is why I am still here. You are intelligent and spirited. Which I need. I find most women of the aristocracy retain no sense of character or strength the moment they are subjected to any form of hardship due to their sheltered upbringing. And I confess I will bring you hardship, though not in any form you would ever expect. So what sort of woman are you? Will I be able to trust you in a way I cannot even trust myself? Or will you pull away when I need you most?"

Victoria swallowed and looked away. "You are making me very uncomfortable, Lord Moreland."

"Good. That means you understand what it is I am saying. Let it be known that I refuse to marry a woman who intends to place her affections elsewhere. I don't expect you to love me, but I want my wife to be *my* wife. No one else's. Whatever your involvement with Lord Remington is or was, do you really expect me to be accepting of it? What man would tolerate his own wife already having a history with another man? Hmm?"

Dearest God, it was as if he could see right through her. She sighed and tossed the parchment over the sofa, letting it flutter out of sight. She reached out a hand across the small expanse between them and grabbed his hand, squeezing it tightly, feeling as though she needed to offer him some measure of assurance. "You needn't worry. He and I are no more."

Lord Moreland paused, noting her hand on his, and lifted a brow. "So you do share a history with him?"

Victoria willed herself not to scream. It was as if

Remington had branded his name upon her skin. And it was anything but fair. "Yes."

He patted her hand. "I appreciate your honesty. I am not slighted, I assure you, but it doesn't bode well for us. I confess I am not one to—"

"Please." She tried to keep the panic from her voice at the thought that he was her only choice aside from Remington. "Please assume nothing. Our association was respectable."

Lord Moreland covered her hand with his, his dark eyes searching her face. "Very well. Tell me more so I may be the judge of that."

She tightened her hold on his hand, willing herself to remain calm and convince him to remain so, as well. "You cannot expect me to reveal details regarding my personal affairs."

The clock on the mantel chimed. And kept on chiming until it clicked back into silence.

Lord Moreland blew out a breath. "Time waits for no one. And it most certainly won't wait for you. 'Tis an enormous decision that awaits you come midnight. To choose a husband or lose all? Had I known this is what your father had in mind, I would have never included myself. I do not approve of this."

"I do not approve of it any more than you do. It is what it is. My father has always marched to his own tune."

He shifted toward her and lowered his voice. "We are friends. Are we not?"

She nodded. "Of course. Since youth."

He nodded. "Good. As such, let me offer you this. If you tell me your history with Remington, I will set aside my misgivings and submit to whatever you decide. But if you don't tell me your history, Victoria, I leave. For you cannot expect me to enter a lifetime commitment without knowing what I am committing to. Those are your choices in this and I will not repeat them again."

She lowered her chin in complete disbelief of the ultimatum he was setting. He wanted her to tell him everything? She'd never once disclosed the details of her relationship with Remington to anyone. Not even Grayson.

Then again…what choice had she? Moreland was a good, reliable path through an open field whose horizon she could see. Even if that horizon was a tad crooked. While Remington? He was a cliff with jagged rocks and a raging ocean at the bottom. Moreland she could survive. Remington? Not so much.

Victoria tightened her hold on his hand, trying to draw strength from it. "If you swear never to discuss my history with anyone, I will disclose everything."

"Agreed." He leaned toward her and poked at her hand, which tightly held his. "Might I request you release my hand? In case Remington interrupts this conversation?"

She feigned a less than enthused laugh and slowly retrieved her hand, drawing it back onto her lap. "I wouldn't worry about Remington."

"Have you seen the size of his hands?"

She glared at him. She didn't remember the man being this annoying.

He shifted, propping an elbow against the carved wooden edge of the sofa behind him. "It is an unprecedented honor. Proceed."

She drew in a shaky breath. "The connection between Remington and myself was instantaneous. When it came to our words and glances, we were like children forever passing a ball back and forth with an amused, playful need to never let the ball fall. Needless to say, we grew very fond of each other, and the day he was leaving England, he asked me to marry him. Though I did not entirely submit, I eventually did during our time of correspondence."

Lord Moreland let out a whistle. "And therein was your first mistake. Never put anything in writing. Much can and will go wrong."

She sighed. "In that, Remington cannot be faulted. He never used my words against me. In fact, toward the end, he didn't make use of my words at all. I lived for his letters. I truly did. They made me happy, gave me hope, and made me believe I was meant for the sort of relationship my parents shared. Then his finances disintegrated—or so he said—and in my desperation, I told my father everything, hoping he would allow us to marry and in turn mend Remington's finances that way. My father threatened to disinherit me. Not that I cared. I would have done without everything for Remington. Only…Remington disappeared without bothering to offer me any words."

She dropped her hand onto her lap. "And now, after five long years, he reappears and expects me to return to what we once shared." She snorted. "Pardon me while I refrain from gagging."

Lord Moreland's brows came together. "Every man deserves a second chance."

"This isn't about second chances."

He rolled his eyes. "Balderdash. Life is all about second chances. Who ever gets it right the first time? Or the second or third time, for that matter?"

She brought her hands together, clasping them. "In that, I will agree. No one ever gets life right, and no one knows that more than I. But there are times when a wrong simply cannot be righted. And this is one of those times. What little remained of the person he knew, he crushed. He filled an entire fountain full of his affection and promises that I grew dependent upon. Something I had vowed never to do, after I saw the way it destroyed my father. And when I truly did thirst, and I needed peace, he refused to even offer me a single drop. Which is why I…" She shook her head, unable to finish. She had never put so much into words. And it hurt. It hurt hearing them and knowing it had all once been real. Though no more.

Moreland sighed, slid closer and wrapped a muscled arm around her, pulling her toward him with a firm tenderness that didn't make her feel in the least bit awkward. She allowed herself to be nestled against his warmth. The musky scent of cardamom drifted toward her from his clothes, further lulling her and making her feel less restless. He smoothed her hair with a gloved hand, the way a father would, and finally murmured, "Marry him."

She stiffened and refrained from grabbing hold of his evening coat. "*Marry him?* Did you not—"

"Victoria." Moreland released her and caught hold of her shoulders, squaring them firmly toward himself. "'Tis obvious he is still in great amours with you, and there is something to be valued in a flame that cannot be extinguished. If he is here, it is only because he is unable to move on with his life and will only suffer unless you forgive him and grant him peace. And I can tell you feel the same, though you may not realize it. Allow him to right his wrongs. Every man deserves another chance."

Her eyes widened. "This has nothing to do with my inability to give him another chance. This has to do with my inability to become the woman I know he wants. The woman he has always wanted, but one I was never fully capable of being. Though I had once tried to be that woman for him, I only suffered for it, and will not suffer through it again. Remington is not like you or any other man. He never settled for less than the moon and the stars and always lived and breathed through his own emotions like a child unable to control what it is he feels and thinks."

"Knowing what divides you is what will bring you together." Moreland rubbed her arms affectionately. "It is with regret, I must withdraw my name."

Her breath caught. "No. No, you can't. Moreland. If you withdraw—"

"*Yes*. Exactly." He released her and rose, his lean face tightening. "If you had allowed yourself to love him once, Victoria, you can allow yourself to love him again. Despite what you think."

Victoria threw up her hands and let them drop in exasperation, wondering why she ever told him anything at all! It was as if he had purposefully asked for her entire history so he could better use it against her.

He crossed his arms over his chest. "You will love him as you once had. You will see."

The scoundrel! Who was he to play God with her heart?

Victoria rose to her feet, leaned in and poked him in that solid chest of his, right below his cravat and between the buttons on his waistcoat, above his crossed arms. "You seek to subject me to misery."

"Misery brings forth enlightenment."

She glared at him. "Since when did you become a philosopher?"

He tsked. "Grow up, Victoria. Life isn't about always getting what you want. And if you ever thought otherwise, you are not living in reality."

She swallowed and stepped back. It stung to hear those words. It really did. Because he was right. She had never been one to get what she wanted. And that was indeed life. That was indeed reality. "You owe me an apology."

Moreland dropped his folded arms to his sides and drawled with faint amusement, "I owe you nothing."

"Oh, yes, you do. You promised that if I disclosed my history with Remington, you would set aside your misgivings and allow *me* to decide how I should proceed. Only now you are walking away!"

"I know when to walk and when to stay." He leaned in and dabbed at her nose. "And you, my dear, need to learn the art of staying, for you have already perfected the art of walking away. Good night." He casually rounded her and strode toward the door.

She honestly didn't know whether she was to be impressed by his unprecedented understanding of her as a person or whether she should start screaming in overwhelmed paranoia at the fact that she was being thrust back into Remington's arms.

Pulling open the door, Moreland paused and swung back toward her. As if sensing her confusion and misery, he sighed and strode back, pausing directly before her. "Victoria."

She glanced up to meet his dark gaze.

He softened his voice. "You will thank me in time."

"Not in this lifetime," she grouched. "May you come back a woman, Moreland, and may you be subjected to the vile passions of a man such as Remington."

He let out a laugh, shook his head and gathered her into his arms, squeezing her tightly against himself. "Men don't have it any easier, despite what you think. Man. Woman. We all suffer. We merely suffer in different ways."

She pinched her lips together at the unexpected words and affection, her right cheek forcefully mashed against his waistcoat. She instinctively tightened her hold on his waist, desperately needing some form of assurance that everything that was happening to her could somehow be righted, and that she would somehow survive.

The open door banged hard against the wall behind them, causing Moreland to release her. Victoria choked back a yelp as she scrambled back and away.

Remington loomed in the open doorway as the clock on the mantel of the hearth started chiming. He narrowed his icy blue gaze, flexing his gloved hands at his sides. "I thought I would announce myself," he said in a strained, clipped tone. "Considering the both of you were *far* too occupied to notice that your time is up."

Mr. Parker leaned in from behind Remington.

Victoria cringed.

Moreland cleared his throat. "Remington. I can assure you—"

"I would rather not hear it." Remington met Victoria's gaze. Vivid anger bubbled within that piercing look. "Victoria." His voice was rough. Almost breathless. "I wish to address Lord Moreland. Alone."

And leave the poor man to die? This was exactly what she didn't want! Endless complications brought on by Remington's insufferable idea of what *passion* was, that blind, raging passion he couldn't control, which had made her life so damn unpredictable and miserable.

Victoria set her hands on her hips. "I suggest you not overreact, Remington. This isn't what you think."

"No. I dare say it is probably much worse." Remington stalked into the room, heading toward Lord Moreland. "I will not relinquish her. Not to you. Not to anyone."

Moreland glanced back at Victoria, his brows rising. To her surprise, he winked. He then smirked, swung back to Remington and drawled saucily, "I do beg your pardon, but she just promised to have all ten of my children."

Victoria's eyes widened in disbelief, before she altogether burst into laughter.

Remington paused, then turned and stared at her, his lips parting. "Do you find my situation amusing? Is that it?"

She straightened and cleared her throat, trying to regain an ounce of composure. But it was no use. "No, I—" She laughed and shook her head in disbelief that she was actually still laughing at something so stupid. "Forgive me, I—" She laughed and laughed, wishing she could stop. "I can't seem to—" She gasped and pointed at Moreland. Repeatedly. "Drat him!"

A muscle flicked in Remington's shaven jaw. He half nodded, turned and stalked out, shoving past Mr. Parker.

Victoria's laughter died within her throat. She eyed Moreland in complete exasperation. "You ought to be hanged."

Moreland slowly grinned and jabbed a quick thumb toward the door. "I recommend you save your inheritance. Convince that fool. Not this fool."

She drew in a ragged breath, disgusted to no end

by all the men trying to manipulate her, and whisked past. She paused in the corridor and turned.

Remington was already at the far end. He veered toward the staircase and out of sight.

Why did he always, always have to allow emotion to rule every aspect of not only his life but the lives of those around him? It was what she hated most about him. He couldn't let anyone live in peace. Not even himself. And to think, he was her security. It was either marry him or live with Grayson. Dearest God, her father had given her a choice between hell and hell.

To the devil with trying to catch up to legs as long as Remington's. She cupped her hands to the sides of her mouth and shouted, *"Remington! I am not done with you!"*

Her voice echoed across the length of the corridor. She was being exceedingly rude and to the point. But then again, that was exactly what the man deserved. She lowered her hands, set her chin and waited for him to reappear.

Within moments, his large frame edged back into the corridor. He turned and faced her, his stance rigid as he stood there, staring her down. Waiting for whatever she had to say, but stubbornly unwilling to move.

He really should have been an actor.

Seeing he had no intention on coming over to her,

she supposed she had no choice but go to him. She lifted the hem of her skirts and closed the seemingly enormous distance between them, her shoes echoing rhythmically. She eventually paused before him, her gown rustling around her body. It appeared the bastard was getting everything he had ever wanted: her.

Remington stepped back, as if she stood too close for his liking. "I have nothing more to say."

"There is nothing more to say."

He angled toward her and gritted out, "You truly seek to perpetuate my suffering, don't you? Damn you, Victoria. Damn you for always making me crawl. I have been crawling and crawling ever since you and I first met."

He really *should* have been an actor. "This isn't about making you crawl. Right now you represent an inheritance I am unwilling to part with."

He stared. "A certain word comes to mind for women like you."

As if he could hurt her anymore. "Let us be done with this. You wish to marry me? Fine. Marry me. You win. I lose. La la la." She dug into her bodice pocket and retrieved his ring. It slipped from her fingers and made a *tink* against the floor as it rolled off to the side.

Victoria held up a finger and then scurried off toward the ring. Plucking it back up, she straightened and huffed out a breath, preparing herself for the inevitable. Veering back toward Remington, who continued to watch her silently, she grabbed his gloved hand and shoved the ring into it. She then presented her hand to him and boldly met his gaze, praying no other words were necessary. Because in that moment, she didn't have any more words to offer, knowing she was committing herself to matrimony. But just because she was marrying him didn't mean she was handing everything over.

For this time, things would be different. This time, she wasn't going to hand over her heart, her mind, her soul and her entire life. Oh, no. This time, *she* would be setting all of the rules. This time, *she* would ensure she never suffered again.

SCANDAL NINE

The manner in which a gentleman offers matrimony will deeply reflect the sort of husband a lady can expect. If there are no flowers and no effort gifted during the proposal itself, she should not expect flowers and effort to be gifted during matrimony. It is as simple as that.

How To Avoid a Scandal, Author Unknown

JONATHAN OPENED his fist, revealing the ring Victoria had placed into his palm, and eyed the hand she held out to him. A fool he was not. Only moments ago she had been in the arms of another, her entire cheek pressed against Lord Moreland's chest. A cheek that had never once been pressed against his own chest. "You appear to be confused about the amount of men you can involve in your life."

"Lord Moreland and I are friends. That has always held true."

"Friends? So what does that make us?"

"Engaged. Because I am obligated to the duty set upon me by my father. Now, I am asking you to place your mother's ring back onto my finger. 'Tis mine and the only thing of worth ever given to me by you." She pushed her hand closer.

The floor beneath him swayed. "You chose me?"

"Yes. I would like to point out, however, that my submission does not denote love. Because that emotion has long flown and I assure you it will not return. This would merely be a marriage of convenience for which *I* will be setting all the rules."

He lowered his chin. "I do not engage in anything for mere convenience, and I most certainly do not abide by *anyone's* rules."

"I am not about to start arguing another one of your pathetic points about what *you* want. There are other people living in this world aside from *you,* Remington." She rattled her hand. "Now be done with it. I'm tired and wish to go home."

Her continued indifference toward him and their union choked him. He didn't want her to be indifferent. Not about him. It was as if Victoria had truly murdered the last of whatever softness she was capable of.

Although…she was giving them a chance. That was worth something, was it not? Yes. Yes, it was.

Jonathan clasped her soft hand and lifted it, pressing his lips against her skin, willing her to feel that her disdain brought on by pride would never triumph over the tenderness and the love he had to give. Closing his eyes, he gently breathed in the tantalizing scent of soap and continued to hold his lips against her hand, wanting to believe that in time, she would learn to love him again. The way she once had. But before he could earn such love, he knew he had to earn her trust by telling her everything.

Opening his eyes, he lowered himself onto one knee before her, still tightly gripping her hand. He held up his mother's ring by the tips of his fingers. "This will always be yours. Whatever becomes of us."

She stared down at him coolly, showing him about as much emotion as a corpse before it was laid to rest.

Jonathan clenched his jaw in an effort to control his overwhelming regret, bitterness and agony. To think that the Victoria he'd once known and loved could be this emotionless was as evil as it was heart wrenching. He had abandoned her for too long. He only hoped he could right this. He only hoped he could right her and reattach her emotions to her soul.

Jonathan lowered his gaze to Victoria's left hand and focused on slipping the ruby ring onto her third finger—a finger believed by Venetian superstition to lead straight to the heart. His ring slid into place effortlessly, as if it were always meant to be there.

He brushed his lips against the stone, and in honor of his mother, who had insisted he always carry her ring in his pocket until he found a wife worthy enough to wear it, he whispered against the ruby, "I have found the one I wish to wed. Give me your blessings, Mother, and may nothing ever come between us. Not even the words I am about to speak in an effort to illuminate the secrets that remain between us."

Jonathan glanced up at Victoria, remaining on his knee, and tightened his hold on that soft hand, hoping she would finally understand and forgive him for abandoning her all these years ago. And he didn't care if Mr. Parker, Lord Moreland or the rest of the world bore witness to his shame and testimony. All that mattered was revealing who he really was and what he had really become.

"Victoria." For some reason, damn his soul, he could only manage a hoarse, low tone. "Five years ago, I commenced service as Cavaliere Servente in return for amnesty against all of my debts. I was approached by a Venetian widow who was set to remarry a powerful nobleman, who agreed to her taking a *cicisbeo*. With debtor's prison hanging over my head for my debts of ten thousand lire, I was desperate enough to agree to anything. I signed a five-year contract that bound me as their servant."

He lowered his gaze to her hand, unable to look at Victoria, who stared intently down at him, no longer appearing quite so indifferent.

He forced more strength into his voice. "After I'd passed several amiable months of service, the *marchesa* grew fond of me. Overly fond. Cornelia and my stepmother were thanking me for lavish gifts I never sent and soon I found myself being asked to dine with the *marchesa* whenever her husband was unavailable. Eventually, the mandated livery I wore was replaced with extravagant clothing. At the time, I assumed I was being extended respect due to my nobility, for she never once indicated amorous interest. Until one night, my belongings were casually moved from the servant's quarters to the room connected to her bedchamber."

He shifted his jaw and struggled to keep his voice steady. "I informed her that nothing could persuade me to degrade myself in so vile a manner. I also informed her that the moment her husband returned from his travels, I would seek to remove myself from their service. I was true to my word. Upon her husband's return, I informed him of my resignation, requesting all debts be returned to my name. Out of respect for their marriage, I offered no explanation, only apologies. *Marchese* Casacalenda was not by any means pleased. He—"

Victoria gasped, her hand tightening against his. "Marchese *Casacalenda?* The man responsible for the merchant rape?"

Jonathan drew strength from the squeeze of that hand. He wasn't in the least bit surprised Victoria knew the man's name after the notorious rape of a

British merchant's daughter a little over a year ago. "Yes. I take it you've heard of him."

"His vile deeds were printed and reprinted in every rag across London. Even my father, when he was still of sound mind, was outraged when the Austrian government in Venice only fined him a thousand pounds and waved him off after what he did to that poor girl. She was barely fifteen and will never be the same."

"Yes. The Austrian government is good at looking the other way when crimes are committed by men as powerful as the *marchese*."

She leaned down toward him, shaking his hand. "So what happened? You didn't remain in his service, did you?"

"Yes. I did. All five years."

"Oh, Remington. How could you? How could you take his money and—"

"Allow me to finish, Victoria," he bit out in riled agitation. "At the time, I was unaware of the sort of man I was dealing with. Until I tried to leave his service. After refusing the money he threw at me, the *marchese* retrieved a pistol and set it against my head. He announced his wife desired very few things in life and that it was my duty, as her *cicisbeo,* to oversee those desires."

"Oh, dear God," Victoria whispered.

He swallowed, remembering the feel of the metal digging into his temple all too well. "He assured me that if I ever tried to leave before my contract was over, Cornelia and my stepmother would find themselves at the bottom of the Adriatic Sea. That is when I ended all forms of contact with you, in fear he would discover my attachment to you and use you against me, as well. And so I...stayed. What was my sense of honor and pride compared to the deaths of those I loved? I had no financial means to protect them or a means to send them away and I—"

Victoria's other hand jumped to his lips and pressed them firmly together, preventing him from saying any more.

He stiffened and glanced up.

Her tear-glossed jade eyes met his.

He stared up at her in astonishment, unable to believe he had finally shattered that stone façade of hers. It gave him hope that perhaps the Victoria he'd once known and loved was still buried within that soul somewhere, and was merely waiting to be rescued. Much like him.

She sniffed against tears that trickled down her face. Releasing her quivering fingers from his lips, she squeezed his hand with both of hers. "Stand. There is no need for any more of this. Stand. I forgive you."

He drew in a harsh breath. She...forgave him? Already? When he had yet to forgive himself for his own stupidity in entrusting his entire family into the hands of a savage?

Jonathan grabbed hold of her arms and dragged her down onto the marble floor. He forced her onto her knees before him in the corridor, spreading her gown against his thighs and the floor around them. He didn't have the strength to stand in that moment. "You are forgiving me?" he demanded achingly, searching her face.

She sighed and nodded, but would not look at him. "Since I last saw you, I have learned many things. I have learned that sometimes we must turn away from ourselves and what we hold to be true in order to survive. You learned to survive as best you could and I learned to survive as best I could. Hold your head up again, Remington, and know that I do not judge you for it."

Jonathan tried to swallow against the tightness in his throat. But couldn't. He felt as if a huge burden had been lifted from his soul. One he had not been able to dislodge all these years.

With his strength returning tenfold, he circled an arm around her waist and rose, yanking them both onto their feet. He dragged her closer, bringing her entire body against his own, wanting to remember this moment for the rest of his life. Upon whatever was left of his soul, he vowed that nothing would ever come between them ever again. *Nothing.*

She tilted her chin up toward him, her gathered blond hair falling away from the sides of her face and swaying. "This changes nothing between us. Understand that I have nothing left to give."

Disappointment bit into him, although he sensed himself beginning to understand her more. He tightened his hold on her, digging his fingertips into her curves. "You are misleading yourself into thinking there is nothing left within you. You offer me forgiveness, and *that* requires an astounding strength few have."

Someone cleared his throat. Twice.

Jonathan glanced up, his arms tightening around Victoria, pressing her softness against him. She tried to scramble out of his embrace, but he only tightened it savagely, causing her to gasp against him.

Grayson shifted from foot to foot and adjusted his evening coat, glancing sheepishly toward Lord Moreland, Mr. Parker and Sir Thorbert, who were all awkwardly loitering in the corridor barely a few feet away.

Jonathan didn't even want to know how long they had all been standing there. Of course, it wasn't as if he had any pride left. He swallowed and released Victoria, sensing she did not wish to be held anyway. He coolly stepped away.

Lord Moreland set his hands behind his back and grinned. "Good night." He offered a curt nod to everyone and disappeared toward the staircase.

Victoria touched a hand to Jonathan's arm. "He withdrew his name. In your honor."

Jonathan glanced toward her in astonishment and though he fought it, disappointment bit into him all the same. That was why she'd chosen him. Not because she was giving them a chance, but because she'd been forced to take him. Her inheritance depended upon it. Just like she had said.

He nodded, trying not to let the tone of his voice betray what he felt in that moment. It should have been enough to know he was going to be her husband and yet... "I suppose I should thank Lord Moreland."

Without meeting her gaze, Jonathan rounded her and stalked toward the staircase. "Lord Moreland?" he called out.

The man paused on the staircase and turned toward him, his dark brows coming up. "Yes?"

Jonathan cleared his throat and made his way down toward him, jogging down a few steps. He paused directly before him and stiffly held out a gloved hand. "I wish to apologize for my earlier behavior. I did not realize you withdrew your name. Might I ask why?"

Lord Moreland grabbed hold of his hand and shook it. "Need there be a reason? It is what it is. Good night." Lord Moreland released his hand and trotted down the remaining stairs, rounding out of sight.

Some men, like Lord Moreland, were born with admirable qualities that saved them from the noose known as folly. Whilst some men, like himself, were born with damnable qualities that sent them straight to the gallows in the name of stupid love.

Jonathan blew out an exhausted breath and pushed himself away from the railing. He made his way back up toward the small crowd gathered at the top of the stairs. "Is it midnight?"

"Not quite," Mr. Parker announced, yanking on his chain and pulling out his pocket watch. He glanced at it and shrugged. "But all is as it should be. The earl expected her decision to rest with you."

Jonathan refrained from growling. Victoria's decision hadn't rested with him. She had been forced into accepting him. And he couldn't help but feel betrayed by her. He expected more from her. Not this.

He paused on the landing beside Grayson and eyed him. "I require some time with Victoria. There are many things she and I have to discuss. Am I allowed to escort her home and allot that time for that purpose? Or would I be overstepping my bounds by assuming I can do so without a chaperone?"

Grayson swiveled toward Victoria and snorted, waving a hand toward her. "She's her own damn chaperone from this night forth. Go on. Take her. And use the carriage I arrived in. After you escort her home, if you're up for it, I have a few snifters of brandy waiting."

"I will require more than a few snifters."

"Yes. So will I." Grayson spun back toward Victoria and spread his arms apart wide. "Who is your favorite cousin who oversees your every need and desire?"

Victoria lowered her chin. "Grayson, I doubt you understand *any* woman's needs or desires. Let alone mine."

Grayson dropped his hands to his sides and huffed out a breath. "A more ungrateful, heartless creature I've never met."

Jonathan smirked and refrained from agreeing aloud.

Sir Thorbert smoothed both sides of his curling gray mustache with a hand several times and sighed. "May my brother rest in peace when his time comes. All is as it should be."

"Amen." Mr. Parker slipped his watch back into his pocket and set his gloved hands together. "Lord Remington. Tomorrow morning, at exactly ten, you must apply for a special license from the archbishop. He will be waiting. A week has been allotted to allow for any complications in attaining said license. The moment license is approved, we will proceed with an informal ceremony before the earl, as was his wish. You will still be mandated to record your marriage within a parish."

Jonathan cleared his throat. "I will ensure it. Is there anything else?"

Mr. Parker shook his bald head. "No. All other obligations shall fall upon me."

Jonathan nodded. "I thank you."

Now all he had to do was survive the rest of his life being married to a woman who didn't want to be married to him at all.

SCANDAL TEN

The moment a lady is engaged, she should conduct herself with even more dignity and grace than ever before. Above all, she must avoid gossip. For although an engagement provides security of a match, nothing is ever guaranteed. Which is why it is best to ensure there is no reason for a lady to find herself at the mercy of a broken engagement.

How To Avoid a Scandal, Author Unknown

JONATHAN DREW in a deep, soothing breath. Gritty coal smoke tinged the cool night air.

Steps approached from behind, forcing him to push that large breath back out. He swiveled toward Victoria, who bustled toward him, her white satin slippers peering out with every step from beneath the hem of her verdant skirts.

Damn her for always looking so delectable and making him weak in the head and the knees. He swept a hand toward the open door of Grayson's black lacquered carriage. "Where to?"

"Twenty-eight Park Lane." She tightened her shawl around her shoulders with the tips of her bare fingers.

She had never fetched the gloves he'd earlier removed. "The longest route possible," she added. "You and I have quite a bit to discuss before you apply for that license."

His left brow went up. The woman was going to get herself into trouble. Setting himself against the side of the carriage opposite the footman who held the door open, Jonathan swept up Victoria's hand. Fingering her warm bare palm, he assisted her up the small set of steps.

She paused, her slippered foot resting on the last step leading into the carriage, her gown spilling across the length of the steps. She searched his face from where she was perched slightly above him. "I hate to admit it, but you do still look well."

Jonathan lowered his chin against his cravat, suddenly feeling as if she were the rake and he the virgin. "That sort of talk will bring the devil to your door. Be mindful not to excite him too much."

She gripped the edge of the doorway with one hand, whilst her other hand tightened its hold on his. She leaned closer down toward him. "I meant nothing amorous. 'Twas an observation, is all. I haven't seen you in five years."

He tightened his own grip on her hand as those green eyes penetrated his soul, and though he knew he ought to move back, he couldn't help but revel in the way his breath drew in that sensuous hint of lavender that drifted up from the heat of her skin. "Admit it. Captain Blue Eyes has seized the illusive mermaid and has at long last brought her ashore."

A smirk curved her full lips as if the opposite were true. "Though a wolf may howl at the moon with never-ending devotion, it doesn't mean the moon is going to fall from the sky. The moon knows its place, Remington. Do you know yours?"

Well. At least the witty banter remained.

She swung back toward the opening of the carriage, her heat and scent dissipating. Releasing his hand, she ducked and disappeared, sweeping into one of the seats inside.

Jonathan smoothed his bound cravat against his throat with the tips of his fingers, feeling unusually warm despite the cool night. An hour wasn't going to be enough. He needed more time to dig into that head of hers and understand what the hell he was up against.

Leaning toward the young footman, he announced, "Twenty-eight Park Lane. Allot two hours from departure to arrival. No more. No less."

The footman offered a civil nod. "Yes, my lord."

He pulled himself up and hopped into the carriage, settling into the seat across from Victoria. He leaned back and blew out a heavy breath, setting his gloved hands onto his knees.

"Two hours?" Victoria drawled.

"What? Did you require more time? I can offer you the rest of the night, as well. All you need do is put in your request."

She glanced away and said nothing.

Jonathan smirked and shifted in the upholstered seat as the footman folded the steps and secured the door. Nothing kept him from touching and kissing Victoria now. Nothing but his own pride. He dug his fingers into his knees to distract himself from his need to grab her and prove to her that since he'd last seen her, he'd grown far more artful in the ways of love.

The carriage clattered forward into the night, causing them to sway against its movement. The dim light of the lanterns set outside the carriage illuminated the small upholstered space that now confined them.

She smiled and patted the small space beside her. "Come. There are a few things you and I need to discuss."

He eyed her. She was being unusually amiable. Which meant the woman wanted something from him. And he doubted it was the same something he wanted from her. "I would rather sit here and ensure we not complicate this."

She rolled her eyes. "I'm not seventeen anymore."

"I did not insinuate that you were."

"You might as well have, with those words and that tone." She sighed, fingering the ends of the shawl gathered in her lap, and eyed him. "I do not foresee either of us surviving this. You would forever be twisting your stubborn blade, expecting me to yield, while I would forever be resisting. It would never end. So I need to know. If we marry, would you agree to separate lives in separate households?"

His breath hitched. She might as well have ripped his heart out through his nostrils and then waltzed about with a bottle of champagne in honor of the insult. "A husband may mean nothing to you, *bella,* but a wife means everything to me. Whatever your reasons for wanting this marriage, I can assure you I will *not* allow us to lead separate lives in separate households. I intend to be a devoted husband and expect you to be a devoted wife."

"Surely you don't intend to bind me to a marriage I am being forced into out of my duty as a daughter?"

"Welcome to the world of being a woman. Though I should probably point out that I am not by any means *binding* you to anything. If you have objections to this marriage, which clearly you do, I suggest you take a more practical approach. I suggest we not marry at all."

She shook her head. "No. That would mean relinquishing what is rightfully mine."

He snorted. "I ask you cease imposing your pathetic notion of matrimony on me."

"Gifting you my fortune along with the freedom

to do whatever it is you want for the rest of our lives is not exactly what I would call pathetic or imposing. In truth, I think it generous."

"Generous?" He shifted against the seat, growing all the more agitated. Why was it everyone seemed to think all he needed to sustain himself was money? It was degrading. "I have my own money, Victoria. More than enough to live comfortably. That said, even if I didn't have a single farthing, I could *never* marry for a worthless sack of coins. I already played the part of a whore and will never play that role again. Not even to you. I want a relationship. I want to return to what we once shared and will not agree to anything else."

She gestured toward him in exasperation. "You cannot reappear in my life and pretend five years haven't passed. I am too disillusioned to entertain the sort of relationship you seek."

"A loving relationship can offer opportunities to heal. Do you not want to be healed? Do you not want to be loved?"

"I know nothing of love. And clearly, neither do you, if you insist on imposing it on me." She was quiet for a long moment, her features tightening. "So you aren't willing to discuss the possibility of a separation?"

It was as if he hadn't said a goddamn thing! He pointed rigidly to his own face. "Do I appear willing?

Do I? I beg your pardon, but it appears you need me far more than I need you. Because I do not *need* to marry you to secure an inheritance. You, on the other hand, *need* me to secure yours. So if we are going to do this, it will be done my way. Not your way. My way. Which means no separation. You and I will live together, the way a husband and wife should. Do you need me to repeat that for you?"

She muttered something to herself as if it was insulting to have her situation pointed out to her. "I cannot imagine going through this angst with you day in and day out for the rest of my life as to what I should and should not feel. I would rather lose everything and live with Grayson."

He fisted his hands, digging them into the upholstered seat beneath him, wishing he could somehow dig them straight into the heart she apparently no longer had. "I didn't realize you loathed me enough to toss aside a hundred thousand pounds."

"Better a hundred thousand pounds than my sanity."

He squinted at her, trying to understand her better. "Why are you not giving me an opportunity to redeem myself? Do you think me incapable of making you happy? Is that it?"

She observed him with a lethal calmness that was reflected in her tone. "Yes. I do. And I do not say it to be unkind, for I have no doubt you could make other women *very* happy."

"I do not want other women," he ground out. "I only want one. I have only ever wanted one. And yet, cursed as I am, she is forever outside of my grasp. Why? Answer me that. Why are you forever outside of my grasp, even though you now sit before me?"

She sighed. The sort of sigh a parent would bestow upon a child before a lecture. "I will tell you why. Because you have failed to recognize that we have *never* been alike. Ever. For heaven's sake, you fall upon your knee when you speak, wanting the entire world to fall upon its knee right along with you. Have you ever considered that perhaps the world does not revolve around you? Do forgive me, but I will not lead my life according to your interpretation of passion. I already tried that once and it nearly destroyed me. I am not doing it again."

He narrowed his gaze. So. She wanted to wage a war against his passions and his ability to fall upon his knee in earnest, did she? So be it. He'd wage his own war, and in turn, gather all spoils, including every last shard of that heart. A heart that had clearly forgotten its purpose in life. Because a life without love and without any passion was a life without breath. "So you will only marry me if I agree to us leading separate lives? Is that what you are informing me of?"

"Yes."

"And this has nothing to do with you despising me?"

"Of course not. I could never truly despise you, Remington. I will always harbor a certain fondness for you. Always."

A *fondness?* Bloody hell, there was the death knell to their relationship if he ever heard one. "So you will not marry me under any other circumstance?"

"No."

He'd endured worse.

He nodded, fully accepting this amorous war she had set between them. He was going to convince her she was wrong. He was going to convince her that he was the man for her with every last breath left within him, and by the end of it, *she* would be the one falling upon her knee. Not him. "Very well. I will marry you and agree to the separation you seek."

She straightened, shifting toward him. "You will?"

"Yes. Though only under two provisos. Are you prepared to meet them? Or am I wasting my time?"

"I will oversee whatever you set. I will also ensure you receive half the estate. You will never want for anything again."

"If that much is true, then you might as well hand yourself over to me now. For you are all I want out of this."

"Remington, please. Learn to respect what it is *I*

feel and what it is *I* think. You cannot force someone into loving you merely because you want them to."

He shrugged, knowing she was right. "I am acknowledging what you feel and what you think, Victoria. But that doesn't mean I have to accept it."

She huffed out a breath. "What are the provisos? Do you intend to name them? Or am I supposed to guess?"

Little did she know that by agreeing to his conditions, she was already agreeing to be his. He spaced his words evenly. "One. The moment we are wed, you will travel with me to Venice. Two. Once there, you will remain at my side and play the role of a dutiful wife for a month. When your month is over, if you still wish to live a life apart from mine, I will remain in Venice whilst you travel back to London. We will do so and there will be no further contact. Any questions?"

She blinked several times, then whispered hoarsely, "You cannot expect me to leave. Traveling to Venice, even on a private steamship, will take at least two weeks. My father may not live to see my return."

He leaned farther back against the seat. "For this to be fair, Victoria, sacrifices will have to be made on both sides. I will be destroying any chance of taking a wife if I marry you and then agree to a separation. I will also be sacrificing you against my will. What do you intend to sacrifice? Money? That is not a sacrifice. That is a donation. Your father has had you at his side for two and twenty years. I am only asking for one month of your life."

Her eyes widened. "What if my father were to die whilst I am abroad? What then?"

"I would never ask you to leave his side, Victoria, if I believed he was on his deathbed. I have already visited with your father several times and have spoken extensively to his physicians. They assure me that despite his mental lapse, he is still physically very strong and will last for at least another six months. Which is why I am only asking for a month. From what I was told, your father doesn't even know you exist and therefore you can easily excuse yourself without affecting him mentally or physically."

Her gaze narrowed. "The Remington I once knew would have *never* demanded this of me."

"Regrettably, the Remington you once knew was drawn and quartered back in Venice." Being in service to the Casacalendas had certainly seen to that. But the one good thing to have come of it was that unlike the old Jonathan, who forever submitted to defeat in the name of what was right, the new Jonathan didn't know how to accept defeat. He'd choked on enough defeat.

She slowly shook her head. "I can only grieve for the Remington I once loved."

Jonathan tsked. "Before you grieve too much, I

ought to point out that the Victoria I once loved also appears to have disappeared. She had a measure of compassion and understanding within her that you do not have at all. So in that, we are equally matched in our grief."

Victoria squinted at him hatefully and shook her head from side to side, her features twisting in silent suffering. She kept on shaking her head.

Jonathan refused to submit to guilt. Not in this. Not when it came to relinquishing the only thing he'd ever wanted: their happiness. "I will give you until the end of this ride to decide what it is you want. As you know, I have been instructed to apply for our license with the archbishop tomorrow morning at ten. I have no intention of doing so if we are not in agreement and therefore will sit here in silence until you inform me as to how I should proceed."

With that, they sat in silence.

Every single passing minute stabbed at him as the carriage swayed. Hell if he knew how much time had actually passed, but he did know he would have preferred slitting his own throat than suffering through any more of this.

Victoria closed her eyes and half nodded, her face softening. Eventually, she opened her eyes. Leaning back against the seat, she replied in a choked tone, "I agree."

He searched her face in astonishment. "You agree?"

"Yes. I agree." She nodded solemnly. "I will ensure my uncle charters a private steamship so that our travels are expedited. All expenses incurred will be pursed by my father's estate. After my obligated month to you is over, I will return to London without further contact or expectations other than those relating to the estate. I will ensure you receive half. Are we in agreement?"

"Yes." He lifted an inquisitive brow. "And how are we to consummate our marriage? It won't be legal unless we do."

She rolled her eyes. "I did not by any means forget. Might I ask what you intend to do if you get me with child? Or is that your plan?"

He shifted his jaw. What if he couldn't convince her she belonged with him and he did get her with child? What then? "I will raise our child in Venice."

She shook her head and kept shaking it. "No. You must ensure no child comes of this. I refuse to separate a child from either of us. It would be cruel."

So she wasn't as heartless as she appeared. His Victoria was still buried in there. Somewhere. "I will ensure my seed never touches your womb. Will that please you?"

She glanced away and nodded.

"Good. So you will travel with me to Venice?"

She sighed. "Yes."

By the end of the month, she would be his. All his. He smiled and patted the seat beside him, wondering if she would let him kiss her. "Now that we are friends, come here."

She stared at him. "I would rather not."

"I ask that we seal our alliance with a kiss."

She choked. "I... No."

"Why not?"

"I prefer we not do anything that involves touching until *after* we marry."

"Coward." Jonathan trailed his gaze across Victoria's full lips and down the soft, pale curve of her exposed neck toward those full breasts. He grew hard, knowing she was no longer a fantasy, but at long last, a reality. "Why do you have to be so damn beautiful? Hmm?"

She brought her shawl tighter against herself as if that would somehow shield her from whatever advances he had in mind. "Do not say such things or look at me like that."

He smirked. "You cannot tell me what to say or do, Victoria. Though it may irk you, I am beyond your control. And that is exactly what intimidates you about me, isn't it? Your inability to control me and my so-called passions."

"I could care less about your inability to control yourself around me. That is your problem, not mine.

And despite what you think, I am *not* intimidated by you."

"Oh, yes, you are."

"No, I am not."

"No?"

"No."

He casually held up a finger, silently preparing her for a demonstration. He cleared his throat, then enthusiastically patted the carriage seat beside him and smiled graciously. "Come here, Victoria dearest. I want you to drape your arms around me and kiss me the way you kissed me that night. Will you? Please?"

She lowered her gaze, her fingers playing with the fabric of her gown. "Cease."

He pointed at her. "You see. Everything about me intimidates you. Even a mere kiss."

She set her chin. "I am a lady."

"I know full well what you are, but that is not why you deny me. You deny me because I represent the very thing you prefer to avoid: emotion. But from this night forth, and every day you have allotted to me, I vow to make you swallow emotion at every turn. You will swallow every kiss, every word, every touch and every hour we make love. Rest assured, *bella,* after a week, you will like what I offer. After two weeks, you will love what I offer. And after three weeks, you will not only love what I offer, but will find yourself unable to breathe without me. And after those four weeks, you will never leave my side and this will all seem like a dream."

She stared him down. "You really need that ego of yours castrated. You seek to coo, kiss, touch and bed me, thinking that is what it will take to make me love you?" She feigned a laugh. "Go on. Tell me how much you love me, then grab me and kiss me and bed me if it will please you. Simply know that I will endure all of it, whilst counting aloud the days until our month is done."

How he wished he wasn't a gentleman. "You must be willing to be grabbed, kissed and bedded, Victoria. Otherwise, I am not in the least bit interested in doing anything with you."

Her gaze sharpened. "Then I suppose this marriage will never be consummated."

He lowered his chin. "Your unwillingness to engage in intimacy does not surprise me. Because you and I both know that if you were to submit physically, in time, you would also submit emotionally. Which is why I am at an advantage and you are at a disadvantage. Because unlike men, you women lack the ability to separate emotion from physicality."

She sat up, clearly provoked. "You speak as if I represent every female you ever met."

He tsked. "Your pride is showing, *bella*."

She pointed at him. "We will see whose pride gets hanged by the end of this, you romantic sop."

"Is that a challenge?"

"You had best believe it. I intend to laugh and laugh at your attempt to woo me."

Pride was such a wicked thing. Hell. He might as well start breaking her and that damn pride now.

Jonathan leaned over to each side and yanked the brocaded window curtains closed, leaving only enough of an opening to filter in the soft light from the lanterns attached to the carriage. Enough light to allow them to see one another. "How about a real challenge, Victoria? I will prove to you here and now that you have no understanding of the level of intimacy that can exist between us. That your understanding of intimacy is completely different from reality."

She glared. "Why am I not surprised that you are already looking for a vile opportunity to ravage me? You men are all so disgustingly predictable."

"You have no idea what I have in mind."

She snorted. "Shall I sit on your lap and raise my skirts for you? Is that what you have in mind?"

"No. That is not what I want. This is not about taking you physically, Victoria. This is about challenging you to look at intimacy in a way you refuse to."

She eyed him. Although she said nothing, he knew she sought to understand his meaning.

He leaned forward slightly. "What I want will not require touching or kissing at all. You will retain your chastity and I will retain my honor until we are both wed. How is that for predictable?"

She dropped her hand to her side and stared. "You wish for us to be intimate without involving any touching or kissing?"

"Exactly."

She blinked. "I don't understand."

"I do not expect you to. You have led a very sheltered life and know very little about what really goes on between a man and a woman."

She snorted. "I know enough to make you moan."

He bit back a growl, having no doubt whatsoever. "Yes. But can you do it without touching or kissing me? Can you do it without words? Because those are the rules."

She squinted at him. "No touching?" she echoed.

"No touching."

"No kissing?"

"No kissing."

"At all?"

"At all."

"That cannot be possible."

"Anything is possible with Captain Blue Eyes." He grinned, fully enjoying how genuinely flustered she appeared whilst trying to understand him.

She dropped her hand in exasperation. "There is no such thing as a man and a woman being *physically* intimate without them *physically* touching or kissing."

"There is such a thing." He sat up and shrugged off his evening coat from his shoulders and arms, letting it fall behind him and around his waist. "Would you like me to remove my shirt and waistcoat for you?"

She shifted against the seat and glanced toward his chest then toward the covered glass windows of the carriage. She shifted against the seat again. "Please don't take off your shirt and waistcoat."

"Why not?"

She crossed her arms over her chest in agitation and drawled, "You might as well remove your trousers instead. I would think that would be of better use to whatever you have in mind."

His erection tightened. "I hate to disappoint you, but my trousers stay on. But I will make you wet and I will make you moan. Without a single touch."

She wrinkled her nose, dropping her arms back to her sides. "Has no one ever told you what really goes on between a man and a woman? Or do you need me to elaborate?"

He let out a laugh and wagged a finger at her. "You had best not provoke me, woman. You will not like it."

She eyed him tartly. "You are the one provoking

me. If what you seek to do allows me to retain my chastity and does not involve you touching or kissing me, *have at it*. You'll not see me resisting. In fact, I am beyond curious as to what immaculate conception looks like."

By God, she'd gotten bold. If only she knew what she was getting herself into. "So you are giving me full permission to proceed?"

"Yes."

"And you promise to cooperate with whatever I tell you to do for the next half hour as long as I do not touch or kiss you?"

She hesitated, as if weighing what the advantages and disadvantages of her situation were, then spoke matter-of-factly, "Yes. As long as there is no touching, no kissing, and I retain my chastity, have at it. Those are the rules. Now go on. Let the Holy Ghost descend."

"You will regret saying that." Jonathan gave her body a raking gaze, wishing upon his soul he could touch her and make her realize what she made him feel. "Do you know how to pleasure yourself? Have you ever done so in the privacy of your bed? Or do I need to educate you on this?"

Sitting back against the seat, he removed his gloves and tossed them aside. He slid his hands to the buttons on his trouser flap, unfastening all four. Watching her, he shoved both the flap and his undergarment beneath down and freed his hard length. Its heat pulsed against the cool air. "I want you to pleasure yourself. So I can watch. And I will do it right along with you, so you can watch me, too."

She gasped, her lips parting and her eyes remaining firmly affixed to his face. "What on earth did they teach you over there in Venice? This goes beyond a mere dalliance and is anything but civil."

"How quickly your sails doth turn against a mighty wind." He intently met her pretty jade eyes, his chest heaving, and purposefully slid his hand over the tip of himself. A bolt of pleasure shot down his body and his legs, tightening his muscles in response. "This is between you and me, Victoria, and we are about to become husband and wife. Therefore I say it is very civil. We are not touching. We are not kissing. And more importantly, you will retain your chastity until we are wed. Now lift up your skirts, push your hands up between your thighs and touch yourself. I'll show you what to do. You told me you would cooperate this next half hour. So cooperate."

"I..." She bit her lip and eyed his exposed erection, which he purposefully held out before him. Her expression was one of curiosity and agonized tolerance in trying to comprehend what it was she was seeing.

She wasn't telling him to put it away. That was a start.

He wet his hand with a few quick slides of his

tongue and watched her face as he stroked his length, his moist palm focusing on the rounded, soft tip. His gut tightened as sensations throttled his body. "I did this to myself that night you kissed me."

She stared. "You...*did?*"

"Yes. After our unearthly kiss." He kept stroking himself. "I had to resort to this. And in that, nothing has changed. I am still resorting to this."

She pinched her lips together, still watching the movement of his hand. Her chest visibly rose and fell as if his display was having the desired erotic effect on her body.

He clenched his jaw and jerked faster, fearing he might not last if she resisted him much longer. His pulse heightened as sensations shot down the length of his thighs. "Intimacy can be very intimidating, I know. But once you get past the intimidation, your soul will melt." He stilled his own hands and whispered, "I want you to remember this and me for the rest of your life, Victoria."

She let out an impish laugh. "Oh, I will certainly remember this. Let there be no doubt about that. And despite what I earlier agreed to, you are *not* getting me to do *that* to myself in front of you."

Christ, she was made of ice.

Jonathan sat up, shoving his stiff cock beneath his undergarment and back into his trousers. It was obvious she needed an incentive to be willing. And he was going to generously offer it. "I will eliminate two weeks with me in Venice if you do this. That means instead of tolerating four weeks of my advances, you will only have to tolerate two weeks." He eyed her. "You have ten seconds to decide. Ten. Before I remove the offer and we are done for the night. You decide."

Her chest rose and fell more steadily. After an agonizing silence that was inching and inching its way toward ten seconds, she blurted, "Close your eyes and I will. But only if your eyes remain closed."

Holy— "Done." He closed his eyes and willed himself to keep them shut. He hadn't thought she'd do it. He really hadn't.

"Two weeks less in Venice, yes?" she insisted.

"Yes. Two weeks less."

She hesitated. "Keep your eyes closed."

"I will."

"Until we are done."

"Yes."

"That is all I will agree to."

"My eyes are closed and will remain such until we are done. I vow upon my soul."

"Good." The soft rustle of her skirts made him draw in a ragged breath. Every muscle in his body tightened and burned in anticipation.

"I feel like I am about to do something I oughtn't," she muttered.

Still keeping his eyes shut, he grinned. "There is no shame in pleasuring yourself, Victoria. None."

"It isn't the shame I am so worried about."

"I promise not to open my eyes until we are done, if you promise to actually do it. Can you even do it? Or are we back to our four weeks?"

She was quiet for a long moment. "We never speak of this or do this again."

"Never again. Unless you want us to."

"I assure you, that will never happen. Now keep those eyes closed."

"They are closed."

"Keep them closed. The entire time."

The woman was a bit too insistent for his liking. Did she think he was stupid? "Victoria?"

She was quiet for a moment. "What?"

"Don't you dare fake this. Despite these eyes being closed, I will know. Believe me, I will. And if I conclude at any point you are lying to me, I will add an additional two weeks to the four as punishment. And if you know anything about arithmetic that amounts to six weeks in Venice. Do you understand?"

She hesitated, as if that had been her intention all along, then muttered, "Fine, fine."

"Admit it. You were going to swindle me out of my God-given two weeks like a wayside thief. Weren't you?"

She huffed out a breath. "Are we doing this or not?"

He smiled, still keeping his eyes closed. "I am ready whenever you are. And remember. I have ways. Inform me the moment you are ready to proceed."

She sighed. "Now."

He swallowed, his pulse thundering knowing she was actually submitting to him. "Touch yourself," he commanded hoarsely. "Do whatever feels natural." With his eyes still closed, he pulled his solid length back out and slowly rubbed his hand up and down. Though he wanted to open his eyes and indulge in seeing her, he knew he had to respect her request. She was already allowing for much more than he had ever expected and he was trying to gain her trust, not destroy the last of it.

The tip of him leaked, wetting his hand. He slowed his strokes, knowing he wasn't going to last, and wondered if she was pleasuring herself or merely watching him. He would test her after a few more strokes.

He envisioned watching her features submit to pleasured anguish. He imagined her losing command of her body, her mind and soul for one breathing moment. Like he wanted her to. In the way she refused to.

He stilled his hands, holding himself tight, trying to listen to anything that might reveal that she was in fact touching herself.

Soon, soft, secret moans began drifting steadily

toward him. "Hmm," she gasped, her breaths coming in soft pants that were almost muted by the clattering wheels of the carriage. "Oh, God," she softly choked out.

It was too choked and too soft and too unrehearsed to be fake. He almost spilled his seed realizing she was in fact behaving as he'd asked. Of course, he had to be sure. "Are you watching me?" he ventured hoarsely.

"Yes," she breathed.

Damn, but he wanted to explode knowing that. "Tell me how much you are enjoying watching me and how you desperately need to watch me while you pleasure yourself."

After a few breaths, she choked out, "I need to."

"Do you?"

"Yes." She gasped. "I do."

He jerked himself a few times, unable to keep his hands away. "Tell me that you wish I was between your thighs. Tell me."

"I…" she choked out. "You. Between my thighs."

She wouldn't be submitting so easily to these wicked words if she wasn't in the throes of true pleasure. Nor did she sound coherent. Of course, he wanted there to be no doubt left. "Louder. I want to feel what I cannot see."

"Remington!" she cried, that refined tone losing the last of its control. "I feel—"

He clenched his jaw and quickly clasped himself, pushing his own body to catch up to hers. How he wanted to be between her thighs, pounding his lust and his love into her.

A long, well-pleasured moan escaped her.

He'd never experienced anything more erotic in his life. His body tightened as pleasure exploded forth. Seed spurted out with every breath, pulse and jerk.

"Victoria," he groaned, throwing back his head. "God, how I have waited for this. For you." He writhed, blinded by the beauty of that moment. At last, he knew true, untainted pleasure. Pleasure in the company of the woman he had always loved, wanted and needed. If only she felt the same.

He tried to make his climax last, but with a few jagged breaths, it was over. He gasped and settled back against the seat, his hand falling away from himself. He slowly opened his eyes and met Victoria's gaze, his chest still heaving in disbelief.

They continued to stare intently at each other as the clattering of wheels against the cobblestones and the rhythmic hoofbeats of the horses echoed all around them.

She slid her hands out from beneath her lifted skirts and yanked the bundled fabric back down her shapely stockinged legs. "I cannot believe I just did that."

Nor could he.

Jonathan sat up and shoved himself back into place,

wiping his hand on his undergarment. He buttoned his trousers, surprised to find his hands shaking.

Sensing her unease, he eyed her and hoped to God he hadn't gone too far. For as he himself knew all too well, there was a very thin veil between pleasure and degradation. "Assure me I did not shame you. For that is not why I wanted you to do it."

She smoothed her hands awkwardly against her skirts. "No, I...was willing." She winced. "Surprisingly."

He pulled on his coat. "You should always be willing, no matter the challenge I set. If you ever feel uncomfortable about anything we do, inform me of it and I will stop at once. I want our time together to be erotic. Not miserable and degrading. I have lived the latter and would never wish that for you."

She drew her brows together, observing him.

He adjusted his coat around his chest by the lapels, opened both curtains of the carriage and settled back against the seat. "Do you have a question? I sense that you do."

"You seem...comfortable with your body. Far more comfortable than I ever imagined someone would be."

He shrugged. "I was not always this comfortable with myself, or my body, for that matter. It is something I have learned."

She glanced away and stared out the window

toward the passing buildings. Buildings whose darkened glass windows hinted at other lives neither of them would ever be privy to. "Why do you insist on Venice? Surely it cannot harbor anything worth returning to after what you have endured. What if this *marchesa* wants to become a part of your life again? What then?"

"Unlikely. She and I have become friends, despite everything, and parted amicably. She even terminated me sixteen weeks before my contract was officially over so I could come to London and vie for you. I have no reason to blame an entire city for what happened to me. Venice has become my home, Victoria. And although my stepmother has since passed, I still want you to meet Cornelia, her husband and their three children. I want you to get to know me in a way you would never be able to if we remained here. I also promised to take you to Venice after we married, and though you may not remember when I made that promise, I remember it quite well."

"'Twas the first letter you wrote." She placed her bare hand on the glass and kept it there, her eyes fixed upon it. "You wish to woo me whilst we are in Venice and persuade me to stay. Don't you?"

He smirked. "Wish to, *bella?* No. I will."

"I don't want to hurt you," she whispered. "I really don't."

"Then I ask you not hurt me. I ask you to love me. Like you once did."

The carriage rolled to a halt, causing them to sway. Her hand fell away from the glass as the driver called out their destination.

Victoria secured her shawl more tightly around her shoulders. "Please, do not escort me in."

"I will remain here in the carriage and wait until you are safely inside."

"Thank you."

The door opened and the footman unfolded the steps.

"Good night, Victoria," he offered quietly. "I look forward to seeing you again. As my wife."

She stared at him, then turned and whisked out of the carriage with the assistance of the footman.

Jonathan leaned forward and watched her pass through the iron gates and up the stairs toward the large entryway. When the door opened and she disappeared inside, he leaned back against the seat and knocked on the roof of the carriage to take him back to Grayson's.

He only hoped to God he knew what he was doing. For he couldn't help but feel he was playing a dangerous game that could very well destroy whatever was left of not only their hearts but their lives.

3:57 a.m.

IN THE QUIET darkness, Jonathan stared at the outline
of his leather trunk from where he sat on the floor
beside the four-poster. Cornelia had tucked a vial of
laudanum into one of the compartments, insisting
he would need it. But he was not bloody ingesting a
single drop of what she or those Venetian physicians
kept telling him to. Even if it meant never sleeping
again. Having watched the *marchesa* consume it on a
nightly basis during his years of service, he knew full
well how addictive and destructive it was.

He would rather not sleep.

Not that he could with thoughts of Victoria as-
saulting him. What must she think of him after what
they'd done in the carriage? That he was perverted,
obsessed and touched in the head, to be sure. Which
he supposed he was. He was so desperate to return
to what they had once shared that he was losing all
reason and all pride.

"Merda." Jonathan pushed himself up from the
floor beside the bed, the silver pendant around his
neck swaying against his bare chest. Swiping a hand
over his face, he grabbed his robe from the twisted
bed linen and shrugged it on over his naked torso.

He tied the robe into place around his waist and
seethed out an exhausted breath. Settling onto the
mattress, he forced his eyes shut and lay there listen-

ing to the steady intake of his breath and the beating of his heart. Three hours. That was all he needed to survive. Three hours.

SCANDAL ELEVEN

The fatigue a bride undergoes during preparations for a wedding as well as during the wedding itself will astonish even the most prepared. That fatigue, however, is but a symbolic introduction to a new life she must shoulder. But if a lady can survive the expectations of both families and the wedding itself, she can survive anything.

How To Avoid a Scandal, Author Unknown

Six days later
Late morning
The Linford townhouse

"No!" THE EARL kept shouting through strained sobs. "No!"

Victoria refused to look at her father, fearing the last of her strength to stand would desert her.

Her father shrieked. It was a shriek that sliced through the air with a fierceness that pierced Victoria's heart and clutched her stomach. She glanced up toward the high ceiling above in an effort to calm herself. She was beginning to regret not agreeing to have her father sedated. She hadn't wanted him to be part of the ceremony at all, because of this very reason, but her uncle, damn him, had insisted her father deserved to be present.

The old clergyman standing before her and Remington paused from the last of his sacrament and glanced toward her father.

Her uncle and Grayson shifted, using their weight to forcefully hold her father against a chair, their straining bodies locking the earl into place. Mr. Parker scrambled toward them from across the drawing room to assist, his forehead beading with visible moisture.

Victoria squeezed her eyes shut so she wouldn't have to look at the clergyman or Remington or anyone else.

This was not a wedding, but a funeral.

She willed herself not to cry.

"Hell awaits thee!" the earl shouted, his voice growing louder and stronger, the chair clattering. *"Hell!"*

Victoria slapped shaky hands against her ears, unable to listen to any more. She didn't even know what his syphilitic mind was seeing.

Muscled arms slid around her and firmly dragged her over. She didn't resist as Remington's large, gloved hand pressed against her hair, setting her cheek against the warmth of his solid chest. A chest enrobed in a soft, embroidered waistcoat.

The soothing scents of mint, soap and hair tonic engulfed her. She let out a sob that had been buried deep within her, her hands dropping from her ears, and fell against him, allowing herself to lean into the comfort he offered.

She drew in several savage breaths, trying to push each breath back out evenly, and nuzzled against him, needing to wrap herself in this…*warmth*. She had almost forgotten how it felt to be held and comforted.

"Enough!" Remington demanded, his voice rumbling against her ear, his breaths heavy. "I will not allow her to endure any more. Either you remove him from this house at once, or announce that we are married and be done with it."

Victoria swallowed, secretly cherishing Remington's fiery concern. Nothing he ever did was without passion. Everything, including his wicked methods of seduction, had a scorching heat that seared everything he touched. Including her.

The clergyman paused. "You are both already bound in matrimony, my lord. May God bless you both in your union. The parish will require—"

"Josephine!" her father screeched. "Dearest God, why? Why?"

Victoria choked back another sob that clenched in

her throat at hearing her own mother's name. A name she hadn't heard uttered from her father's lips in years. Tears overwhelmed her and she sobbed. Why was he able to recall the dead but not the living?

She clutched the sides of Remington's solid waist, wishing she could escape this never-ending madness of being caught between the present and the past. Neither of which she seemed able to escape.

Remington kissed the top of her head, his arms tightening as he secured her more firmly against himself.

It was too much. All of this. Nothing ever lasted. Everything always disappeared. And in time, she knew Remington would, too.

Victoria scrambled out of Remington's embrace, pushing his arms away in an effort to distance herself from the torrent of emotions overtaking her. She staggered as the yellow drawing room whitened and her limbs felt light.

She tried to focus on Remington's face, but he faded into a white fog as her wobbly limbs slipped from beneath her, erasing everything.

JONATHAN'S HEART bucked to his throat when his arms instinctively shot out and caught Victoria. As her soft, small frame fell heavily against him and her blond head sagged, hiding her face completely, he realized she had fainted.

"Victoria!" Jonathan scooped her up off her slippered feet, burying his hands within her abundant, champagne-colored gauze-and-silk gown, and protectively lifted her into his arms.

The earl's shouts faded into a drone as he dipped his head toward Victoria. "Look at me. Victoria. Say something. Please say something."

She rolled her head toward him, a daisy falling from her blond chignon and fluttering to the floor. She blinked, her pale oval face slowly filling with color again. Her green eyes lifted from his chest to his face and sharpened with a renewed strength he had not expected to see so soon.

"Set me down." She took in a deep, shaky breath.

That intake of breath made his eyes instinctively veer toward the fullness of her breasts displayed by her gown.

He searched her face, noting she no longer appeared dazed. "When did you last eat?"

"I cannot remember. I have been so…overwhelmed by everything that I—" She shifted in his arms and pushed at his chest. Her feet kicked out, once, then twice. "Please. Set me down."

"Shh." He tightened his hold, squeezing her warm softness against him. He glanced toward Grayson. "She needs rest and a good meal if we are to make our journey this afternoon."

Grayson nodded as he darted back to the earl, who staggered up to his booted feet, muttering.

Victoria stiffened and pushed against Remington again. "Let me go. You holding me will only upset him. Please—"

"I am not setting you down. We will remove ourselves." Jonathan turned and carried her out of the drawing room. His steps echoed as he made his way down the corridor and up the stairs. He didn't look at her for fear of bringing more intimacy to an already intimate position. "Where is your bedchamber?"

She hesitated. "The third door. On the right."

Once on the landing, he readjusted Victoria in his arms, his fingers digging into the soft curves hidden beneath her gown, and headed toward the door she had indicated.

Her small hands smoothed his cravat. "I didn't want to be there anymore. I didn't. I didn't want to—"

"I know, *bella*. Believe me. I know. I didn't want to be there, either. I am so sorry for your loss. I truly am." He tightened his hold on the soft warmth of her body, enjoying the unexpected attention she was bestowing upon his cravat. If only she could be equally interested in him.

He paused at the third door and balanced her against the upper half of his body so that he wouldn't have to set down. The scent of sweet lavender and fresh daisies filled his nostrils as her curled, pinned hair lingered close. His body tightened as he fought to keep from burying his face into the scent. Instead, he grabbed hold of the knob in an effort to distract himself.

She kicked out her legs and leaned far forward, causing him to lose his grip on her entirely. She stumbled down onto her feet and caught herself against the wall of the corridor. Straightening herself, she stepped away, placing a hand on her corseted stomach, and announced, "I was overwhelmed and became lightheaded, is all. There really is no need for all of this."

He grabbed the knob and twisted, pushing the door open. "Even so, I am asking you to rest. In an hour, we record our names with the parish, then leave for Portsmouth. You will not survive without—"

A high-pitched bark made him glance down as paws raked his leather boots in greeting. He slowly grinned at the short-legged terrier he recalled all too well.

"I remember you." He bent and scooped a pudgier, graying Flint into his arms. He set him in the crook of his arm and rubbed the small, furry head that nuzzled against his hand. "Still as friendly as ever. Are you coming with us to Venice, old boy?"

Having received his share of affection from him, Flint twisted toward Victoria, looking for more.

Victoria dragged Flint out of his arms, cradling him

in her own, and wandered into her room. She kissed his head. "I decided to leave him with Grayson."

The earl's shouts echoed in the distance.

Jonathan entered the room after her and slammed the oak-paneled door shut. He didn't want her to listen to any more of it. How had she survived in his presence at all? It was as if she had learned to completely separate herself from reality. It eerily reminded him of how he himself had to survive while with the Casacalendas.

Leaning heavily against the door, he eyed her. "I feel it is best you spent some time away from him. You do not want to remember your father in this way, do you?"

"No. I don't." She turned away and wandered toward the four-poster bed. She set Flint onto the bed, then gathered her skirts above her ankles with both arms.

Jonathan's breath hitched as two shapely legs encased in snowy-white stockings appeared. He pressed himself harder against the door, reminding himself that now was not the time to notice or want such things.

She climbed onto the large mattress beside Flint, who was already curling into a comfortable position. Stretching herself out, she buried her legs once again beneath her skirts, then turned on her side, giving him and Flint her back. She plucked out the daisies woven into her bundled hair and tossed them one by one onto the pillow beside her, thus ending her acquiescence to his request for her to wear flowers in her hair during the informal ceremony.

Jonathan pushed himself away from the door and set his hand hesitantly against his coat pocket, where he'd hidden her wedding gift. It was a simple gift, but one he hoped she would like.

He cleared his throat, letting his hand drop to his side, and decided to wait for a more opportune time to present it. Glancing around the sizable bedchamber, he noticed a row of trunks packed for their travels. Curiosity took him to the other side of the room, toward Victoria's dressing table.

As a *cicisbeo,* he had learned everything there was to know about a lady's boudoir. He had also learned that her dressing table bespoke everything about her. How much time she spent before it, whether she was extravagant, conceited or fussy. He didn't expect any of those things from Victoria, but he wanted to reacquaint himself with her in any way he could. Ways he knew she would fight to the end to keep him at a distance.

He paused before the white marble top of the dressing table, reflected in the gilded oval mirror attached to it, and slid his hand along its smooth edge. An open, carved wooden box filled with colorful satin and lace ribbons. Two neatly folded handkerchiefs. A silver-handled brush, set perfectly straight. Curl papers. A sachet full of dried lavender set between two slim perfume bottles. A glass bottle of strawberry water for the skin and hands.

He smiled. She appeared to be everything he already knew her to be. Neat, humble toward her own appearance and simple in her tastes. No rouge, no Spanish wool, no Chinese boxes of colors, no white paints, powders, almond paste, talc or creams. None of the senseless things he had slathered Bernadetta with on a daily basis. While such things made a woman pretty, yes, they did nothing for her soul.

He only hoped he could salvage whatever was left of Victoria's. He hadn't realized how horrid her situation was until today. Absolutely nothing remained of the spirited, boasting man Jonathan once knew as her father. Even worse, the man was unable to acknowledge the daughter whom Jonathan knew he loved very much.

Turning back toward the bed, Jonathan noted Victoria was quietly watching him from where she lay. Her eyes no longer appeared swollen or red from tears. She looked peaceful. Which brought him some measure of comfort.

Flint had already fallen asleep, tucked against the back of her skirts. Somewhere Jonathan himself wouldn't mind being.

Making his way toward Victoria, he paused beside the bed. "How do you feel?"

"Better. Thank you." Her green eyes met his. "I feel as though this time away from him will be good. That doesn't make me a bad daughter, does it?"

"How could you think that? You have already shouldered so much on his behalf."

The rushing of heavy footsteps and a crash resounded from somewhere within the house, sending a tremor reverberating up through the walls around him. He blew out a heavy breath, knowing he should probably help.

He leaned toward Victoria, placing both hands against the softness of the satin coverlet. "I will leave you to rest, after which you will eat. You require strength. It will take us two days just to get Portsmouth, and then another sixteen days to Venice. If the sea is favorable, that is."

She nodded against the pillow.

He eyed the scattered daisies and raked them all toward him into a small pile. "You should have left them in your hair. They looked pretty."

"They did?" she whispered.

"Yes."

She lowered her eyes to the coverlet and smoothed a bare hand against it. "Remington?"

This was turning into an intimate little conversation. Something he did not expect. He scooped up the daisies and sat on the edge of the bed, trying to pretend he was more interested in the pile of delicate white petals in his hand than anything else. "What is it?"

"I am so sorry. I really am."

He struggled to remain indifferent, even though his heart pounded uncontrollably. "For what?"

"I do not mean to treat you with disdain. I really don't. Not when you are being so kind. I simply feel as if…with each loss I have endured, I lose a larger and larger part of myself. There are times I don't even recognize who I am."

He glanced up at the unexpected words and shifted toward her, searching her pale face. "Victoria. Know that I understand much more than you realize. You are adjusting to a lot. Your father's illness, his impending death, me, our marriage, what is expected of you. I have been adjusting to a lot myself and confess it has been overwhelming and challenging trying to balance having you and my freedom delivered to me all at once."

Her hand continued to skim across the surface of the coverlet. "How did you survive being in that man's service all these years? Didn't you ever think to… escape? Did you not try?"

He flung all the flowers from his hand onto the floor, distancing himself from his own emotions. "I was dealing with an animal, not a man. There were so many stories surrounding him, he became more of a myth than flesh. Prior to my arrival, there had been a pretty, young servant who disappeared. Most likely because she had refused to share his bed. No one ever knew what happened to her and whatever inquiries her family had made were silenced. There were other stories that included a newborn babe floating in the laguna that many claimed belonged to one of his many lovers. Though whispers cannot usually be trusted, I had no doubt that most, if not all, of the rumors were true. A few months into my contract, Cornelia had married and was with child, which further complicated my situation and bound me into service. I had more to think about than just her. She had a family."

"Did you ever tell Cornelia? About what happened to you?"

"No. No one but you and Grayson know of it, and I am asking you to keep it that way. I do not ever want Cornelia to know. She would only end up blaming herself for it. The Casacalendas and I parted amicably after my service. I would not even be here if it were not for the *marchesa,* who sought to right what had been done. She contacted your father and convinced him to reconsider giving me an opportunity to vie for you, hailing my success in Venetian society. She knew how much you meant to me and for that, I will forever be grateful to her."

Her hand stilled as she observed him. "Were you ever mistreated? Aside from being forced to…" She left the unsaid hanging between them.

He swallowed, realizing there was so much he had not yet told her. But he had every intention of proving to himself and to Victoria that his soul was greater than the humiliation his pride had endured. "Not in the way you think. Though I avoided the *marchese,* for he was an eerie soul that unsettled me to the core, the *marchesa* herself was very kind and attentive. She fancied herself in love with me, though I could never define the way she treated me as love. I was more of a trinket she paraded in society."

"Did you know her prior to going into service?"

He cleared his throat. "Yes. She, uh…she was a close acquaintance of the family Cornelia was originally supposed to marry into. The *marchesa* and my stepmother became good friends. Very good friends, in fact. She was much older than I, and according to whispers was a sad soul who lost every child she ever carried. So when she offered me the position as a means of settling my debts, I assumed she was extending kindness and a form of compassion toward a family she was never able to have. I discovered soon enough that it was nothing more than lust. Nonetheless, she was intelligent, extremely popular and hailed by Venetian society for her contributions to the arts."

"Was she pretty?"

Jonathan's brows went up, noting Victoria's pale features were flushed. Was she actually jealous? "I had no attachment to her, even after I became her lover. It was like any other task I was set to perform."

She averted her gaze. "So she was pretty."

He shrugged. "Yes."

Victoria raised herself onto her elbow and stared at him, her blond chignon shifting to one side. "I don't understand how Venetian society would have permitted her to not only have a lover but to flaunt him. London would have torched their house, dragged her husband into the street and taken a brick to his head and then hers."

He laughed and leaned toward her. "Do not overexcite yourself. You need rest." Touching her soft face with one hand and her shoulder with his other, he gently guided her back down onto the pillow.

He sat back, distancing himself, lest he become too distracted with the idea of touching her again. "Venice is not London, as you will find. No one is addicted to censuring their neighbors. And though having a *cicisbeo* is no longer widely practiced, there was a time when every respectable married woman in Venice had one and would have never dared to step outside her home without him. She paraded him everywhere. Even Mass."

"Mass?" She snorted against the pillow. "You lie."

"I do not."

"You mean to say married women in Venice retained lovers and flaunted them in church? Before the eyes of God? I refuse to believe it."

"London's definition of a *cicisbeo* is much different from what it is in practice. A true *cicisbeo* is not meant to be a lover at all. Which is why I entered into the agreement in the first place. 'Tis a respectable position entailing an honorable man serving a married woman, defending her honor in public whenever her husband is not available to do so. I was designated to be her chaperone in society and a servant in her home, tending to duties similar to that of a footman and a lady's maid."

"A lady's maid?" she echoed, her eyes widening. "You were a lady's maid?"

He cleared his throat and shifted against the mattress. "I prefer you not call it that, as I am no maid. But, yes, some of my duties were similar to those of one."

"So you dressed and undressed her?"

"Yes."

"Daily?"

"Daily. But that was menial compared to all of my other duties. I ensured her servants carried out their tasks, assisted her with anything and everything she needed and accompanied her everywhere. I was both servant and chaperone."

"Heavens above, you were more a husband to this woman than her own husband was."

He shrugged. "That is how she and I eventually became friends. I came to realize she wasn't as heartless as her husband was."

"How could her husband have even tolerated such a thing? Was he not at all jealous of his own wife?"

"I am certain he was jealous at times, but he had his own array of coquettes to occupy him. His way of thinking was neither rational or traditional. The Casacalenda marriage in and of itself was a mutual alliance of power. Nothing more. The *marchese* led his life the way he pleased and the *marchesa* led hers the way she pleased. They were associates, of sorts."

"Associates," she muttered. "More like rapists."

He sighed. "Enough." He poked her arm. "I cannot wait to show you Venice. You and I will ride gondolas all day and feast on mussels and cod until our sides burst. Cornelia will be beside herself when she discovers we are married. I have not sent word as I intend to surprise her upon our arrival. She always believed we would be together. And right she was."

Victoria smoothed the coverlet again, watching her hand. "Whatever does or does not happen, Remington, my life will always be here with my father. I hope you understand that."

His stomach dropped but he shoved his disappointment aside. "You need the company of more than a dying man. What do you intend to do with your life once your father passes? Have you given thought to that? You need me. You need me to take care of you and I intend to. But it will be in Venice. Not here."

She glared up at him. "Do not assume because you are now my husband you will dictate my life. Cease pretending I have already offered my heart. I have not."

He looked away, her words biting into him. He supposed this was just the beginning of what he could expect. "Forgive me for ever wanting your heart."

He rose, dug into his pocket and retrieved the wedding gift, which he had wrapped in a lace cloth. He set it on the edge of the bed. "This is my wedding gift to you. I apologize for not having it bound. There was no time for the shop to do it." He rounded the bed and strode toward the door, yanking it open.

"Remington," she called out, pushing herself up. Flint sat up along with her, eyeing him.

Jonathan paused and fully turned toward her. "What?"

"Forgive me," she said softly. "I did not intend to be so cruel. Please don't be angry with me."

"I am not angry. I am disillusioned. You are far more than this shell of a woman you have reduced yourself to. If I were meeting you now for the very first time, I don't think I would have even bothered. Now…rest. I will return when it is time for us to leave." He stepped out, shut the door behind him and blew out a heavy breath, eyeing the closed door. Why did he have this horrid inkling that a month was all he was ever going to have with her?

Under the circumstances, they really needed to reacquaint each other by starting all over again and rebuilding not only Victoria but also himself. They needed to be friends first. Lovers last. Or their relationship would never survive. Not with all the doubts and pride eating Victoria alive. Until she agreed to be his, all his, he refused to have her submit to anything. Not a touch and most certainly not a kiss.

FLINT ROUNDED Victoria and settled himself against her legs, closing his eyes. Oh, to be a dog. Life would only gloriously consist of food, sleep and occasional trysts with no attachments.

Victoria shifted toward the rectangular object Remington had left on the bed, reached out and dragged it over toward where she lay. She carefully unfolded the lace cloth and blinked down at an unbound copy of a book. And not just any book, but *The Fortunes and Misfortunes of the Famous Moll Flanders* by Daniel Defoe.

Tears stung her eyes.

It was the only book by Defoe she'd never read.

Even after all these years. She had once pestered Grayson for a whole eight weeks, desperately trying to acquire it, only to be denied due to its scandalous content. And yet…Remington had somehow remembered that. He had remembered who she had once been, while she herself had completely forgotten. How was that possible?

A tear trickled down her cheek. She swiped it away with the shaky tips of her fingers. When she was seventeen, she had wanted to travel the world and see all of the cities she had read about in the books Mrs. Lambert always piled before her. Cities like Madrid, Warsaw, Saint Petersburg, Cape Town, Paris, New York and…*Venice*. Venice above all others, for she had wanted to visit the plain and see all the trees Remington had carved with her name, and wanted to ride in a gondola all day watching the entire city float by.

When she was seventeen, she wanted to be eighteen, so she could be Remington's wife and a mother to his children who would all have eyes as blue as his. More than anything she had wanted to surround herself with the joys of having a family again. Her own family. The sort of family that she had once had before tragedy after tragedy had taken it away.

Victoria gathered the unbound book Remington had given her, hugging it lovingly to her chest, and lowered herself back onto the pillow. Her life was slowly edging away from youth, and what had she done with it thus far?

Nothing. Absolutely nothing. It was the first time in her life she was disappointed with herself as a human being. If she continued down this path of pushing everyone away, including Remington, she knew she would be destroying the last of who she really was.

SCANDAL TWELVE

Some women are content to leave their characters unformed. Sadly, those are the same women who eventually suffer from the shattering of fortitude. As a result, these women are unable to function in the manner society expects them to. Which is why a lady should never leave herself unformed.

How To Avoid a Scandal, Author Unknown

Eighteen days later, evening
On a private chartered steamship en route to
Venice

SHE HAD TO make this trip twice? Oh, dearest God, no. She'd rather stay in Venice for the rest of her life.

Victoria staggered alongside Remington, allowing him to guide her toward the bolted bed in the cabin. The glass lanterns swayed and creaked in slow, steady motions, shifting golden light across the wooden boards beneath her traveling boots. Falling away from Remington's hands, she flopped onto the unevenly stuffed mattress, her cobalt gown spreading around her. She swallowed the remaining spicy, fibrous bits of ginger in her mouth, waiting for it to fade her nausea. Though she now lay still, the world continued to sway back and forth, back and forth.

Vomiting every hour throughout their voyage at sea had not been the grand adventure she had envisioned. But at least Remington wasn't taking advantage of her delirium. For some reason, the man hadn't even bothered with a single advance, aside from friendly pats and hand-holding.

She actually preferred their association to remain civil and simple. It allowed her to focus on getting to know him again, instead of focusing on what he did or did not expect of her as a woman. Though he was notably more serious than the Remington she'd once known, there was an alluring maturity and purpose in everything he said that was rather inspiring.

The boat lurched and nausea rolled through her gut and chest again. She squeezed her eyes shut and fisted the coverlet on the bed, fighting it. "I would have made quite the sailor," she grumbled. "They would have tied me to the side of the railing just to keep the ship clean."

Remington sat beside her, his trouser-clad thigh resting against her back. He rubbed her shoulder affectionately. "The first journey is always the worst. Do you require more ginger before I go on deck for air?"

"Land. I require land."

He chuckled. "We arrive in Venice tomorrow morning."

"I believe I will kiss every single stone I see out of pure joy." She opened her eyes and rolled back toward him. She paused, searching his shadowed face, which observed her in the swaying, dim light of the lanterns.

The dark circles beneath those handsome blue eyes were hauntingly more noticeable than they had been in recent days. They etched into his cheekbones and the tone of his olive skin. And though his voice and mannerisms throughout their voyage never once eluded to it, his features looked increasingly frayed. As if there was something physically wrong with him.

She swallowed at the thought. "Are you… unwell?"

"Aside from constantly worrying about you, I am very well. Thank you. Why?"

She drew her brows together. "The darkness circling your eyes makes you appear quite ill."

He snorted. "I am not ill, I assure you."

"Is it…exhaustion, then?" She blinked, trying to remember when she'd last seen him sleep. She blinked again. Why was it she couldn't remember him ever sleeping beside her? "I am always asleep long before you ever come into bed, and yet you are always up long before I wake. When do you sleep?"

He shrugged. "I lie beside you every night."

"You do?"

"Yes."

"When?"

He shrugged again. "Here and there. I sleep."

"It mustn't be very long. I know I have yet to see you dress or undress, and our cabin is anything but large."

He lifted a dark brow, his hand sliding up the corseted waist of her traveling gown. "I didn't realize you had an interest in watching me dress and undress. Do you?"

She groaned and swatted at him. "You exaggerate my point. I am merely expressing my concern. You look a bit ragged. Exhausted. Are you not sleeping?"

He pointed to himself. "You are expressing concern? For me?" He lowered his chin. "Shall I fall upon my knees and thank the Lord for finally gifting you with an ounce of compassion for Captain Blue Eyes?"

He was making a theatrical out of this. "Have you seen yourself in a mirror?"

"Every morning while I shave."

"And you are not concerned with what you see?"

He smiled, that adorable dimple appearing on his shaven cheek. "You love me. Admit it. You have never stopped loving me."

She glared at him. "You are avoiding my question. Are you sleeping or not?"

His smiled faded. He shifted against the bed. "I admit to being restless. I am still adjusting to a life outside of the one I had led in service. I had endless amount of duties that rarely allowed much sleep."

"So you aren't sleeping?"

"I am. But only two to three hours at a time."

How on earth could she not have noticed he was sleeping so little? A more self-absorbed witch she'd never known. In an effort to distance herself from him, she had also overstepped her bounds as a human being. Dear God. This could not go on.

"Come." She gently patted the space beside her. "I will ensure you sleep. Lie beside me."

He shook his head. "A dose of sea air is all I require."

"You require sleep. Now lie down."

"Sleep does not come to me that way. I require air first."

She sighed. "Then take in your air and return to me at once. I will not have you evading the rest you require."

"You worry needlessly."

"Someone has to worry." She jabbed him. "Fifteen minutes on deck. No more. Or I will find you and drench you in vomit. Which you know I am more than good for."

He rumbled out a laugh. "Yes, *bella*. Are you certain you don't want anything before I leave?"

Even though she was feeling much better, thanks to the ginger, she became an actress and rolled away onto her side, groaning. "Land. Sweet land."

"And you will get it. Tomorrow morning. I vow." He was quiet for a moment. "Your concern is endearing."

He leaned in and kissed her cheek, his lips surprisingly cool. He lingered, the scent of wine and fresh sea air drifting from his skin. He kissed her cheek again. Only this time, his hand skimmed the length of her skirts, from knee to waist and waist to knee and back again.

Victoria drew in a shaky breath, the frantic pounding of her heart making it almost impossible to endure. His touch and his lips upon her cheek made her drift back to a time she never could seem to escape. Even after all these years, she could still remember the way his hot, wet tongue had ardently touched and circled hers in the quiet darkness while she stood at the foot of the stairwell in her home at Bath. Here she was, two and twenty, and it was still the only kiss she had ever known.

Would it be the same?

Could it be the same?

She didn't know if it was the sea air or the swaying of the ship or her weak constitution, but she desperately wanted his lips on more than her cheek. She wanted them on her own lips.

Victoria shifted back toward him, causing him to lift his dark head from her cheek.

He smiled and patted her hip. "I should go."

"No," she murmured, reaching out for his arm and dragging him closer. "Stay."

"I will only be gone for a short while."

"Kiss me. On the lips. Like we did that night. Will you?"

His shaven jaw tightened, shifting the muscles visibly. He searched her face. "No."

She stared up at him in disbelief. "No? I... Is there a stench I am emitting? Or is it the fact that I am more beige than attractive?"

He leaned toward her and cupped the side of her face with a large, warm hand. "There is no stench. And though you are indeed beige, that is not why I am denying you."

She focused on him, his hand and his words. "Then what is it? Am I not treating you well enough? I...I have been trying to be kinder to you. Believe me, I have."

He slid his thumb across her lips. His eyes trailed the movement. "You are treating me exceptionally well compared to when we were back in London, and for that I thank you. But that is not enough for me. As you know, I am foolishly sentimental and will admit that the last time these lips had ever touched another's, I was nineteen. It is the only kiss I ever wish to know."

Her breath hitched. "You mean…you never kissed anyone after you kissed me that night? Not even your *marchesa?*"

He tilted his head to better observe her, causing strands of dark hair to slip across his forehead. "Not her. Not anyone. Though I became her lover, I bound her to one simple rule she willingly granted. That my mouth never touch hers. It made our physical interactions…interesting, but it was the only way I could honor myself, knowing what I was submitting to. I wanted you to be the only one to have that part of me."

Victoria swallowed, the erratic beat of her heart fluttering to her throat. He had wanted to save himself for her? It was… "Oh, Remington," she breathed out. "Am I allowed to say that is the most romantic thing I have ever heard of?"

He slid his hand away and sat back. "You are allowed to say it if you mean it. But I will admit there was nothing romantic about bedding one woman whilst always wanting and thinking and yearning for another." He sighed. "Now, if you will excuse me, I must take in my air."

"No. No, you can't." She struggled to sit up, but the room swayed again, reminding her that she was not in control of her body. She sank down against the mattress again and caught his arm. "Remington."

"Jonathan," he corrected.

"Jonathan," she offered.

"Yes? What is it?"

She shifted her hand toward the lapel of his traveling coat and yanked him down toward her, willing him to stay. "You cannot tell me such things and then leave me to my own thoughts in this creaky cabin."

He gently pried her fingers from his coat and laid her hand back to her side. "I fear the sea is overtaking the last of your senses."

Perhaps it was. She couldn't explain it, but it was as if his words had revived a small part of herself that had been buried all these years. "I want you to kiss me. Please."

He stared at her. "You want me to kiss you?"

"Yes."

"Now?"

"Yes. Now."

He grinned, clearly reveling in his newfound glory as a man. "Whilst I am endlessly flattered, it is with much regret that I must still deny you."

"You still intend to deny me?" she echoed.

"Yes."

"Of a kiss?"

"Yes."

"I do believe I must have heaved out my brain over

the side of this ship and misunderstood. Are you not the same man who made us pleasure ourselves in a carriage whilst rolling through London? What is this? Do you wish to punish me for the way I have been treating you?"

"A real man does not punish the woman he loves. Not under any circumstance." He leaned over her and placed both hands against the headboard above her, his wide chest blocking her view of the cabin.

She sucked in a breath and gawked up at him, eyeing his mouth. "By denying me, I assure you, you are, in fact, punishing me."

"No. By denying you, I am ensuring neither of us gets hurt." He drew in a ragged breath and stared down at her, his blue eyes observing her. "I will not permit you to taint the memory of our kiss and then walk away. When you kiss me, Victoria, it will only be because you have decided to spend the rest of your life with me. I will not settle for less. Not when it comes to us. I can assure you, not touching you has been… *beyond torturous.* All I have been wanting to do ever since we've been wed is—"

He shifted, throwing a muscled, trouser-clad leg over her, and slid his lower half down her lower half, rubbing his erection and hard body against her. *"This."* He lowered both his gaze and his hands to her breasts, skimming his fingers along the edges of her neckline and the curves of her breasts hidden beneath. *"And this."*

She gasped and slid her hands down his solid chest toward his waist hidden beneath his coat. She yanked his shirt from his trousers and slid her hands against his warm, smooth skin, savoring the feel of him.

He sucked in a breath and repositioned himself above her again, setting both of his hands above her shoulders, and stared her down, as if trying to penetrate her soul. "No," he rasped.

Her heart pounded. "No?"

His chest rose and fell in heavy takes. "I will not kiss you or bed you until you are mine. When you are mine—the way you used to be—I will kiss you and you will kiss me."

He pushed himself away and slowly stood. Shoving his shirt back into his trousers, he cleared his throat and adjusted his waistcoat. "I will return in fifteen minutes." Striding toward the cabin door, he opened it, stepped out and shut it behind him.

Victoria lifted a heavy, wobbly hand straight into the air above her and then let it drop onto the mattress beside her where Remington—or rather Jonathan—should have been. He wasn't even going to let them kiss. Not until she announced she was his.

The man truly was not of this earth.

Though it shouldn't have surprised her. Such an ultimatum was exactly the sort of thing a man who once believed in magic rings would issue. Damn him and damn herself. Was it possible she was wrong in denying him an opportunity to heal whatever remained of her soul? Was it possible she had been wrong all along about her understanding of him, of love, of life?

Yes. Yes, it was very possible. And Remington, her dear Remington, was beginning to illuminate those dark corners of her life yet again. Just as he had once upon a time when she was seventeen.

JONATHAN HADN'T quite made it up on deck. Hell, not even past the cabin door. He continued to lean against the wall of the ship's narrow passageway, standing opposite the closed door that separated him from Victoria. The boards against his back and beneath his boots creaked as the kerosene lamps hanging from the low ceiling swayed, shifting sparse light.

He was bloody deranged to deny her what he wanted most. But he refused to kiss her or consummate their marriage until he felt it would mean something to her. He sensed her softening, little by little, but it was not enough, and he refused to settle for anything less than her heart. Especially after the life he had led all these years. He was not going to bed Victoria only to discover it had earned him nothing but the same goddamn thing the Casacalendas had offered him—*money at the price of his worth and his pride.*

Nonetheless…it was endearing to know that his Victoria appeared to be concerned about him. She had actually noticed he hadn't been sleeping very much, despite him trying to hide it from her. The schedule he had kept as *cicisbeo* and all its never-ending duties—not even including the sex—had stayed with him. He knew it would take time before that life completely faded away, and it still weighed upon him in many ways, but the last thing he wanted was to burden Victoria with his problems. Not when she still shouldered so many of her own.

Knowing he had about ten minutes that needed to be spoken for—for he had no desire to go on deck or rush into a room that had a bed he was trying to avoid—he reached into his coat pocket and yanked out Victoria's little book, *How To Avoid a Scandal*. A book he had vowed to read in honor of not only the earl who had given him the incredible opportunity to be Victoria's husband, but in honor of Victoria herself.

Jonathan flipped to the page he'd last been reading and smirked. All and all it was an intelligent book. Witty and even amusing. It encompassed the epitome of what every man wanted from his wife. A loving, doting, dutiful, yet not by any means mindless woman. Mindless—he knew Victoria was anything but. Whilst loving, doting and dutiful? Well…he had two weeks.

He drew his brows together and read on:

Allowing a man to kiss or touch you at any time during your courtship, even before a set wedding, is allowing for too much. After all, it is a lady's duty to give a man a genuine reason to run down that altar aisle. It is a lady's duty to give a man a genuine reason as to why, on his own wedding day, he should smile.

A loud creak made him slap the book shut and look up.

Victoria hovered in the open doorway. "What are you reading?" She squinted at the book. Her eyes widened as she glanced up at him. "Is that my etiquette book?"

He shoved the book into his pocket and awkwardly adjusted his coat by the lapels, smoothing it over his chest. It was humiliating enough having to disclose that he'd been a whore and a "lady's maid." He didn't need her thinking he also had a penchant for women's etiquette books. "Why the devil would I be reading an etiquette book? 'Tis a book of poems, is all." He cleared his throat. "So. Has it been fifteen minutes?"

She eyed him. "No. Did you take in your air?"

He shook his head. "No."

"Do you plan to?"

He pushed himself away from the wall. "No."

She gestured toward the bed in the cabin and set herself against the open door. "Then rest."

He would rather be making love to her on deck against the mast with the sea roaring around them. Of course, he'd never tell her that.

He brushed past her, aware that she watched him, and drifted toward the bolted bed. He sat, yanking off his leather boots. He tossed them, sending them skidding, then removed his wool coat, folding it carefully to ensure the book within its pocket didn't fall out. He set it on the floor beside him.

As he unbuttoned his waistcoat, Victoria paused before him and presented her back and the long row of buttons of her traveling gown that hid a set of hooks beneath. "Will you assist me in this? I prefer not to sleep in my gown."

His fingers stilled against the last button holding his waistcoat together. A damn saint he was not.

He stood. "Allow me to fetch the servant from the other cabin."

Victoria turned toward him and closed what little distance remained, her skirts brushing against the length of his trousers, covering his feet. "Anne hasn't been feeling any better than I. She needs rest. You and I can undress each other without feeling awkward, can we not?"

Words eluded him. All he could think about was what undressing each other would lead to.

She smiled, her hands skimming toward his waistcoat. She unfastened the last button for him. "There."

She slid her hands beneath and slipped his waistcoat from his shoulders, dropping it onto the bed behind him. "That was simple enough. Something new for me, I assure you. I have never undressed a man. Which I am quite certain you will be pleased to hear."

His pulse thundered as her fingers drifted toward his lace cravat and unknotted it. Her green eyes met his and she smiled again.

His breath grew jagged as he traced his gaze down to her full lips. How he wanted to ravage those lips and then ravage the rest of her. But he refused to settle for anything less than what he deserved. He was not going to be a marionette for any woman ever again. Not even to her.

He grabbed her soft, warm hands against his loosened cravat. "No. Cease."

Her hands stilled beneath his. "I am undressing you as politely as I know how and ask you do the same for me." She hesitated and slowly withdrew her hands from beneath his, eyeing him. "I...do not wish to make you uncomfortable. I was merely being amiable."

Who was he to resist what little she offered? This was his Victoria. His beautiful, innocent Victoria.

He lowered his hands to his sides, set his chin and leaned toward her. "Proceed."

She lowered her gaze and hesitated.

"Go on," he insisted. "Undress me and I will undress you. We can be civil, can't we?"

She bit her lip and nodded. Raising her hands back to his throat, she pulled away his cravat. She folded it and momentarily leaned away, setting it aside. She turned back, settling before him once again and paused, her brows coming together. She leaned in and eyed his exposed throat. Her hand drifted out and gently gathered the silver pendant he wore, lifting the silver chain from beneath his shirt. She squinted at it. "What is this? It looks like a winged lion."

He lowered his gaze to the pendant she held, trying to focus on something other than the heat of her body and the fact that he was in a state of undress before her. "'Tis the patron saint of Venice. Saint Mark. Or *San Marco,* as the Venetians say. Cornelia bought it for me when we first arrived in Venice. The entire city is actually emblazoned with lions. Statues, gates, doors, even gondolas. 'Tis all in honor of *San Marco.*"

She fingered it, swaying the chain against his throat. "'Tis beautiful. You wear it well."

Noting the way her eyes admired the pendant, he smiled, gathered the chain and pulled it up and over his head, removing it from around his neck. Lifting it over her head, he drew it down and adjusted it around her throat, where it settled between her breasts. "It is yours now."

Victoria placed her hand against the pendant. "No. I… It's yours. Cornelia gave it to you."

"And I am giving it to you. My wife. It is my right. Now turn around. You are done undressing me. If you take off any more of my clothes, you might as well commit to staying in Venice altogether."

She hesitated.

"Turn around," he repeated.

She bit her lip and slowly turned, exposing the long row of buttons from the back of her neck to her waist.

God help him, he wanted to yank that dress from her shoulders, rip it down to her hips and thighs, swing her up into his arms and carry her naked to the bed. He wanted to make love to her using every sway of the ship to his advantage and show her exactly what she made him feel every time he looked at her, and how she put him into a state of weakness he had been cursed with ever since he was nineteen.

She glanced back at him from over her shoulder expectantly, a long curl cascading out of her chignon.

He moved closer, blew out a breath to keep his body under control and started to unbutton the back of her dress, starting at her neck. His fingers brushed against her chemise. The warmth of her soft skin hidden beneath it made him fumble. As he exposed more and more of her back, he uncovered a pale blue corset with an ivory chemise beneath it and glimpses of more pale, smooth skin. Ever so slowly, he slid the long sleeves of her gown from her shoulders, revealing slim, graceful arms.

Every muscle in his body tightened, and though he fought his desire, he had already grown so damn hard he could barely breathe. He shifted his jaw. Unable to resist, he sensuously rounded his palms against the bare skin of her shoulders, grazing the thick straps of her chemise.

She stilled beneath his touch and he knew by the intake of her breath and her stance that if he wanted it, she would let him touch far, far more than just her shoulders.

It made him want her all the more.

His hands skimmed down the length of her arms, his breath now coming in uneven takes. He lowered his hands to her corset, memorizing the size of her waist and how the smooth satin and rough lace felt against his skin.

She turned toward him, causing his fingers to graze against her hips. He lowered his gaze to the rounded tops of her full breasts, which her corset pushed up, his pendant now nestled between them.

If he didn't stop touching her, he wouldn't stop at

all. He pulled his hands away and stepped back, the back of his legs bumping into the bed.

She stepped farther back herself. "You have far more self-control than I do."

"But unlike you, my body will be suffering all night."

Her eyes trailed the length of his body and paused on the flap of his trousers.

Jonathan instinctively set a hand against his erection, uncomfortably reminded of the way the *marchesa* had always eyed the flap of his trousers as a way of signaling she wanted him to remove them.

Victoria glanced up, as if sensing his unease, and cleared her throat. "Uh…forgive me. I didn't mean to look. That is…I did, but—" She wrinkled her nose. "I supposed I ought to be flattered knowing I have such an effect on you."

He yanked out his shirt from his trousers and covered his erection. Little did she know just how wicked his need for her really was. Those first few times, when he'd had to perform on command like a dog, the only way he could manage the sort of erection he needed to pleasure himself and the *marchesa* was to imagine Victoria gloriously naked beneath him. Envisioning her naked, writhing, panting, moaning and at his command had miraculously carried him through.

Victoria turned away and shimmied out of her

gown, her curvy bum waggling at him through her thin chemise.

Jonathan swung toward the bed, wide-eyed, and sucked in a breath, wishing he hadn't seen that. It was difficult enough pretending he could survive not touching her and kissing her and bedding her.

He yanked back the coverlet, trying to occupy his hands and thoughts, but he knew he wasn't going to get any sleep tonight.

SCANDAL THIRTEEN

It is said laughter is a demonstration of one's good breeding and that a lady ought to cultivate her laugh. This author, however, has met many well bred women whose laughter ought to be left in the wild, yet are perfect in every other way. So heed this advice: all that matters is that one's humor is genuine and in place. For without any humor, one is merely a face.

How To Avoid a Scandal, Author Unknown

ONCE VICTORIA had draped her gown against her trunk for Anne to tend to in the morning, she became very conscious of the fact that she was only wearing a chemise and a corset. She rounded the bolted bed and crawled into it. She could sense Remington's own unease by the way he raked his hand through his hair as he watched her push her bare legs beneath the cool linens and coverlet.

For his sake—not to mention her own—she scooted herself as far over to the edge as possible. She even rolled onto her side, away from him, so as to encourage him to get into the bed he was clearly avoiding.

The necklace he had so tenderly bestowed upon her slid against the skin of her throat, the silver chain gathering into a pile around the pendant against the mattress.

She fingered the pendant. She could sense that the physical submissions Remington had engaged in with the *marchesa* had affected him immensely. The way his hand had jumped to cover his erection was but a whisper of what he had suffered. Because after what they had shared in the carriage, she knew the man was anything but coy.

Though pity was not the emotion she would have ever wanted to feel for Remington, she couldn't help but pity him. For what he had endured at the hands of the *marchesa,* with her own husband's blessings, was no different than rape. Remington had naught been more than a boy of nineteen at the time he'd been manipulated into accepting what he'd thought was in best interest of his family. She blinked back tears.

The creaking of floorboards and the dragging sounds of trunks made her realize he was reorganizing their belongings. She bit back a smile, knowing he was probably only doing it in an effort to put off getting into bed.

After a few more creaks of the floorboards, the mattress shifted and Remington sat on the edge of the bed on the other side. She pinched her lips together and gripped the edge of the tick, willing herself not to turn toward him.

He shifted, causing her body to tilt, and she knew he had pulled his legs onto the bed. He shifted closer toward her and paused. He huffed out a breath. A large hand then reached over her and took up her hand which was against the mattress. He dragged it back toward himself, causing her to roll onto her back.

She swallowed as his long, warm fingers entwined hers, the heat of his skin penetrating her own. She closed her eyes, reveling in his touch. Nothing mattered in that moment but that touch. She actually felt… at peace.

He released her hand, shifted his body and, using his other hand, took hold of her hip and dragged her closer toward him. He draped his arm around her and murmured into the curve of her shoulder, "Good night."

Even though he was fully clothed in a shirt and trousers, Victoria felt as if he might as well have been naked, the way she was drowning against the hardness of his warmth and flesh. She tried to shift away from the growing heat of his soap-scented body, but he yanked her back toward himself. Something hard dug into her bum.

"Pardon my friend," he whispered in an amused drawl. "I can't get him to leave."

Her eyes widened. As if his erection digging into

her wasn't alarming enough, his fingers were now tracing the curve of her throat, back and forth, back and forth, in soft, playful strokes.

Her heart pounded. It was unbearable. "Remington?"

"Jonathan."

Why did she keep forgetting? "Jonathan."

"Sì, mia cara?"

Heavens above, hearing him speak Italian was like licking sugar cubes. "I feel likely to faint."

"What irks you about me now?"

"Aside from your...*friend?* You keep touching me and it is hardly fair, considering you have no intention of even giving me a kiss."

He chuckled. His hand slid from her throat, past her breasts and down to her waist where he tightened his hold on her. "Sleep on the floor if my touching bothers you." He nudged her with his chin. "Or on deck."

She giggled and swatted his hands away. "I believe neither of us is going to get any sleep tonight."

He raised himself onto his elbow toward her, beneath the linen and coverlets. "You win. Put an end to your misery and kiss me. Go on."

Her heart pounded at the unexpected offer. She shifted toward him, rolling entirely to her back, and glanced up at him. Only...she could tell by that pompous smirk and the playful glint in those eyes she wasn't getting anything at all.

She squinted up at him. "You weren't really offering me a kiss, were you?"

He grinned. "No. But you want it, don't you?"

She laughed. "You brute."

He lifted his free hand and dabbed his finger against her nose. "Sleep."

She refrained from nipping his finger. "I am not the one who needs to sleep."

Remington rolled further into her. "How about a story?"

Victoria rolled her eyes. "I am not a child in need of bedtime tales and would prefer you place all effort toward rest. Now sleep."

He shifted onto his back, crossed his long legs and stared up at the timbered ceiling. "Once upon a time there was an incredibly wealthy and privileged nobleman by the name of Bartholomew." He paused. "Shall I go on? Or are you already bored?"

She smiled, rolled onto her back and stared up at the timbered ceiling along with him. "If I listen, do you promise to sleep afterward?"

"I will do what I can."

"I want you to promise. Because you and I both know you are a man of your word."

"That I am. I will sleep. I promise."

"Good. Proceed."

He cleared his throat. "Now this wealthy and privileged man was unlike any of the others in the kingdom. Bartholomew looked upon life as if it were a puzzle he could easily solve, and he had an incredible talent for cutting and shaping gems like no other. Such was his talent that by the time he was seventeen, royalty sought Bartholomew out on commission. Needless to say, he learned to use his talents to his advantage. He shaped and polished an exquisite ruby and had it set into a beautiful gold ring. He then placed this ring into a velvet-lined box, which he sent to a beautiful noblewoman who had for many years refused every man in the kingdom. His gift arrived with a missive warning her that the ring held magical qualities that would provoke her to love him against her will. She was charmed. They courted, fell in love and married, thus proving the ring held a measure of magical merit."

Victoria glanced over at him, noting his profile was as solemn as any statue. Why, he was disclosing the history of his mother's ruby ring. "Is this a true story?"

His blue eyes captured hers. "Yes."

She glanced away and stared back up at the timbered ceiling. "You used your father's methods to procure me."

"At nineteen, I didn't have methods of my own."

"True. So what happened? Do go on."

"Long after they were married, and much to their utmost joy, a strapping boy of unprecedented quality was born unto them."

Victoria giggled. "Strapping? Let us not embellish too much, my dear sir."

"I ask that you not interrupt the storyteller."

She giggled again. "Forgive me, but were you referring to yourself? Or do you have a brother I have yet to meet?"

"I will ignore that devious slap against my honor and proceed with my story. Now, throughout the years, this strapping boy—being me, of course—had fallen fancy to the idea of embarking upon grand adventures. So much so that he was forever sneaking out of the house and getting into trouble for senseless things, like shooting all of the apples off the branches of every single tree with his pistol. Trees that were not on his father's property. He also liked the challenge of shooting fish in all the ponds instead of using a hook. It was incredibly difficult to do, by the by, and took him weeks upon weeks to do it."

"They should have taken away your pistol."

A deep laugh escaped him. "They did. All six. The gamekeeper was threatened with the loss of his position if he were to ever provide me with anything involving gunpowder. So I turned to knives instead, without my father knowing. They were easier to hide and made no sound when in use. Then one day, I got my dagger stuck to the ceiling of my father's study and could not get it down. I hoped unto God he would not notice."

Victoria burst into snorting laughter, imagining little Remington looking up at the handle of a knife sticking out from the ceiling and being quite distressed. She slapped a hand over her mouth, realizing she was snorting.

Remington laughed along with her. "My father noticed within the hour. After a good whip to the backside, my father sat me in a chair and said, *'In a world such as ours, boy, there are three dozen scoundrels for every one good man. Challenge yourself to be something more than what everyone else can be. It requires far greater skill to do the right thing at the right time than to aim a damn pistol at a moving fish.'"*

"A very wise man, your father."

"Yes. He was. I thought his words were remarkable and have taken them to heart ever since that day. Even more so when my own mother succumbed to a fever shortly afterward. The doctors did not seem to understand what was wrong with her. All they knew was that she was dying. Knowing this, she removed her ring from her finger and gave it to me, asking that I live the life of a gentleman and find the same sort of love she had shared with my father. She insisted that I should never settle for less and that is all that would ever make her happy. From the age of twelve, I carried that ring with me everywhere, waiting to meet my girl, and wondering what she would be like."

Victoria kept staring up at the ceiling, an aching tenderness overwhelming her knowing she was and had always been that girl. She had simply forgotten how to be that girl.

"After my mother's death, I was toted off to Eton against my will. There, I found more scoundrels than gentlemen, which only reaffirmed my father's words and my dedication to perfecting my character. To my astonishment, not even a year later, my father married a widow. I was not pleased with him at all. I felt as though he had betrayed my mother's memory. I hated his new wife, as she was annoyingly superficial, but I did grow very fond of her daughter, Cornelia, who was only a year older than me. I actually looked forward to holidays, merely so I could spend time with her. We always argued about who was more of a romantic, she or I. She always won. Then one day, whilst back at Eton, I came upon seven boys punching the wits out of a helpless chap I knew from the eating hall. I jumped in and fought them all off as best I could. And though neither of us could walk without wincing for a week, he and I bonded. That chap was Grayson."

Victoria couldn't help but smirk. "You should have let those boys carry on."

His knee nudged against her leg. "I will defend

him to the end. He has always been a good friend to me. When you sent him to Venice, Grayson sought to buy my contract back from the Casacalendas. As I had warned him and had predicted, the *marchese* turned him away with a request he never make an appearance in Venice again. Because it wasn't about the money. It was about control. Grayson was outraged and sent countless letters to every Austrian government official who held power in Venice. He was told to take it to his king or better yet, the Basilica, as the crime appeared to be one only the church could address. Grayson was finally forced to accept what I already had."

Victoria shook her head in disgust, turned and propped herself on an elbow to get a better look at him. "Why wouldn't you let Grayson tell me? *Why?*"

Remington lifted his hand and placed a large, heated palm against the side of her face. "Part of it was shame. I had been stripped of my worth as a man because of my stupidity in involving myself with the wrong people. But in the end, I also knew you would have boarded a midnight ship and hunted me down, and in turn, exposed yourself to a harm I would have never been able to live with."

"You still should have told me," she whispered in earnest.

"And I now regret that I didn't. But that cannot be changed, can it?" His hand left her face and trailed the outside of her arm, sending a skittering sensation throughout her body. His hand traveled down to her waist, hidden beneath the coverlet. His thumb sensuously rubbed in a circular motion, searching for a place just below her stay, making her catch her breath.

Her heartbeat throbbed in her ears. She could feel his need and his expectations in that touch. It weighed heavily upon her soul. Was she ready to be the woman he deserved? Would she know how to match his passions? His love? She feared disappointing him. "You should sleep."

He drew away his hand and nodded. "Yes. Good night."

"Good night." She settled against the pillow beside him and glanced toward the lanterns, which waned, giving way to darker shadows in the room.

Aside from creaks and the sea rushing against the sides of the ship, it was quiet for a very, very long time.

Too quiet.

"It is much too quiet," Remington blurted, as if privy to her own thoughts. "Even with the sea roaring."

She smiled. "Are you requesting a lullaby, my lord?"

"Are you offering?"

"No."

"Why ever not? I have yet to hear you sing."

"If I sing, you will never sleep again."

He chuckled. "I will heed the warning. Recite something for me, then."

"What would you like me to recite?"

"Anything. Though nothing sad."

"That eliminates every poem I know."

"Oh, come. You must know one poem of good cheer."

"No. I don't. My father preferred poetry he could relate to. Sorrow. Death. Loss." She paused, remembering the book Remington had been reading. A book she was quite certain wasn't filled with poems at all. She'd recognized her etiquette book the moment she'd glimpsed it. Though she didn't know why he would deny it or how he had even come across it. "What about that book of poems you were reading earlier? Is there anything of merit that perhaps I could read?"

He was quiet for a moment. "Victoria?"

"Yes?" she innocently prodded.

"That was not a book of poems."

"No?"

"No. It was, indeed, your etiquette book."

"I see. The etiquette book you denied having."

"Yes."

"And were you actually reading it?"

"Yes."

"Why?"

"Well… I… Not because the idea of female

etiquette appeals to me, but because…it was yours. And it has my name all over it. I like looking at it and knowing that at one time you held that book with a love I now seek to reclaim."

He would have to remind her of all the countless hours she spent thinking about him and getting ink all over her hands. "And where did you get it? I distinctly remember tossing it."

"Your father confiscated it and gifted it to me. He even wrote an inscription within its pages pertaining to your mother. Would you like to read it?"

She swallowed and shook her head against the pillow. "No. Not now." She didn't want to think about death or her father or her mother in that moment. Only this. Only Remington.

Remington sighed. "How do you expect me to sleep, Victoria, when the tone of your voice makes me want to hang myself?"

"Forgive me. My mind had wandered." She squinted for a moment, digging into her thoughts for something to recite. "I do know one ditty. If you want to hear it."

"Out with it. I would love to hear it."

"I should warn you, though. 'Tis a bit vulgar."

He was quiet for a moment. "And where would you have learned something vulgar?"

She bit back a smile, noting the concern in his voice. "Grayson always sang it whenever he visited and insisted he would keep singing it until I married. Sure enough, he was true to his word. He sang it all the time and annoyed me so much, I eventually paid attention to the words and then annoyed him in turn by reciting it myself. My father really was quite livid about the whole thing. Not only with Grayson, but with me, seeing as the words were so crass."

He adjusted the pillow beneath his head. "This I must hear. Go on. Recite it."

She snuggled against the pillow and set her chin to the air, remembering the words. "*'I, a tender young maid, have been courted by many men as ever was any. A spruce haberdasher first spake me fair, but I would have nothing to do with small ware. My thing is my own and I'll keep it so still, yet other young lasses may do what they will.'*"

Remington rumbled out a laugh. "Grayson never shared this one with me."

"Because he likes you more than he likes me."

"I disagree. But do go on."

"*'A sweet-scented courtier did give me a kiss, and he promised me mountains if I would be his. But I'll not believe him, for it is too true, some courtiers do promise much more than they do. A fine man of law did come out of the Strand, to plead his own cause, with his fee in his hand. He made a brace motion, but that would not do, for I did dismiss him, and nonsuit him, too.'*"

"Are you certain Grayson taught you this? This maiden sounds remarkably like you. Turning away suitors and all."

Victoria smacked his forearm with the back of her hand from where she lay. "You are supposed to be sleeping. Now where was I?" She drew in a breath. *"'Next came a young fellow, a notable spark, with a green bag and inkhorn, a justice's clerk. He pulled out his warrant to make all appear, but I sent him away with a flea in his ear. An usurer came, with abundance of cash, but I had no mind to come under his lash. He proffered me jewels and great stores of gold, but I wouldn't mortgage my little freehold.'"*

"This is profanity at its best. Enough. I have heard enough."

"Oh, hush. You are no maid. Now allow me to finish. *'A blunt lieutenant next surprised my placket, and fiercely began to riddle and sack it. I mustered my spirits up, and became bold, and forced my lieutenant to quit his strong hold.'"*

"I intend to pummel Grayson for reciting such vile rubbish to you."

She laughed. "You really need to stop interrupting me. *'A fine dapper tailor, with yard in hand, did proffer his service to be at command. He talked of a slit I had above my knee, but I'll have no tailor to stitch it for me.'"*

He choked. "This is *not* helping me sleep. At all."

She smirked. "You wanted to hear it."

"And I am regretting that I did. Are you done?"

"No. Not quite. *'Now here I could reckon a hundred or more, besides all the gamesters recited before, that made their addresses in hopes of a snap, but young as I was, I understood trap. My thing is my own, and I'll keep it so still, until I be married, say men what they will.'*" She paused, oddly realizing Remington was right. It really did sum her up.

He hesitated. "Is that it?"

"Yes. Would you like me to recite something else?"

"Uh…no."

"Are you ready to sleep?"

"Yes."

"Good."

He drew in a breath and let it out. "Good night, Victoria."

"Good night, Remington."

He shifted toward her. "I was really hoping you would be calling me Jonathan by now. Remington is what everyone else calls me and you are not everyone else."

Her heart fluttered. "Good night, *Jonathan dear.*"

He settled back against the pillows again and let

out a breath. "I am in love with the way your voice dips whenever you say my name."

Heavens, would her heart ever cease fluttering like a butterfly caught at sea? In that moment, she actually considered forcefully grabbing his face and kissing him. Only…she knew she'd most likely make him angry for going against his wishes. That, or she would end up riling him and neither of them would get sleep.

"Good night," she offered.

"Good night."

Silence lulled them. Eventually, all light left the cabin and there was nothing but the creaking of boards, the rocking of the boat and the incessant noise of water pummeling the ship outside. In the darkness, she listened to Jonathan's breath, finding comfort in knowing he was beside her, while pleading he would find rest.

After a very long while, his intake of breaths grew steady and slow. She didn't know how long she lay in the darkness—maybe an hour or two or three?—but eventually, she also succumbed to peace.

SCANDAL FOURTEEN

A lady with too much enthusiasm toward everything and everyone becomes a lady well known for being kept in the nursery for too long. There is an art when it comes to exhibiting emotion. Whilst some prefer a lady squelch all emotion, this author insists only enough be exhibited to allow others to appreciate what you think and feel, without making them assume you were bred by squirrels. Be refined in conveying your thoughts and emotions and they will become your greatest assets.

How To Avoid a Scandal, Author Unknown

Early morning
Venice, Italy

STEP BY STEP, Victoria descended from the plank of the ship out onto the narrow stone landing before her. The cool morning wind rushed against her face, causing the silk ribbons of her pleated bonnet to flap against her chin. She tightened her hold on her beaded reticule and drew in a deep breath, savoring the moment. The air was tinged with the acrid salt of the sea mixed with pungent fish, and an unexpected sweetness that reminded her of melons.

Though the land seemed to sway beneath her after she had been confined to the ship for so long, a renewed strength overtook her. She felt as if she had awakened to find herself in a Renaissance painting filled with never-ending periwinkle skies scattered with mountainous clouds angels could doze on. And at the foot of such an illustrious sky, an endless sea shimmered green, reflecting the blinding brightness of the sun peering through the clouds.

Amidst all of this remarkable beauty, towering above and around her, left and right and as far as her eyes could see, were grand marble, stone and brick façades of age-worn palaces and buildings pressed side by side. A grand bridge of white stone, the Ponte de Rialto—which Jonathan had earlier pointed out from the deck—joined both sides of the city in a single, magnificent sweeping arch.

Flower boxes and iron balconies dotted some of the arched windows, and in the distance, two elderly Venetian ladies dressed in lavish French morning gowns of white and green casually chatted against the railing of one of the balconies, gazing out onto the Grand Canal. Their matching pale pink fans fluttered every now and then. Several gray doves floated past and veered up toward rusty, ceramic-tiled roofs before disappearing entirely from sight.

If magic were ever to exist, it would exist in a place such as this. But the most astonishing thing to behold in Venice was all the buildings that rose up out of the water like lily pads in a pond. All of them, Remington had explained, were held up precariously by endless piles driven into the clay beneath the water.

Remington paused beside her. The curved brim of his top hat shadowed his blue eyes against the brightness around them as he glanced down at her. He held out an arm, his gray morning coat shifting against his muscled arm. "Welcome to *Venezia, signorina*."

Her stomach flipped. She was really here. In Venice. With Remington. She grinned and placed her gloved hand against his solid forearm, allowing him to lead her down the narrow stone pathway beside the muddy green water lapping against the edge behind them.

"First, we secure a gondola. Otherwise we will never get anywhere. I already arranged for our trunks to follow. Come." Remington gestured ahead toward a group of narrow black boats whose ends curved dramatically upward like the shoes of a sultan. All the bows were embedded with oddly shaped iron blades and in the middle of each boat was a small, enclosed black cabin with curtained windows.

She drew her brows together as they approached. "Is that a gondola?"

"Yes."

"It looks more like a sultan's hearse."

Remington chuckled and released her arm as they paused before a young, dark-haired gentleman towering above them from atop the rear of a gondola.

"Signore Remington!" the young man exclaimed, the muscled arm that wasn't holding his long oar popping into the air, lifting his coat. "London no good, eh? *Venezia* better."

Remington rumbled out a laugh and touched his hand to the rim of his hat. *"Sì,* Antonio. *Venezia* is better. But I have brought something *Venezia* could never boast." Remington turned toward Victoria, swept up her gloved hand and propelled her toward the man. "Victoria, this is Antonio. One of many, many gondoliers I have gotten to know throughout the years. Though he will argue with me on this, he specializes in knowing more about languages than women. Antonio, *mia moglie, Signorina* Victoria."

"Moglie?" Antonio echoed, his dark gaze sweeping Victoria's length as if she stood before them completely naked. Antonio hopped down onto the stone stoop, causing the attached gondola he had left behind to teeter and rock against the water. He let out a long, low whistle. *"Tutti i ragazzi vogliono incontrare una ragazza come lei."*

Victoria's brows went up. Surely, even the boldest of men would have shown a bit more restraint. And as she could only infer what the man said, by the seductive tone of his voice, she found herself wishing Mrs. Lambert had insisted on Italian all of those years ago, not French.

Victoria glanced toward Remington. "I am assuming you introduced me as your wife and he approved?"

Remington grinned and tightened his hold on her hand. "He is under the impression that every man must dream of meeting a woman like you. Something I already knew years ago."

Heat crept into her cheeks as she turned back toward the man, who grinned at her with crooked, but very white teeth. *"Grazie, signore."* That was about all the Italian she knew.

Antonio removed his cap from his head, revealing long black curls any woman would have swooned for.

He bowed sweepingly.

Remington released her hand and said something more at length to the man in Italian, his voice cheerful, warm and smooth.

Antonio rolled his eyes, shook his head and replied something in turn with a flurry of words, securing his cap back in place. He waved them toward the gondola.

Victoria dug into her reticule to retrieve money.

Remington leaned toward her, his gloved hand covering hers and stilling it against the cord of the reticule. "Antonio insists you ride free for the first few days. He hopes you will enjoy his services enough to secure him for however long you stay."

She glanced up in surprise as Remington released her hand and stepped toward the gondola. She turned toward Antonio and shyly smiled at him.

Antonio waggled his dark brows and grinned.

Remington veered back toward Antonio and stared him down. "Try not to ring that bell of yours too much around my wife. I just might hang you up on a church spire."

Victoria smacked Remington's shoulder. "He is letting us ride free. Let him ring all he wants. He's earned it."

Remington dropped his hand to his side and eyed her. "I do not want you feeling uncomfortable. The men here are a bit more forward than what you are accustomed to."

"So I have noticed. It has its charm." She approached the gondola excitedly and glanced back at Remington. "Might I...?"

"Of course." He parted the ivory curtains for her, gallantly assisting her into the covered cabin.

Victoria sank into a plush cushion. Smoothing her skirts around herself and the seat, she glanced around, feeling the buoyancy of the gondola, and yet feeling surprisingly secure and more comfortable than in any carriage.

Remington settled beside her, his large frame taking away some of her space and squeezing her against the side of the curtain he drew open and tied into place.

He removed his hat, set it at his booted feet and then to her surprise, wrapped his arm around her shoulder and yanked her closer. "We will be more comfortable this way," he murmured against her bonnet.

She bit back a smile and nestled against his solid warmth. She couldn't imagine riding about Hyde Park with her husband's arm draped around her. It would be the scandal of the Season. She had to admit, she liked Venice based on this moment alone. It felt like she was finally free of all pretenses.

The gondola slid out upon the Grand Canal and the lapping water filled the air. The cool wind pushed in through the open curtains, swinging the fringed, silken cords that held them open and feathering against their faces.

She felt as if she were floating between the earth and sky as they began weaving around the other countless gondolas that cluttered the canal. She glanced up toward whitewashed, arched windows passing alongside them and then back down toward the thick, green water where the buildings were reflected in distorted ripples.

Antonio bellowed out something in Italian as they veered around the corner of a building and into a narrower area. The buildings seemed to close around them. She could now see the water lapping against the stones, the movement displaying fresh and blackened seaweed and moss. Various wood doors with stone stoops set against the water drifted by, barely an arm's length from where she sat with Remington. To think one could step from one's home straight into water was as odd as it was charming.

Between the beauty of the buildings, the water, the gondola and Remington's warmth affectionately surrounding her, she felt a soft flame of happiness. A true happiness she had not felt in years. Everything seemed so...*perfect*.

Eventually, the gondola veered toward the stone stoop of a towering, narrow brick façade. The gondola came to a halt. She sat up, glancing toward a bright-red doorway with a large iron knocker in the shape of a lion.

Remington drew back his arm, snatched up his top hat and climbed out onto the stoop, causing the gondola to sway. His gloved hand reappeared before her. "We will see more at night. We visit Cornelia first."

Her heart soared at the thought of finally meeting his stepsister. She grabbed hold of his hand, gathered her skirts and stumbled out of the gondola onto the stone step. She straightened and cleared her throat, slipping her hand away from Remington's.

"Return when the moon is highest, Antonio!" Remington called out.

"*Sì, signore!*" Antonio called back. With a graceful swing of his oar, he and his gondola floated away down the water pathway.

Victoria glanced around. She and Remington now stood between deep, murky-green water and a building, with nowhere to go except through the closed red door before them.

She eyed him. "I hope Cornelia is at home or we may have to swim."

Remington stepped toward the door and used the iron ring against the block located beneath the lion's mouth. "'Tis early. As such, I know we are assured entrance."

Victoria settled nervously beside Remington and arranged her skirts about her. "What if Cornelia doesn't approve of me?"

"Then I will have to get myself a new wife."

She smacked his arm as the door edged open.

A thin, gray-haired man, his face heavily aged by the sun, peered out at them. His dark eyes widened as he stepped out toward Remington. "*Signore!*"

"Marcello." Remington tapped his gloved finger against his lips. "Have Cornelia and Giovanni come down at once. Tell them nothing. Only that I have arrived and that it is extremely urgent."

The man nodded, tapping his own finger against

his lips. He pulled the door open wider and waved them both inside.

Remington ushered her into a large, open marble and gold-painted hallway that opened onto two enormous side rooms with soaring ceilings.

The doors closed, darkening the foyer, leaving the scent of sea and wine noticeably hanging in the air. Several lit candles softly illuminated honey-colored silk-brocaded walls that decorated the expanse of the dim hallway.

The butler held out his hands. *"Signorina?"*

She turned toward the man. "Oh. *Grazie.*" She untied the gauze ribbons of her bonnet, removed it and handed it to him. She unclasped her velvet mantelet and removed her gloves and reticule, handing those to him, as well.

Shuffling past, he gathered Remington's hat and gloves. Setting everything onto a side table, and patting it into place, the old man trudged up the staircase with a swagger that a butler in London would have been tossed for.

She fidgeted with her fingers and eyed the stairs. She had always wanted to meet Cornelia, though certainly not under such unannounced circumstances.

Remington stepped toward her and yanked her back firmly toward him, wrapping his arms around her. His hold tightened. "She will adore you."

Victoria nodded awkwardly, her stomach in a knot. She felt as if he was about to put her on display.

"Jonathan!" a female voice exclaimed. "Why ever are you back so soon? I thought surely…"

Victoria's gaze lifted toward a full-figured, curvaceous woman standing at the top of the staircase.

Long, unbound chestnut hair lay in waves, framing a very pretty, round porcelain face. Cornelia adjusted the red sash around the waist of her clinging golden silk robe. She blinked down at them with inquisitive brown eyes, her arched brows coming together.

"Say nothing," Remington whispered into Victoria's ear from behind, his breath heating her cheek. His arms tightened even more.

Victoria melted against his solid frame. She couldn't help but be enamored by how excited he was to share her with Cornelia. She brought her own hands up toward his forearms and squeezed them, assuring him she would remain quiet.

Cornelia descended the staircase, her pearl-studded satin slippers peeking out from beneath her robe with each hurried step. She paused directly before them, her eyes widening. "Is this…?"

Remington playfully rocked Victoria from side to side with his own body. *"Yes,"* he drawled. "This is Victoria. The new Lady Remington. She and I were married back in London."

A high-pitched screech escaped Cornelia as she

clapped her hands and jumped up and down, causing all of her curls to bounce up and down along with her. "Oh, this is…*marvelous!* Absolutely marvelous! Oh, Jonathan. Why did you not write and tell us? You really should have…" She froze and clasped her robe together at the base of her exposed throat. "Fie. I am not even dressed to meet her."

Remington released Victoria and started pulling her back toward the door. "I suppose we should leave. Come along, Victoria. We will find ourselves a hotel."

Victoria giggled and scampered after him in an effort to play along. This reminded her of the Jonathan she had first met.

"Jonathan!" Cornelia exclaimed, hurrying toward them. "That is not in the least bit amusing. I will not have you and your new wife staying in a hotel. You will stay here with me and Giovanni. *Oddio.* You could not have arrived at a more harried time. Giovanni's birthday is next week and though the brute resisted to the end, I'm hosting a masked ball in his honor. We will have to find you both something to wear and visit a *mascarero* at once. Only I—"

Cornelia paused. She spread her arms out toward Victoria and smiled, her cheeks rounding. "Enough with my incessant talk. I wish for your affection, sister dearest. I deserve it after having endured years of Jonathan's rantings."

Victoria hurried forward, oddly feeling as if she already knew this Cornelia. She pressed the woman's lily-scented softness to herself and murmured against her shoulder, "Your brother has told me so much about you."

"Oh, has he now?" Cornelia pulled away and searched her face with bright brown eyes and flicked Victoria's hair with an exploratory finger. "She really is beautiful, Jonathan. *Corpo di baco.* I do believe she will overturn every gondola in Venice."

Victoria let out a nervous laugh.

Cornelia swept out a hand and rattled it. "Come. Whilst we wait for my husband to join us, I will show you my redecorated ballroom, which I intend to debut quite soon. Giovanni thinks it's exceedingly pompous, but then, he has no taste whatsoever."

Cornelia grabbed her hand and hurried them both past Remington and through the open doors of the archway on their right. Cornelia released her and gestured toward the expanse of the room with a great sigh. "What do you think? Is it fashionable enough?"

Victoria glanced around the large rectangular room, noting how on one side its large windows faced the canal and at the far, far end they faced a small cobbled courtyard. Why, the room was the expanse of the entire house!

Her eyes widened as she slowly turned to get a better view. The room was simply furnished with an array of upholstered chairs and French clocks. The impressive length of the sweeping walls was painted a soft, pale green and bore dozens of oversize gilded mirrors and sconces that not only expanded the room, but allowed the light from the outside windows to brighten the space all the more.

"'Tis beautiful," Victoria breathed. "Stunning. Especially with the views of the canal and the courtyard."

Cornelia waved her hand about. "Yes, I think so, too." She sighed heavily. "I must see what is taking Giovanni so long. The poor man would be late for his own funeral." She spun around and hurried out of the ballroom, her robe floating around her as her slippers shuffled against the marble.

Silence hummed.

Victoria wistfully glanced around the ballroom again, wondering what it would be like to own something like it. Something she could call her own and use to enliven not only her life but the lives of others with dance and music. She headed back toward the entryway.

Remington leaned against the open archway, setting his hands behind his back. He eyed the ballroom and then her as she approached. "What do you think of her?"

"She is everything I expected and more." Victoria settled herself against the archway opposite him, smiled and arranged her skirts.

His blue eyes met hers across the short expanse between them. After a moment, he asked in a low tone, "And what do you think of Venice?"

It was a question that she knew asked far more than the obvious. He was asking her if she could see herself staying. She drew in a shaky breath. "It is truly enchanting."

"We can make it our home. Raise our children here."

Children.

Silence hung between them.

"*Remington!*" a deep sweeping voice boasted from the top of the stairs. "*Congratulazioni!* You are now a man. A real man."

Startled, Victoria pushed away from the archway and turned toward the staircase. A distinguished-looking gentleman with thick, silver-streaked black hair descended the stairs. A red silk cravat hung loosely around his neck. And his shirt was scandalously open, exposing the intimate curve of his throat and the dark hairs of his chest. Fortunately, everything else, including his gray trousers, was properly affixed.

Remington touched a hand to Victoria's waist. "Victoria, this is Baron—"

"No, no, no. We are *famiglia*. I insist she call me

Giovanni." The man held up a hand and paused at the bottom of the staircase. He smiled and eyed Victoria, then leaned against the iron banister, setting his collar up. "I hope you and Remington do not have any plans. 'Tis obvious *mia* Cornelia intends to take over your entire schedule whether it pleases you or not. She has already added you and Remington to the guest list for the party in honor of my being *very old*." He wrapped his cravat around his collar and knotted it, the sapphire ring on his finger winking at her with each quick movement.

Victoria smiled, fascinated by his unconventional approach to their conversation while he dressed in front of her. He was so worldly and charming. He seemed as if nothing could disrupt his good mood. "I am so pleased she did. I have never attended a masked ball before."

"Never?" Giovanni smoothed down the front of his cravat, crossed his arms over his chest and tsked. "If only Austria would reinstate Carnival. It would put our pathetic attempts to shame."

"There is no more Carnival? Since when?"

Giovanni's eyes widened as he huffed out, "Since the Earl of Hell known as Napoleon swept through *Venezia,* is when." He rattled a hand about. *"Merda!* Do the British not inform their people of anything?"

"Giovanni!" Cornelia scolded from atop the

staircase. "We all know what you think of Napoleon, but please try to refrain from turning into him yourself. Cursing at our new sister-in-law? Whatever are you thinking?"

Giovanni sheepishly eyed Victoria. "You must forgive this wild brute. I am still being tamed."

Victoria smiled. "There is no need to apologize."

Cornelia regally descended the stairs and alighted beside them. "Later this week, you must grant me an entire day with Victoria in the city. There is so much I wish to show her. Things I know Jonathan will not, as they involve shopping. You and Jonathan can tend to the children that day if the governess finds herself overwhelmed."

Giovanni snorted and wagged a finger at Cornelia. "No, no, no. Remington and Giovanni will take to the city, whilst you will both tend to our beautiful *bambinos*. That is how it is done. You British have it all wrong, as always. Must I forever teach you everything?"

Cornelia snorted in turn and pushed his hand away. "I do beg your pardon, *Napoleon,* but you and Jonathan have already seen *Venezia.* I wish to show her the city before Jonathan sweeps her out into the plains and I never see them again."

Giovanni dropped his hand to his side and huffed out a breath. "Whatever my Cornelia wants, is what my Cornelia gets."

Cornelia leaned in and nuzzled his cheek with the tip of her nose. "Do not ever forget it."

Giovanni grunted.

They really were adorable.

Victoria leaned toward them, entranced by the way they interacted with each other. "I understand you two have three children? When will I meet them?"

"You will have to meet them right now." Cornelia reached out, grasped her arm and guided her around Giovanni. "And yes. We have three. Jonathan, Marta and Aniela. Come, come. They are all in the nursery and ought to be up by now."

Cornelia hurried them up the stairs, giving Victoria only a moment to glance back down toward Remington.

Remington grinned, then cupped the side of his mouth and yelled, "I forgot to mention that she will exhaust you to no end and will never allow you to say no to anything."

Victoria giggled. She stumbled on the last step as Cornelia tugged her onward. Gathering her skirts from around her feet in an effort to keep up, Victoria darted down the corridor after Cornelia. She had almost forgotten how truly wonderful it was to have a family. A real family of her own. It was something she hadn't been a part of in a very long, long time.

SCANDAL FIFTEEN

A lady's reputation will only fall apart if she lets it fall apart. She must therefore guard her name and her virtue with her very life, because sometimes abiding by all the rules is not enough. Sometimes, a lady will find there are unscrupulous men who seek to not only break the rules, but the very women who are trying to uphold them.

How To Avoid a Scandal, Author Unknown

Five days later
Venice, early afternoon

CORNELIA'S THREE adorable children with their pudgy faces, playful dark eyes, rosy cheeks and curling hair ranging from hues of chestnut to black haunted Victoria for days. Seeing Remington fawn over his nieces and nephew with words, silly faces and laughter made her ache for children in a way she had never thought possible.

Of course, to entertain such a thought would mean staying with Remington forever. Though she and Remington had shared a bed these past five nights, the only thing they had shared in that bed was a flutter of endless words that eventually exhausted them both.

As each day passed, she knew it was inevitable. Them. This. With each day, the excitement and the beauty that possessed everything and everyone around her made her realize life really could be perfect. One simply had to fight to make it perfect. And she had decided that come tonight, when she settled into bed alongside Remington, she would astound him by submitting to him completely. Her heart. Everything.

"The next shop is by far the most divine," Cornelia insisted, patting Victoria's knee with a gloved hand, stirring Victoria from her daze. "London has nothing like it."

Victoria grinned. She couldn't wait to see what Cornelia had planned. They had already spent most of the day floating about from stoop to stoop throughout Venice, stopping their gondolier whenever something was of interest, and exploring endless shops for glass beads, gloves, ribbon-and-lace bonnets, slippers and flowers. There really wasn't much room left in the gondola to hold another parcel.

Their gondola came to a bobbing halt beside a narrow stoop that only held one other waiting gondola. A black door with a brass dolphin knocker loomed before them. A long row of large glass-paned windows was draped with lush, red velvet that had various colored porcelain masks attached for display.

"Come." Cornelia gathered her pale pink equalette skirts and effortlessly hopped out of the gondola's cabin.

Getting in and out of a gondola was something Victoria had yet to master. She gathered her skirts and tried to step out elegantly, only to stumble, as always. It was getting to be quite amusing.

They entered the dim quarters of an enormous shop that hummed in silence and appeared to stretch for miles. A heavy, musty scent clung to the warm air. Large yellow glass lanterns hung sparsely from the vast timbered ceiling, softly illuminating dozens and dozens of alternating aisles in a way the plate-glass windows facing the canal could not. Tall wooden shelves set side by side cluttered every wall in the vast space, creating a fortress-like maze. And astonishingly, every single shelf displayed mask after mask, all of different expressions, sizes and colors. She never realized so many masks could actually exist.

Cornelia swept a hand toward the countless narrow aisles the shelves created. "When Carnival was banned, the *mascareros* were forced to gather their wares. Hence all these masks. Though masked balls are still quite popular, sadly, this shop is always empty. Now I want you to choose masks for yourself and Jonathan. My brother never willingly accepts anything from Giovanni and me, but I'll bully him if he doesn't accept a few wedding presents."

Victoria breathed out an elated sigh and scanned the never-ending parade of shelves and masks. "There must be thousands of masks here. How do I choose?"

Cornelia leaned toward her and said in a low, conspiratorial tone, "The purpose of a mask is not to hide your identity, but to flaunt it. Choose whichever mask you believe best reflects you. Though choose wisely. Others will judge you based upon the façade you wear."

Cornelia nudged her, then winked. "Take your time. We have at least two hours. I intend to look around myself. There are a few masks in the back I've been meaning to buy for myself and Giovanni, though I have yet to decide on which. Find me when you get bored. And if you cannot find me—which I assure you may happen—feel free to bellow across the aisles a few times and make your way toward the very far back. Venetians do it all the time and no one will think less of you. Now have at it."

Cornelia offered her a pert wave, then disappeared with a rustle of skirts down one of the aisles, veering off to the right and into the labyrinth of shelves and masks.

Victoria smiled and drifted to her left, down toward the farthest aisle against the farthest wall. Seeing as they had time, she would go through each and every single shelf and aisle. It would probably take at least two hours…if not three or four.

She scanned the first set of large shelves. Frozen porcelain faces laughed, cried, smirked and smiled. Though incredibly, none of the masks laughed or cried or smirked or smiled in the same manner. There were masks resembling the moon, the sun, flowers, animals. It was endless.

She edged farther down the long aisle against the wall, more and more masks taunting her as she moved deeper into the shop. She veered down another aisle, feeling as though she were an ant crawling through a forest. Eventually she paused and eyed a particular mask that seemed out of place amongst all the pompous, bright feathers and porcelain.

It was an expressionless, all-black velvet oval mask. Smooth, with a sharp nose and no mouth. Only eyeholes. She didn't know why it appealed to her so much—perhaps because it was so simple in comparison to everything around her and reminded her of how she often felt around others. Somber and out of place.

Victoria reached toward the shelf and carefully fished the mask out from the clutter. She tilted her head, the bow of her bonnet digging into her chin, and fingered it. It was soft, yet not by any means fragile. The black velvet was attached to leather. It was very elegant and very simple, yet…how did it affix to one's face? There was no sash or even a ribbon. She drew her brows together, and turned it over, noting a small wooden piece attached to its back.

There was a soft creak from behind her and a deep voice announced, *"Eccellentissimi prima scelta."*

Her heart jumped. She spun toward an older, broad-shouldered man looming in the aisle behind her. Attractive amber eyes pierced the distance between them. His alabaster, seam-pinched waistcoat and snowy-white shirt, which boasted a knotted silver-lace cravat, were all scandalously flaunted by the absence of any coat. Striped gray trousers hugged his solid thighs, the ends of them pulled against foot straps that buttoned beneath polished, black leather boots. His unconventional appearance hinted that he was the keeper of the shop.

He smiled with vibrant, boyish charm, raking away long strands of graying, sun-tinted hair from his forehead with a bare hand. He playfully set a red and gold feathered crow mask against his own face with his other hand.

After peering at her through the large round holes for a moment, he drew it away and carefully set it onto the shelf beside him. His smile faded as he casually slid a heated gaze down toward her breasts and back up to her face again, making no attempt to hide his admiration for her and her newly acquired India muslin gown. *"Non farti passare per un santo."*

Searing heat touched her face as she struggled to remain indifferent. Heaven only knew what the man had said, but the tone of his voice was a bit too erotic for her liking. "Uh…forgive me, I do not understand."

She casually held up the black velvet mask she held, hoping to distract him from looking at anything he oughtn't. "Are you the keeper of this shop? Do you speak English? And if so, can you tell me how this is supposed to be affixed to one's face?"

His dark brows rose. *"British?"* he asked in a heavy Venetian accent.

Oh, good. He spoke English. "Yes. I am British."

He moved closer, the scent of cigars and leather floating toward her as he searched her face. "Visiting? Or staying?"

She swallowed, not at all comfortable with his questions or the way he continued to look at her as if examining a bottle of brandy he was trying to sip. "Your questions are not in the least bit respectable, *signore*. I ask you refrain."

"Ah. I understand."

"Thank you."

He nodded and stepped closer, shrinking the already small aisle with his presence. "Remove your bonnet and open your mouth to me."

Victoria scrambled back, farther into the aisle. "I beg your pardon?" she echoed, her fingers clenching on the mask.

The shop seemed to pulse as he drew closer, towering over her. The plate-glass windows beyond him eerily brightened the color of his golden-brown and gray hair and darkened the space around her. "Remove your bonnet and open your mouth to me. I will assist with your mask. The knob goes into your mouth and is held in place by your teeth."

Oh! Is that what the knob was for? She let out an exasperated laugh, glancing down toward the mask. "I see. I understand. Thank you. Forgive me, but for a moment I actually thought…" She winced, realizing how indecent it would have been to even say it to a man she did not know.

"You flatter me." The shopkeeper gestured toward the ribbons of her bonnet and smiled. "Remove your bonnet. I will assist."

"No, thank you. That won't be necessary. I—"

"One cannot purchase a mask without knowing if it matches the worth of its owner. Come. Remove your bonnet."

She retreated a bit more. Why was he being so insistent? Was he afraid she wasn't going to buy any of his masks? "I appreciate your assistance, sir, but there really is no need. I intend to purchase it, I assure you. I find the knob amusing."

His dark brows came together. He folded his arms across his chest, the broad outline of his shoulders straining the fabric of his white shirt and waistcoat. "It is not meant to be amusing. *Morettas* were once worn by women who visited convents and do not allow their wearer to speak. Is that what you seek for yourself? A mask that holds no emotion?"

She feigned a less than enthused laugh. How depressingly appropriate that she would choose such a mask. She would find another one. She doubted Jonathan would approve of her wearing the sort of mask he'd been trying to metaphorically strip from her. A mask she was done with wearing. "I thank you for pointing out the history of the mask. I suppose that leaves me to find another one. One offering more cheer. Now if you will excuse me, *signore,* I—"

He blocked her from leaving with the width of his body, his arms dropping to his sides. "You are very pretty," he concluded with a tilt of his head. "What is your name? Are you staying with the woman you arrived with? Is she your friend? Or family?"

Victoria blinked up at him in astonishment. Had he been watching her? Her heart pounded as she veered around him. "I am a married woman, *signore,* and therefore I respectably ask that you—"

He grabbed her arm and yanked her firmly back toward himself as if she had said quite the opposite. His dominating eyes held her in place as his grip tightened, pinching her skin beneath the sleeve of her morning gown. He leaned toward her and whispered, "I will ensure your husband never knows. Come with me. I promise to have you returned to him by the evening."

Her eyes widened. Who did this vile imbecile of a shopkeeper think he was? She ripped herself from his grasp, tossed her mask toward one of the shelves and glared at him. "You think much too highly of yourself, sir. I suggest you leave before I call the authorities."

She spun around, gathering her skirts from around her slippered feet and hurried down the aisle in the opposite direction. *"Cornelia!"* she yelled out.

She was not staying in this shop with a man like him in it. As she passed shelf after shelf of frozen masks, she eyed the open aisles alongside her, looking for Cornelia through the musty dimness, but there was not a single customer in sight, much less her sister-in-law.

The older gentleman's shadowed frame stalked steadily alongside the opposite aisle of shelves. He stared her down through gaps between the shelves, his husky features tight as he dug into his inner pocket for something.

Panic seized her ability to breathe. She scrambled frantically toward the end of the shadowed aisle, looking to dash across, but he veered right in and grabbed her.

She screamed as he shoved her hard against the shelf. Using his large body to hold her in place, he ripped off her bonnet, grabbed hold of her face and shoved a bundled handkerchief deep into her mouth with large fingers. She gagged and tried to spit it out, but he only pressed his hand hard against her mouth, forcing it back in.

Though she screamed against the leather-scented handkerchief and the bare palm of his hand, it was naught more than a muted cry. Tears blinded her as she struggled violently against his large frame. Her elbows jarred the shelves at her back, shooting teeth-clenching pain up the length of her arms.

He crushed her against the shelf with his massive body and grabbed an ivory porcelain mask from the shelf beside her head. "This is a better fit," he whispered.

Removing his hand from her mouth, he set the cold porcelain against her entire face, hooding her vision and in turn pushing the wadded handkerchief farther into her mouth.

Her eyes widened as she jerked her head against the mask and his movements, but his fingers had already secured the ribbons into place against the back of her head, pinching her temples and her scalp. She shoved against him with her hands, still trying to move, but couldn't.

He was utterly mad! He intended to ravage her against a shelf? In the corner of a shop?!

He pressed against her harder, now crushing her ability to breathe and move as his erection dug into her corseted waist. Unraveling his lace cravat, he yanked her hands down and behind her, sending the masks at her back clattering. He met her gaze and smiled as he tugged and knotted the cravat tightly around her wrists. Her skin chafed and her hands could no longer move.

She choked on a silent sob and tried to control her breathing to prevent herself from fainting. Her only air was coming through her nostrils, which were pressed tightly against the hard contours of the porcelain mask. The porcelain stuck to her face, growing moist from the silent tears streaming down her cheeks and the perspiration dewing her entire face.

He grabbed hold of her corseted waist and forced her in the direction of another, darker aisle in a far corner of the shop. She stumbled to get away, her legs tangling against her skirts in her effort, but he rammed her against a shelf and pressed his massive body against hers, keeping her from moving.

Bending his head toward her, he trailed soft kisses down her exposed throat, his lips warm. *"Lascia che per sempre inizi stansera,"* he murmured with a staid, haunting calmness.

He jerked up one side of her skirts and buried a

hand beneath them, yanking up her chemise. A large, warm hand was now gliding up the length of her thigh.

Tears overwhelmed her ability to see through the round openings of the mask. She screamed more forcefully against the gag and tried to use her own body to shove him and his hands away, but he only pressed into her harder, impaling her against the shelves behind her, making it impossible for her to move.

Where was Cornelia? Where was anyone? Why—

The man's fingers playfully grazed the outside of her lower thigh, back and forth, back and forth. "You need this," he murmured.

Victoria gagged against the handkerchief, the acrid taste of bile rising against her throat. The endless shelves of masks around them seemed to blur into one another.

He coolly watched her, his chest heaving against hers as though he were restraining himself from doing far, far more. He leaned into her and slid the tip of his tongue down her throat. "I can sense you defy every man who desires you," he rasped below her ear. "Why?"

She let out a muffled sob, his words slashing through her soul. It was as if he was stripping far more than her dignity. He was trying to dig his hands into her soul. Unable to properly breathe, she felt her vision fraying.

"You smell of lavender," he murmured against the curve of her shoulder. The hand touching her lower thigh fell away and her skirts dropped.

He reached behind her head and unlaced the mask, tossing it back onto the shelf beside them. Sliding his hands around her corseted waist, he unraveled the cravat that bound her wrists against each other and draped it around his throat.

He smiled, then gently pulled out the saliva-moistened handkerchief from her mouth and stepped back, stuffing the handkerchief into his pocket. "We will finish this another time."

Victoria gasped, gulping in the air that she had been deprived of as she fell back against the shelf and stumbled away from him. She wanted to run and scream and punch and butcher and maim him for what he just did, but for some reason, her body and her tongue would not cooperate. She only trembled.

"Victoria?" Cornelia called from behind them.

Victoria sagged out a sob, relieved she was no longer alone with him.

The man turned away and faced Cornelia. His deep voice cut into the pulsing silence. *"Baronessa.* I was wondering when you would join us. I must say, you keep such wonderful company. I wish to call upon your *fidanzata* tomorrow night at eight. I understand she has a husband. See to it he is not at home when she receives me. That is not a request." He weaved past them and disappeared down one of the aisles, moving deeper into the shop, his boots echoing heavily.

Cornelia gasped, turning toward the direction the man had gone before whipping back toward her. "Victoria! What happened? Where is your bonnet?" She rushed toward her, shoving the parcel in her hand beneath her arm. "Oh, God. What did he do? Did he hurt you? I tried to find you. I did, but…didn't you hear me calling for you?"

"No." Victoria drew in several ragged breaths, pushing herself away from the shelf, and placed a shaky hand against her stomach, the frantic beating of her heart still not at ease. "Who is he?" she demanded, still gulping for breath. "I want his name. I want that *disgusting* bastard's name! I want him hanged. *Hanged!*"

Cornelia's eyes widened, the parcel slipping from her hands and clattering to the floor. "What did he do? Dearest God, did he…?"

Victoria fought the trembling in her body and the sob clenching her throat as she pointed rigidly in the direction he had gone. "That…*savage* slathered himself all over me as if it were his right. This is outrageous! For a woman of my standing to be—"

Cornelia gathered Victoria into her arms and pressed her close. "We must tell Jonathan at once!

He will resolve this. He will resolve this misunderstanding. You will see."

Victoria flung Cornelia's arms away and stepped back into one of the shelves. *"What sort of misunderstanding do you think this is?"* she shouted. "That—that shopkeeper treated me as if I was not a customer but a Drury Lane whore!"

"Shh! We must leave. Come. Hurry!" Cornelia grabbed her arm and dashed them down aisle after aisle. They veered around a corner and were suddenly at the front of the shop again. Cornelia flung open the door, shoved Victoria toward the direction of their waiting gondola and slammed the shop door behind them.

Victoria scrambled into the gondola and stumbled into her seat. "I did not encourage him! I didn't!"

Settling beside her on the seat, Cornelia eyed her and said in a hushed voice, "I believe you. I do. I am… beyond words. But that…that was not the shopkeeper. That was *Marchese Casacalenda*. Jonathan was in service to him and his wife all these years. Did my brother ever tell you that?"

Victoria's heart about popped from her chest. She gasped, willing herself not to heave up everything she had eaten, and shook her head. Oh, dearest God. Oh, God.

"Jonathan will resolve this," Cornelia insisted. "He and the *marchese* have always had an amiable understanding. Despite the man's reputation, I can assure you, he was always very good to us. Always. We owe him everything we have."

Victoria shifted toward Cornelia, her throat tightening. "*That man*—" Victoria seethed out, trying to keep herself from shouting "—has never done anything worthy of praise. Whilst you may think he saved you and your mother from debt, in truth, he destroyed Jonathan. *That man* forced your brother into becoming a whore to his wife. What happened to me in that shop is nothing compared to what happened to my poor Jonathan. And if you doubt anything I say, go speak to your brother about this. Because I...I am—" Victoria choked, unable to keep herself calm. She slapped a shaky hand against her mouth in disbelief of what had just happened. Out of all the shops in Venice, out of all the women in Venice, why her? Why? Why did fate always have to be so cruel to her and to Jonathan? Why?

Cornelia fiercely gathered Victoria into her arms, an anguished sob escaping her. "I don't...I don't understand," she insisted against her bonnet. "Jonathan never told me. Why didn't he tell me? We tell each other everything."

Victoria swallowed, realizing that in her anger she had betrayed Jonathan's request that Cornelia never know. "Forgive me, Cornelia. I...I shouldn't have told you. Please don't tell Jonathan I told you. He didn't want you to know. The truth is, he wanted to leave their service, he really did, but when your life and your mother's were threatened by the *marchese,* Jonathan chose to protect you instead by cooperating. I sensed there was something revolting about that man long before he even touched me."

Cornelia openly sobbed against her. "I let him do it. I…let him. Mama insisted it was the only thing to do. And Jonathan…my poor, poor Jonathan, he swore they were treating him very well and that—" Cornelia sobbed and sobbed, her arms trembling around Victoria. "Jonathan loves everyone too much. And I hate him. I hate him for it. I really do. Because he is forever getting hurt. And he doesn't deserve it. He doesn't."

Victoria tightened her hold on Cornelia as tears streamed down her face. Jonathan had indeed always loved everyone too much. Including her.

She had always loved him, always, but had refused to acknowledge it, thinking she was protecting herself from another loss. But in the end, she had only been hurting herself and Jonathan. "I will see to it that Jonathan never gets hurt again, Cornelia," she whispered hoarsely against her. "That I vow. I will see to it with every last breath left within me."

They said no more as the world floated by in a blur, taking them back home.

SCANDAL SIXTEEN

When a lady becomes a wife, she is not by any means exempt from the rules of scandal. The rules are simply reorganized to reflect the expectations set by her husband. Sometimes, those expectations will exceed those of society. It can become annoying and extremely daunting.

How To Avoid a Scandal, Author Unknown

"GIOVANNI!" CORNELIA'S voice thundered from the corridor at the front of the house with a heightening hysteria. "Where are you? Giovanni? I must speak with you at once! For heaven's sake, *Giovanni!*"

Jonathan froze, then threw down his playing cards onto the lacquered walnut table and rose, glancing toward Giovanni, who had also dropped his cards and risen.

They both dashed across the length of the drawing room, their boots echoing in frantic beats.

Oh, God. Oh, God. What—

"Cornelia?" Jonathan yelled, his pulse thundering as he sprinted down the corridor toward the en-

trance hall. He stumbled out into it just as Cornelia and Victoria released each other from an embrace.

Giovanni skidded past Jonathan, coming to a thudding halt, as well. *"Ti sei fatto male?"* he demanded.

Cornelia stalked past Giovanni, ignoring him, and veered toward Jonathan. Her round face was flushed, her eyes red and swollen with tears that the shadows from the rim of her wide, pleated bonnet could not hide. Her lip trembled as she glared up at him. "How could you? How could you do it?"

Jonathan sucked in a breath and searched her face. He'd never seen her this angry with him. Ever. "What? What have I done?"

"You cannot claim to love others if you do not love yourself!" she shouted up at him, her throat straining. "I would have preferred death over what you agreed to! Have you no respect for yourself? At all?"

A solid smack across his face snapped his head aside and stung his shaven cheek straight to the jaw. He froze.

"Cornelia!" Victoria rushed over and shoved her aside. "He doesn't deserve such disdain. Not from you. Not from anyone. Leave him be. Leave him be!" Victoria fell against him, her arms tightening around his waist as she pressed against him.

His eyes widened, realizing Cornelia knew the truth about him and the *marchesa*. She knew he had been a paid whore. Whatever had been left of his honor and pride and good name was...*gone*. The only thing he had left. Gone. Because of Victoria. The woman he thought he could trust. The woman he thought he could love, despite her refusal to love him.

Gritting his teeth, he ripped Victoria's arms from his waist and grabbed hold of her shoulders. "You told her? When I specifically asked you not to? Why would you tell her? *Why?*"

Victoria lifted her gaze to his, her eyes also red and swollen with tears. "Please don't be angry. Please. Forgive me. I didn't mean to tell her. I—"

"It wasn't your right!" he boomed, shaking her, causing sections of her hair to fall out of her pins. He shook her again, his fingers digging into her shoulders in an effort to rein in his anger. *"It was my right, Victoria! Mine. Not yours!* Have I not crawled enough for you? Is that it? Now you seek to strip the very last of my honor by degrading me before the only family I have left?"

Victoria's eyes filled with tears as a sob escaped her lips. "Jonathan, please. Forgive me. I—"

"Remington!" Giovanni shoved him away, breaking Jonathan's hold on Victoria. "You are hurting her. Enough! Enough of this."

Jonathan turned away, raking shaky hands through his hair, unable to look at Cornelia or Victoria. He would now forever be nothing more than a worthless whore. Even to his own sister. He could never forgive Victoria for this.

Cornelia stifled a sob. "Giovanni, you must do something. *Marchese Casacalenda* is coming for Victoria. He is coming tomorrow night. What are we to do? Will the authorities do anything, given his power? Surely, they must do something! They cannot allow him to terrorize a woman like this."

Jonathan choked and swung back toward Cornelia and Victoria, his chest heaving. His arms and legs felt numb as he frantically tried to make sense of her words and what was happening. "What do you mean? What happened?"

"The *marchese*." Victoria's teary, anguished gaze met his. "He was in the mask shop. I…I didn't encourage him. I didn't. I don't think he knew who I was. I thought he was the shopkeeper. And then he made an offer to me. When I denied him and tried to flee, he grabbed me, bound me and…" She pinched her lips together, shook her head and looked away.

Jonathan could feel the veins of his neck swell as his mind, his breath, his body and his heart pulsed with a seething agony and hate he had never known in all his God-given years. Never once had he ever entertained the thought of murder. Until now.

Violently stripping his coat from his shoulders to free his arms and his body of the heat rising within him, Jonathan whipped it to the floor. "He will die for this," he rasped in a suffocated tone. He glanced toward Giovanni. "I will need your best pistol, a dozen lead balls and gunpowder."

Victoria swung toward him, her eyes widening. "What is it you intend to do? Kill him?"

"Yes."

"Are you mad?!" Victoria shouted up at him. "He may deserve death, but I will not see you hang for it!"

Jonathan knew it was best not to look at Victoria, lest he altogether lose his sanity knowing he and he alone was responsible for exposing her to this situation. Of all the women in Venice the bastard would want. Out of all the women, the *marchese* would seek to claim his Victoria.

"I will kill the bastard as legally as I know how," Jonathan pointed out in as cool a tone as he could. "In a duel. Giovanni. I am asking you to be my witness and my second should I be unable to finish."

A gasp escaped Cornelia. "Giovanni. No. Tell him no. You cannot allow for this. Both of you could be killed! Serving as a witness, let alone a second, is no different from holding the pistol yourself. You know that! Your own uncle was killed serving as second."

Victoria grabbed hold of Jonathan's arm, pulling him toward her, and shook it. "Jonathan. Jonathan, no. Please. *Please.* I am begging you. If you've ever loved me, please do not do this. There are other ways of bringing a man to justice."

Her words, let alone the anguish in her voice, should have compelled him to relent. It should have. But when the honor of the only woman he had ever loved was being threatened by the same man who had taken his own honor, nothing was about to compel him to change his mind. "There is no other way. I intend to duel."

Giovanni's dark gaze intently met Jonathan's. "I have three children and a wife to consider."

Jonathan stepped closer to Giovanni and said in a low, even tone, "If a man who wronged you in the most heinous of ways whilst using your own family against you wronged you again by seeking to make your own wife a whore, what would you do? Go to the authorities, who you and I both know will do nothing? Or would you protect your wife from a man who will not yield unless dead?"

Giovanni swiped his face and muttered, "I would kill him."

Jonathan half nodded. "Quite so."

Giovanni eyed him. "If you seek to do this, Remington, you must abide by the code of honor or *Venezia* and its courts will incriminate you. He must be given an opportunity to redeem himself. If he does not yield, I will gladly be your second and testify in court if he is killed."

"Giovanni!" Cornelia exclaimed. "No. I will not allow for it. I will not! How can you—"

"Aver detto abbastanza!" Giovanni boomed, sweeping out a rigid hand toward her. "We all know what the *marchese* is capable of. He is better off dead. Let the devil take his soul."

Jonathan set a hand on Giovanni's shoulder and gripped it. *"Grazie.* I need to talk to my wife. Please. Alone."

"Of course. Yes, of course." Giovanni rounded Jonathan, grabbed hold of Cornelia's arm and hurried her toward the stairs. "Come. We will visit with our children, *cara,* and leave Remington with his wife."

Cornelia smacked at the arm that was dragging her up the staircase. "No! I am not leaving until this is resolved in the manner it should be resolved. How can you allow for any of this? Giovanni, he is my brother!"

"And I am your husband!" Giovanni roared. "Which is why you will do as I say and leave them to their business. Now!"

Though Cornelia ferociously argued with him all the way up, they eventually disappeared out of sight, the flurry of angry voices dwindling.

Jonathan turned to Victoria, willing himself to remain calm, despite the trembling of his hands. He wanted so desperately to gather her in his arms and to hold her and tell her how much he loved her and how sorry he was for ever bringing her to Venice to begin with, but he was genuinely afraid he would crack. And that would do her little good. "What did he do?" he whispered. "Did he…penetrate you?"

She blinked back tears and shook her head. She closed her eyes and after a few moments whispered, "No. But he might as well have. He bound me, lifted my skirts and touched my thighs against my will. I have never known such…fear. Such…humiliation. Not ever."

His eyes widened as he sucked in a burning breath. The bastard had ravaged his Victoria with his putrid hands in a manner unfit for even a dockside whore. "I will duel him," he seethed. "And I will kill him. Let there be no doubt about that. He cannot expect to touch any part of you and live."

Victoria opened her eyes and slowly shook her head. She yanked at the ribbons of her bonnet, flung it aside and swept toward him. "Jonathan. Please. Do not do this. Let the authorities see to this."

"The authorities will do nothing. They never do. He lines their pockets with enough to ensure he is always outside their reach. Even when his own servants were disappearing and their families demanded answers, the authorities did not ask questions. They did nothing. *Nothing.*"

"I will not allow you to destroy your life over this, Jonathan. Do you understand me? I will not!"

His gaze narrowed. "You do not know me very well, if you think I intend to let *anyone* defile you in so vile a manner without justice."

She paused before him and lifted her jade eyes pleadingly to his. "Jonathan. My virtue and my honor are not as important to me as you are."

Feeling as though the room were blurring, he roared, *"That fucking prick will not live after what he did to you!"*

Victoria jumped, her eyes widening.

By God. He was frightening her, and in turn, spewing rancid words she shouldn't even be hearing. He swallowed and tried to regain whatever composure he could.

"Forgive me," he finally said, his voice ragged and tired. "Setting aside his intent to return for you, you will never be the same. This will haunt you and in turn, it will haunt us. You already set me at a distance and I…" He looked away, feeling tears pricking his own eyes. "I myself have yet to touch you and make you mine."

Victoria stepped closer. "I am yours, Jonathan. I am and always will be."

She seized him by his waistcoat and yanked him hard against her with a surprising strength that caused him to freeze. Her hand jumped up to the back of his collar and yanked his head down toward her, forcing their lips to collide.

His heart lurched madly as their lips parted in unison and her hot tongue slipped into his mouth before he could even respond. All of him melted against her with an agonizing groan that echoed around them. In that moment, nothing existed except the movement of her tongue against his own. Her luscious, velvet mouth and its soft heat poured against him, making them one.

She loved him.

She wanted him—and she knew what kissing him meant.

She was committing to him.

Forever.

He savagely deepened their kiss and slid his arms around her body, pressing his hands against the soft curve of her back and molding her more firmly against him, forcing her to feel his love, his lust, his very breath. He was already rigid with desperate need.

A torrent of wild, whirling sensations took command of his mind and his body. Another moan escaped him, echoing again within the quiet entranceway. Her hot, wet mouth devoured his, taking away his ability to breathe and think. Her hands gripped his hair hard, tugging him downward toward her, as if demanding he give in to more than the kiss.

He lowered his hands to her full muslin skirts, his palms skimming the length of that soft fabric. She was kissing him. She really was.

He fiercely fisted a large handful of fabric in each hand, yanking her skirts above her ankles to allow her better movement, and then blindly stumbled with her toward the ballroom behind them.

He broke the kiss when they made it through the entryway of the ballroom and quickly turned away, stepping toward the open double doors. His chest heaved as he slammed the doors. The noise echoed in the vast space around them, emphasizing that they had the entire ballroom to themselves.

Spinning around, he stepped toward her with marked determination, grabbed her corseted waist and steered her backward toward the nearest wall.

Her jade eyes never once left his.

"You kissed me," he challenged.

"Yes," she tossed back, allowing him to move her backward. "Which means you are now obligated to oversee my happiness for the rest of your life. And I assure you, my happiness does not lie with a dead man."

"I have been shooting pistols since I was six and hitting every mark since I was nine." Pressing her against the wall with his hips, he lifted her chin upward to better look at her beautiful, flushed features. "I will not die. He will."

"You cannot predict what will happen."

He outlined her chin with his thumb. "Do you love me, Victoria?"

She blinked rapidly. "Why else do you think I don't want you to duel?"

He lowered his head and hovered over her lips, the heat of her breath mingling with his own. "Do not insinuate what you feel for me. Say it. I want to hear you say it. I *need* to hear you say it."

"I love you," she whispered ever so softly.

"Like you mean it."

"I love you, Jonathan," she announced with more bravado and strength. "I love you, I love you, I love you."

His jaw tightened as he dug his erection against her lower half. "How much do you love me?"

She drew in a breath and let it out. "Too much."

"Too much is just enough for this man."

"And do you love me?" she whispered.

He kissed her forehead tenderly, wishing to God he could erase what had been done to her. "I have always loved you. Always. You know that."

He kissed her forehead again and again, brushing away the curling strands of blond hair gathered atop her head. He dug his fingers into its softness and removed one ivory pin after another, tossing them until all her thick hair slid down heavily and tumbled past his arms, her shoulders and down to her waist. Just as he'd joked those many years ago, she now truly looked like a mermaid. "By God, I would die for you."

She pushed at him, her eyes widening. "Do not die for me. Live for me. I have had my share of death."

"Let us not speak of it anymore. I promise you, in time, I will erase what was done. I will touch you in a way to make you mine again. All mine. Not his. I will erase the wrong that's been done."

Her gaze narrowed with savage determination as she tugged him near. "I do not need it to be erased at the expense of your life. You cannot and will not fight this duel. We are leaving Venice. Tonight."

"I will not set aside this wrong. Nor will I run."

Her flushed features tightened. "You will not be running. You will be acknowledging what is more important: *us*. This is about honoring yourself, Jonathan, as opposed to blindly submitting to whatever you feel. Not all emotions are good, and they cannot always be trusted. Even the best men can grow rotten. Turn away from the way you feel this once and do not submit to a savage act unworthy of you."

"Victoria—"

"Let nothing come between us again. Not now. Not ever. Now ravage me. Consummate this marriage. Do it. Now."

The base of his throat pulsed and throbbed as he fought his need for her. "No. I... Not now. We will do so tonight. In a bed. As you deserve."

"I know what I deserve. Now do you, Jonathan Pierce Thatcher, Viscount Remington, want to engage me, Lady Victoria Jane Thatcher, in all physical matters and in turn make us both love each other more than we already do?"

He swallowed. "Of course."

"Then do not make me beg for what is rightfully ours. For what has always been ours. Have we not waited long enough to be happy? Do we not deserve this moment? I am submitting everything I am to you, Jonathan, and ask you to submit everything you are to me."

God save him, this couldn't be real. He gently set her against the wall, lifted her chin toward him and lowered his head. He covered her mouth with his own, wanting her to know that he loved her. So damn much.

Nudging her lips farther apart, he pulled her tongue deep into his mouth and slid his hands down the length of her. He dug the tips of his fingers into the fabric of her gown in a desperate effort to contain his need to rip her dress apart and slam into her. What she needed from him was tenderness. Not more savage lust.

Her hands sagged for a moment, then trailed down the length of the buttons on his waistcoat toward his trousers. He shifted to allow her hands to roam and pushed his tongue rigidly against hers, challenging her to do more. One hand slid toward his backside, whilst the other gently rubbed against his erection, causing him to grind against her hand to increase the tightening sensations coursing through his body.

Her palm opened completely and rubbed the tip, finding it through the wool of his trousers, causing him to gasp against her mouth. He didn't know if she knew what she was doing, but it felt amazing.

Breaking their kiss, he set her more firmly against the wall and slid down the length of her body, savoring every curve that met his hands, until he was on his knees before her. He unfastened his trousers, pushed aside his undergarments and pulled out his heavy erection whose tip was already beading with wetness. He grabbed the hems of her skirts and threw them over his head, disappearing beneath them.

"Jonathan!" she gasped.

"Shh. It will be my lips and my hands you will forever remember." Though he could see nothing, he could feel her soft warmth and smell her moistened lavender skin. He eased her silk stocking–clad legs apart and skimmed his lips past a lace garter toward the inside of her thigh. He drifted toward her warmth and dragged his tongue against her nub, then sucked. Dragged, then sucked.

Her hips started to sway rhythmically against him, moans escaping her. It was beautiful and erotic.

And he knew that if he should die come tomorrow

morning in her honor, he would have died knowing he had finally claimed the greatest love he had ever known.

As JONATHAN's hot tongue lapped at her wet folds, forcing sensations to sabotage all thoughts, Victoria sagged helplessly against the wall and set her palms against it in a desperate effort to steady herself. She gasped for air as his large warm hands firmly held her in place. He was reminding her that such touches were magnificent. Not vile. Not savage. They denoted love. The purest and truest love.

Her knees grew weak against the tightening sensations overwhelming her and despite struggling to remain upright, she simply could not. With a moan, she slid heavily down the length of the wall toward him, causing him to stop. He withdrew from beneath her skirts just as she sagged onto the floor.

With his dark hair ruffled from his adventures beneath the fabric, he rolled onto his back, dragging her along with him. Her long, unbound hair seemed to tumble everywhere around them.

He lifted her and sat her just beneath his exposed erection. She pushed her hair back over her shoulders to keep it from interfering with everything he had in mind.

Holding her gaze with searing blue eyes, he slowly dragged her skirts up and up and pushed the gathered material away, exposing her lower half to him. "You will be carrying our child soon," he whispered up at her. "I will see to it. Tell me. How many children do you want? Do you even know?"

Her skin prickled and her heart pounded, aware of what was about to happen and that a child could indeed come of it. *Their* child. She lifted herself slightly to allow him entrance. "Four," she whispered back. "Promise me four."

"Four you will get." His hand slipped between them as he guided himself to her opening. He paused, meeting her gaze.

Sensing his hesitation, Victoria boldly defied him by forcefully sinking her entire weight down against that thick length. She gasped, stiffening against the unexpected searing pain that stretched and filled her.

Jonathan let out an anguished moan and grabbed hold of her waist, burying himself even deeper. "Dearest God, this cannot be real."

It was real. All of it. Them. This.

She sucked in a breath, trying to control the assault of physical sensations. It was equally as pleasurable as it was painful. "Is it supposed to hurt?"

"You went too damn fast," he breathed out, his chest heaving. "Do it slow for a bit of time. For both of our sakes. Or I will not last and you will not benefit.

Now move against me. Slow. And once you are ready, fast."

She set her hands against his chest and slowly rose against his length and down it, the growing moisture surrounding her folds making it not only more tolerable but even enjoyable. With each slow and steady movement, she found herself growing more and more bold, allowing his rigid length to go deeper and deeper, stretching herself more. Sensations started to build and she began to lose the ability to go slow.

He moved beneath her, his hold tightening on her waist as he fiercely took over each movement. "Look at me, Victoria," he rasped. "I want you to look at me."

Their eyes locked.

Holding her gaze, he thrust against her again and again, each thrust growing more violent and urgent. His shaven jaw grew tighter and tighter, his blue eyes never once leaving hers as he pounded up into her.

"Say you love me," he insisted. "Say it."

"I love you," she choked out, pushing down against his relentless thrusts and sensing she was but a few strokes away from the bliss she so desperately sought.

"Say it again."

"I love you," she choked down at him, her voice echoing all around them in the ballroom.

She held his gaze the whole while, gasping and

swaying and meeting the demands of his raging lust that seemed to grow with each passing second. She wanted to prove to him that he needed her far too much to ever do anything that might force them apart. She thrust down against his thick length repeatedly, her moans mingling more steadily with his grunts as her body trembled and pushed her beyond anything she had ever experienced.

"Look at me," he huffed out, pumping even faster. He kept holding and holding her gaze as if he needed her in order to breathe and to live. "Do not ever once close your eyes. Do not ever let me go. Not even as you fly."

Her eyes widened as she stared down into those love-ridden, penetrating blue eyes. Her entire body at long last bloomed with an agonizing pleasure that made her cry out. She desperately fought to keep her head up over him and do as he commanded. She bucked against him, bliss shattering everything but her breath and those eyes that held so much love. She would never be the same. And she vowed to never hide from her emotions or from him ever again.

JONATHAN'S MIND blanked as Victoria's wet, squeezing warmth tightened around his thick length. She cried out, her body and hair swaying against him, her smooth face flushing, but held his gaze as he had commanded.

Knowing she had found pleasure, he let a tormented groan escape him and quickly rolled her onto her back, ready to submit to his own. He set his hands just outside her shoulders and moved against her faster and faster, once again capturing those green eyes and silently commanding her never to let him go.

His breaths grew more and more ragged as the onslaught of sensations made his world spin. "Victoria. God. Victoria. This is everything I ever wanted and more."

His entire body shook with an explosive rush he'd never known. He choked out moan after moan that echoed around them as his seed spilled into her womb.

When his heart had eventually slowed, he kissed her smooth forehead, her nose and lips and withdrew himself gently, settling beside her on the floor. He closed his eyes for a moment, mentally and physically exhausted, and wondered what the hell had just happened to him. It was as if his soul had been cleansed. He had finally made love. He hadn't fucked. He had made love.

Victoria sighed wistfully. "Jonathan."

Still dazed, he turned to her, wrapping his arms around her, and cradled her against his chest. He nuzzled her abundant hair, the scent of soap and lavender calming his whirling thoughts. He lifted his head and smiled down at her, unable to find the words to express what this moment meant to him. She was finally his. All his. And no one and nothing was ever going to take her from him.

After a few long moments, she whispered up at him, "I don't want you to duel. I want my four children. And I want those children to have a father."

His chest tightened, reality slashing his thoughts yet again. He sat and pushed himself back into his trousers, fastening the flap into place. "There is nothing more to say." He stood, reached down and, taking both of her hands, pulled her gently up onto her feet. Her skirts fell back down around her legs with a rustle. He kissed her hands. "When he arrives tomorrow, you will retire. I do not want him seeing you ever again. I will do what I need to do to protect you and your honor. If you defy me in this, I will ensure your bedchamber door is bolted shut. Is that understood?"

She stared at him, abashed, and violently yanked her hands from his. "You are going to die and you expect me to be accepting of it?"

"I expect you to respect my decision. As a man."

"Whilst you disrespect me as a woman?"

"Enough. We will speak of this no more."

"So be it." She frantically gathered the silver chain from around her throat and yanked it up over her head. Grabbing his hand, she thrust it into his palm. "Take this." She yanked off the ruby ring from her finger and smacked it atop the pendant. "And this."

He drew in a sharp breath. "What are you informing me of? That after you have claimed the very last of me, you intend to toss me? For what? For defending your honor? As is my right as your husband? As is my right as a man?"

She leveled him with a firm stare. "If you fight this duel, I will not be waiting for you, whether you live or die. And all you will have to remember me by, should you live, are the objects you now hold in your hand. For that is how you are treating me, Jonathan. As a possession of yours that some other man has put his hands upon."

Fury choked him. "I have always followed my heart, Victoria. Always. You cannot ask this heart to stop beating for what it holds to be true."

Tears glistened in her eyes and a choked sob escaped her lips. She stepped toward him, grabbed his hand and pried his fingers back and open. She snatched his ring, letting the pendant fall to the floor, and darted past him toward the window facing the canal. She unlatched the large window and pushed it open.

He jerked toward her, his heart pounding. "What the devil are you doing?"

"Freeing your soul." She whipped the ring out into the murky green water outside the window.

He choked and felt like sinking to the floor and never getting up again. His mother's ring. His family legacy. His dreams, his hopes and everything it ever represented. Gone. All because—

Anger swelled within him, almost keeping him from breathing. *"Goddamn you!"* he roared, stalking toward her. "Why do you always seek to rile me at every turn? *Why?*"

She turned toward him, tears streaming down her flushed cheeks. "God. Damn. You. For one moment, cease thinking that I am the reason behind all of your problems. For one moment, consider the possibility that perhaps you are destroying yourself by having no self-control. I am warning you, Remington. You are about to lose far more than a stupid ring. Do what you must in the name of what you define as love and honor. Simply know that I will do what I must in the name of what I define as love and honor. I will leave you if you go against me in this. I will leave you. And even if you should live, I will *never* take you back. *Ever.*" She glared at him, then hurried past toward the closed doors, flung them open with a resounding bang and disappeared.

"You know damn well I will only come after you!" he shouted after her. "Like I always do! Hell, you and I have been playing the same game ever since we first met! You run and I run faster! You think you can outrun me, Victoria? Is that what you think? Yes, well, *try!*"

When there was no answer, Jonathan savagely swung his fist through the air. He punched the air again, wishing he had something to hit. Everything was falling apart. Everything! All because—

He was going to put a dozen bullets into the *marchese* for destroying the last of his life. A dozen bullets. If not more.

SCANDAL SEVENTEEN

A lady's definition of honor differs greatly from a gentleman's. Which not only creates a vast number of misunderstandings, but also a vast amount of scandal.

How To Avoid a Scandal, Author Unknown

The following evening
7:23 p.m.

A LONGER, MORE agonizing day Jonathan had never known. Neither Cornelia nor Victoria would speak to him. They wouldn't even acknowledge him when he entered the room. It made him want to shred himself apart.

He had already talked himself out of wearing his blade or keeping it anywhere in the room where he waited. For he knew he would only use it the moment the *marchese* arrived.

Giovanni set his hands behind his back and stalked the length of the parlor, his riding boots thudding against the marble. "Perhaps he will not come."

Jonathan seated himself on the closest chair and

shifted against the cushion. He leaned back, trying to appear comfortable when he was anything but. "He will come. The man always adds an additional half hour to his schedule. He never likes to wait and therefore ensures others do the waiting instead. A trademark of his."

Giovanni swiped a hand over his face, his sapphire ring glinting in the candlelight. "Rethink what it is you seek to do. Honor means nothing to a dead man."

Jonathan placed his hands onto the chair's armrests and dug the tips of his fingers into the gilded wood. "I am not dead yet."

Giovanni sighed and shook his head. He suddenly paused. His eyes widened as he smacked his hands soundly together. "I have it."

Jonathan eyed him. "What do you have?"

Giovanni pointed at him. "The authorities will do nothing. But the *Sei* will."

"The Six?" Jonathan's brows came together. "What the hell is that?"

Giovanni waved his hands about as he approached. "No. Not what. *Who.* Six men who specialize in seeking out duelists. They banded together long before you ever arrived in Venice and have brought many powerful men to justice. Not just here but throughout all of Europe. I know their contact."

Jonathan stared at him, his throat tightening.

Giovanni stepped closer. "If we inform them of this duel, they will send men to seize the *marchese* on the field at the appointed time and show no mercy. But they will also seize you, Remington. For they always seize both sides. Which means you and Victoria will have to leave Venice tonight. Before their contact is informed of it."

He was not about to yield. Not in this. Jonathan shook his head. "No. I allowed myself to be intimidated by that bastard once before and lost five years of my life. I am not about to—"

The calling bell sounded.

Jonathan stiffened. The butler had been instructed to escort the *marchese* into the parlor, allowing the man to think he was meeting Victoria.

Giovanni's dark gaze met his as the house grew eerily quiet again.

Jonathan leaned back in his chair. "When he arrives, you will leave."

Giovanni blinked hard several times, tension etching into his forehead. "I promised Cornelia and Victoria I would remain at your side."

Jonathan glared at him. "I don't want or need you any more involved than you already are."

"Regardless of what does or does not happen, you must abide by the code of honor."

"I will. I am, after all, a man of honor."

"If you strike him for any reason before the duel is

set and conducted, you will be incriminated in court for being the aggressor should he be killed. You cannot touch him. Do you understand? Not under any circumstance."

"Yes." Even though it was going to take the very hand of God to keep him from doing it.

Steady footsteps echoed in the corridor outside.

The *marchese*.

Jonathan rose from his seat, flexing his gloved hands, and coolly turned toward the closed doors of the parlor, waiting.

The doors of the parlor flew open and slammed against the walls, shaking the large portraits and gilded mirrors hanging throughout the room. The lit candles shuddered, shifting disfigured shadows across the high, crown-molded ceilings.

The man was always one for making an entrance.

A cloaked figure loomed in the doorway, looking like the Black Prince stepping out of hell wrapped in black satin and velvet. Except for those penetrating amber eyes and that set, shaven square jaw, the *marchese*'s face was hidden beneath a well-fitted black velvet mask. The man was known for visiting all of his lovers in masks, though he never wore the same mask twice and collected masks in the same manner he collected women.

"Leave us, Giovanni," Jonathan said tersely.

Giovanni lingered beside him. "Remington—"

"Giovanni," Jonathan repeated. "I will abide by the code of honor. But only if you leave. So I suggest you leave."

"Scopa." Giovanni pushed past Jonathan, bumping him hard with his shoulder, as if wanting him to know that he was not leaving willingly. He strode toward the cloaked figure in the doorway.

The *marchese* stepped aside with a sweep of his velvet-lined cloak and bowed his masked head as Giovanni passed.

Once Giovanni had disappeared, Jonathan shifted his jaw and pierced the *marchese* with a long, unwavering stare he hoped the man would remember whilst taking his last breath. "You are about to regret ever breathing. How dare you come here seeking to claim my wife?"

Sharp, amber eyes met his from beneath the slits of the mask. The *marchese* slowly entered the room, his movements smooth and ghostlike. A gruff laugh escaped his exposed lips. "This is very…how do you British say? *Awkward.* Forgive me, Remington. I did not realize she was yours. Might I say you have very good taste. Is this the same British woman my wife assisted you in acquiring?"

Jonathan narrowed his gaze, restraining himself from dashing at him and snapping his coarse Venetian head off his spine. Widening his stance, Jonathan methodically stripped one glove from his hand. "The code of honor demands I grant you an opportunity to redeem yourself. So redeem yourself. Get upon your right knee, serpent, and beg me for mercy. And maybe, just maybe, I will refrain from killing you."

The *marchese* strode farther into the parlor, his boots thudding across the marble tile. "I never beg for anything."

"You will after what you did to my wife."

"Consider my interest the greatest compliment you will ever know. I never bother with married women. You know that. I despise the complications. Husbands are so…territorial. Irrational. As you are demonstrating."

Trying to contain his anger, Jonathan held up the glove and shook it in warning. "The moment this glove falls—" he bit out "—you are dead tomorrow at dawn."

The *marchese* paused, as if genuinely surprised. That moment, however, was very short-lived. His cloaked figure stalked toward Jonathan, each heavy, booted step shaking the enameled glass chandelier above.

The *marchese* stopped before him, his height almost reaching Jonathan's. Almost. "I assisted you and your family when you had nothing. And this is how you repay me? With rooster pride? Ten thousand lire is not a mere spit. I also shared my pretty wife with you, did I not? Despite your initial resistance, you enjoyed her *figa* very much. I heard you grunting and moaning and pounding against her with incredible bravado almost every night. In truth, I often forgot she was my wife and almost thought she was yours."

Jonathan fought not to react as the muscles in his arm quaked from the rigid, pent-up tension he wanted to let loose, breaking straight through the mass of skin and bone standing before him. But if he struck him, if he touched him in any way, it would be proven in court that he had provoked the duel. And hang for the bastard, he most certainly would not.

The *marchese* leveled his chin so that the slits on the mask were more visible. He tsked. "In the end, this is not about your wife, is it? This is about you and me and your shattered pride. I could have ripped your wife's womb in half with my *cazzo* and this would still be about you and me and your shattered pride."

Jonathan sucked in a savage breath at the insult. He violently whipped the glove to the floor, wishing to the devil it was the *marchese*'s skull he was shattering against the wall and roared, "To the death! That is the only form of satisfaction I will receive out of this. *To the death!*"

The *marchese* sighed and stripped the mask from his face, causing his auburn and gray hair to stand on end. He held up his velvet mask and with the flick of his black-gloved wrist, tossed it at Jonathan's feet. "You clearly wish to die."

Jonathan snorted. "I am not the one who will die. The moment your last breath is taken on that field, I will personally deliver your corpse into the hands of those families whom you have wronged and let *them* decide if you are worth burying."

The *marchese* narrowed his gaze. "You have acquired quite the tongue since you left my service."

"My tongue was always there," Jonathan growled out. "I simply had to bite it for reasons you are well aware of. But you have no further hold on me. Nor will you *ever* have a hold on my wife."

The *marchese* observed him. "To the death? Will that please you?"

"Your death is the only thing that will please me."

The *marchese* nodded. "Very well. Pistols? Or swords?"

"Pistols. I provide both to ensure there is no tampering. The first shot will be decided by coin. Each pistol will be loaded shortly before each fire and will be loaded by my second and my second only."

"Very well. When? Where?"

"Six, tomorrow morning. The plain. By the first patch of mulberry trees off the main road." All the trees he had marked five years earlier with Victoria's name. When Victoria was still his without ultimatums and he was still a man with innocent pride and innocent honor.

"Your fearlessness impresses me."

"Leave. Leave before I make you swallow every last drop of your own blood. Our business is done until tomorrow morning at six."

"If you are not there, I will assume your wife is mine. *Buona serata*." The *marchese* offered a single nod, swiveled on his booted heel and strode out as if they had just finished the most amiable of conversations.

Jonathan seethed out a harsh breath, his clenched throat restricting his ability to breathe. Even as the man faced death on the morrow, he didn't seem to be in the least bit intimidated or humbled. And if death itself could not intimidate or humble a man, whatever would? Whatever would? Nothing ever would. *Nothing!*

Jonathan kicked away the velvet mask from his booted foot, stalked toward the nearest side table and snatched up a large, ornate vase. Gnashing his teeth, he turned and whipped it hard. It shattered against the nearest wall with a thunderous crash, spraying shards everywhere.

He whipped around and snatched up another vase and then another and another, shattering them all one by one by one against the floors, the walls, the doors, until all of it was nothing more than a roaring blur.

"Remington!" Giovanni boomed from behind. *"Enough! Enough!"*

Jonathan froze, his breath coming in ragged gasps, the porcelain figurine in his right hand still high above his head. Damn. He was destroying his sister's home. And not only her home, but her life. And Giovanni's. And Victoria's. Hell, he had yanked Victoria away from her father's side in some selfish, pointless need to prove his ability to claim her. Only to then expose her to harm.

Jonathan sank to the floor with a thud and sat there in complete silence, letting the figurine fall away from his ungloved hand. If he dueled, Victoria would leave him. But if he didn't duel, he would be walking away from himself and everything he ever believed in.

"Jonathan?" Cornelia's soft voice made him glance up.

He swallowed. "Forgive me. I will pay for everything. I promise."

"I am not worried about objects that can be replaced. I am worried about you." She drifted toward him with a pale pink and ivory hatbox in her hand and gently set it before him. "Read the top letter. Then decide what it is you intend to do." With that, she turned back to Giovanni, grabbed his hand and tugged him out of the room.

Jonathan sat there for a long moment. He then slid the hatbox over and lifted the lid, peering inside. He froze, recognizing all of Victoria's old letters. The ones he had never been able to read.

Setting aside the lid, he placed his hand against the folded, yellowing parchment on top, its red wax seal cracked. He drew in a breath, let it out, then plucked it up and unfolded the letter. The words had subtly faded.

September 26, 1825
REMINGTON,
Grayson refuses to inform me of your where-
abouts or what has become of you. He claims
he has been sworn to secrecy. I worry to no
end as to why and despise you and him for
betraying me in so cruel a manner. With the
Season over, I do nothing but stare at books
whose words hold no meaning. At night I cry,
feeling that I have buried yet another person
I love. Why would you condemn me to a life
without you? Why would you condemn me to
never knowing what has become of you? Does
pride truly mean more to you than I do? I only
wish to understand you, not judge you. Within
my soul, I knew this would happen. I knew from
the moment I gave in to this stupid passion I felt
for you that you would only disappoint me and
shred what little remained of my heart. I simply
thought that after having endured all the losses

I have, I would have been more prepared for the
pain you are forcing me to swallow. And yet I
am not. This is beyond anything I ever wanted
to feel again. At the very least, write and assure
me you have not been harmed. I fear for you
and the life you have fallen into.
Ever faithfully and always yours,
Victoria

He refolded the letter and shoved it back into the box along with the rest, slapping the lid back on. Holding a rigid fist against his mouth, he squeezed his eyes shut, her words echoing in his soul. It appeared he was going to disappoint her again. But at least this time, he was being true to everything he ever believed in.

4:26 a.m.

VICTORIA LEANED against the closed door of the guest bedchamber. She splayed her fingers across the cool, smooth wood and swallowed against the tightness throbbing within her throat. Jonathan had not come to her room at all. Not to sleep and not even to say goodbye. In two hours, it could very well be the last time she would ever see Jonathan. Not for a single moment was she going to fool herself into thinking that he would live.

She pushed herself away from the door. How could something so beautiful morph into something so dark?

Gathering her nightdress from around her feet, she drifted over to the dresser, where a small mirror and a basin of water had been set. She glanced at her reflection and cringed at the sight of tired, red, swollen eyes and a tangle of blond curls swept every which way, falling out of its pins.

She looked like Victor had on his death bed. Brave though he had been to the very end, he'd still cried, knowing he was dying. Her brother had cried, even though he believed in God. Fear had a horrid way of breaking even the strongest of faiths.

Victoria frantically readjusted the ivory pins in her hair and smoothed the falling curls. She leaned over the basin and dipped shaky hands into the cool water, scrubbing her face clean of tears. Using the folded cloth set by the basin, she dried her face.

She squeezed her eyes shut and blew out a slow breath. If he wasn't going to say goodbye, she would go and say it for him. Victoria padded across the room, unlatched the door and pulled it open. She froze upon finding Jonathan before her, dressed in full traveling attire and boots.

His blue eyes met hers. His face was ragged, as if he had already fought a hundred duels for her. He held out a gloved hand and unraveled it, revealing his coiled pendant. He stepped toward her and gently draped the pendant over her head. "Wear it. No matter what happens."

He caught her hand, lifted it toward him and kissed the top of her hand, his eyes closing, allowing his warm lips to linger. It was as if he were saying goodbye.

Her eyed widened. "You are choosing honor over me? Over us?"

He released her hand and stepped back. "Forgive me for always disappointing you, Victoria, but this is who I am and who I have always been. Though allowing my emotions to dictate my life has in many ways been a curse, 'tis better to die in the blaze of one's beliefs than to live a life without believing in anything at all." He turned and disappeared, his heavy steps echoing in the corridor until they faded.

Victoria stood there staring at nothing in particular, too many emotions raging through her for her to feel anything but numbness. She staggered, then lowered herself onto the cool floor and sat there for a very, very long time, unable to even cry. There were no more tears left within her.

She could live out the rest of her life drifting, emotionless, and mourning for whatever was about to pass, or she could become the sort of woman she had always wanted to be. The sort of woman who marched into battle in the name of everything she believed in. Like Remington always had and did.

Victoria rose to her feet, her strength fully returning. She was not going to abandon her man when he needed her most. Oh, no. Because despite what he thought, this was her duel to fight. Not his.

6:05 a.m.
The plains

"FIRST SHOT is awarded to the *marchese*," Giovanni announced, tucking the coin back into his pocket. He turned and retrieved one of the matchlock pistols from the velvet-lined walnut box set on the matted grass. "We proceed."

Jonathan stepped toward the wooden stake that marked his position and solemnly watched Giovanni prime the pistol by grabbing the ramrod and loading the lead ball with it. Giovanni pointed the pistol downward and strode toward the *marchese,* who already stood waiting beside his own wooden stake fifteen yards away.

The *marchese*'s second, a hefty young Italian, silently positioned himself off to the side and held up the white handkerchief.

Jonathan blew out a calming breath and set himself sideways, turning his head toward the *marchese.* The less he gave the bastard to shoot, the better.

The *marchese* took the offered pistol from Giovanni and waited for the handkerchief to fall.

The thudding sound of pounding hooves and a tremor beneath Jonathan's boots made him pause.

He turned toward the direction of the noise as two figures riding on hellish black horses drew near.

The horses jerked to a halt barely a few feet away. The riders dismounted with a single thud and removed a set of ropes from their saddles, which they looped onto the shoulders of their morning coats.

Jonathan's lips parted in astonishment as Cornelia and Victoria marched toward him in unison, both dressed in oversize male attire. Giovanni's attire.

What the blazes were they doing?

Victoria slid the looped rope from her arm and tossed an end toward Cornelia. Cornelia caught it with graceful ease, and together, they snapped the rope straight and dashed straight at him. The two rounded him so fast, he didn't even have time to think or dodge the hemp rope that caught his upper arms.

"Jesus Christ!" He stumbled as the rope looped and tightened around his arms and waist with each sprinting round they made. He grabbed at the ropes to free himself, but it kept slipping against their swift, sparring movements, burning against the palms of his hands.

"Victoria!" He jerked against the ropes that tightened, causing them to stumble momentarily. He whipped toward her, only to find he was already looking at Cornelia. "Enough of this. Enough!"

But the two merely sprinted around him faster and faster, looping and yanking on the ropes tighter and tighter, causing his skin beneath his linen shirt and waistcoat to sting at every movement. Gritting his teeth, he fought against the ropes, only to find the muscles in his arms and chest tensing and burning in vain. His anger spiked. The only way out of this was to physically hurt them with the weight of his own body. And that he refused to do. Even if they deserved it.

He jumped toward Victoria, the hemp rope digging into his sides. "Untie me. *Now*."

"No. I am finally going to live my life the way you do, Jonathan. By embracing what it is I feel instead of always running from it." Victoria stepped farther back as Cornelia knotted the rope more firmly into place behind him. "Take him off the field," she ordered, her green eyes staring him down with a heated intensity he'd never known.

His eyes widened as the rope jerked him from behind with a force that made him stumble. He jerked in the opposite direction, causing Cornelia to gasp and stumble back toward him.

"Giovanni!" Cornelia boomed.

Giovanni dashed toward them and skid to a halt, his dark eyes darting to each of them in bewilderment.

Jonathan staggered forward and growled out, "Giovanni. Untie me. Now."

"Giovanni," Cornelia chided in an equally predatory tone, yanking on the rope and tightening her hold,

"if you assist him in any way, I swear upon whatever love I have for you, I will take a lover into my bed. I will."

Giovanni rumbled out a laugh and held up both hands. "I apologize, Remington, but my wife means more to me than you do. She has never threatened to take a lover before. Which means she means it." He rounded Jonathan and grabbed the knotted end of the rope hard. "Come. Off the field."

He was never going to forgive Victoria for ending this duel. Ever! Jonathan wrestled against the strong movements, leaning as far forward as he could to resist. Though he dug in his heels and threw his weight forward, he still skidded backward, being dragged farther away.

In the distance, he could see Victoria remove her oversize coat and toss it onto the ground. She strode toward his own marked stake and positioned herself beside it, facing the *marchese*.

His eyes widened in disbelief. Victoria wasn't ending the duel. She was fighting it. Christ! He lunged forward. *"What are you doing?"* he shouted across the field, his throat straining. "Victoria!"

She glanced back at him over her shoulder, her face too far away for him to make out her features. She shouted back, "This is my duel, Jonathan! Not yours! Whatever happens, know that I love you!"

He choked. Dearest God. No. No! He lunged

forward again, yanking Giovanni with him. "Victoria! No! *Nooooo!*"

Giovanni grabbed hold of him and shoved him facedown onto the field in the opposite direction, so he couldn't see anything but the long grass around him.

"No!" Jonathan roared, violently jerking and rocking his body from side to side. "Giovanni, let me go! Giovanni!"

"Sit on him, Giovanni," Cornelia drawled.

Giovanni sat on him, his hefty weight pushing out whatever air was left within Jonathan's chest. *"Mia* Cornelia. Assure Jonathan that Victoria is not actually going to—"

"Jonathan has a choice in this," Cornelia said tersely. "He can announce the duel is over or he can watch Victoria fight the duel for him. It is as simple as that."

Jonathan felt everything momentarily fade. He didn't even know if he was breathing anymore. All he knew was that if anything happened to his Victoria, he would put a bullet through his own skull. For it would be her blood on his hands. He had challenged her to live by his rules and now she was going to die because of them.

Giovanni leaned toward Jonathan, shifting against his shoulders. "I will untie you, my friend. But I am still waiting for an answer."

Jonathan swallowed hard. He finally understood that honor and pride meant nothing without Victoria. "Untie me. I will not fight. *Now untie me!*"

VICTORIA STARED down the *marchese* from where he imposingly stood opposite her, dressed in only a white shirt, black boots and gray wool trousers. She was about to discover what he really was. An animal. Or a man. "I am here to defend my honor."

The *marchese* lowered his pistol to his side, his eyes sweeping the length of her body, which was clad in trousers. "I will not duel a woman."

"Yet you have no qualms about violating one?" she called back, widening her stance. "You either have morals, my lord, or you don't. Which is it?"

The *marchese* strode toward her, his long legs whipping away grass and wildflowers with a refined grace that did not reflect his savage ways. He paused before her, lingering so close that the scent of cigars and leather choked her. "This is not your fight," he said in a rough, accented tone.

Victoria fisted her hands at her sides to keep them from shaking and refrained from swinging at him. "No. It was *my* honor and *my* pride and *my* body that you violated and therefore it *is* my fight."

The muscles in his shaven jaw tightened as he half nodded. He hesitated, then held out the pistol, directing the handle toward her. "Take it. The first shot is yours."

Though she knew nothing about pistols, and had never even held one, it didn't matter. All that mattered was that Jonathan was safe. She reached out and grasped the smooth end of the pistol. It weighed heavily in her hand, eerily symbolic of death.

The *marchese* jerked up her hand and set the muzzle of the pistol against the middle of his chest. "Now shoot, *cara*."

Her hand trembled as her hold tightened on the pistol. She stared up at him, her breath coming in uneven takes, as he intently held her gaze. All she had to do was slide her finger toward the trigger and pull it back and it would all be over. He wouldn't be a threat to anyone anymore.

His amber eyes mocked her. "Why do you hesitate? Am I still too much of a man in your eyes? Even after what I did?"

She clenched her jaw as her finger instinctively slid toward the trigger. She wanted to kill him. She did. In the name of everything he ever did to her, to Jonathan and anyone else, but it was obvious that was what he wanted. He wanted to drag her down into the pits of hell with him.

"You are not even worthy of hate," she seethed out, lowering the pistol. "I pity you. I truly do. For you will never know a day of the sort of love that I share with my husband. With my Jonathan."

His smile faded. "You are wrong. Love created the man you see standing before you." He lowered his chin. "Now give us both peace. Shoot." He reached out and grabbed her hand, jerking the pistol to the edge of his right shoulder. He mashed her finger against the trigger.

Her eyes widened as an acrid puff of smoke filled the air and thunder clapped from the pistol, jarring her arm back. She screamed and scrambled back, the pistol falling from her hand and landing in the grass between them.

"Victoria!" She could hear Jonathan charging in their direction from across the field.

The *marchese* staggered back, the right shoulder of his white shirt blackened with gunpowder as bright-red blood bloomed and soaked his shirt within seconds. *"Bartolomeo!"* he roared toward the Italian gentleman scrambling toward them. "We leave. This duel is over."

The *marchese* yanked his shirt up over his head, his defined muscles shifting. He gasped as he stripped it from his body, exposing the gaping flesh on the edge of his shoulder. Wincing, he dug his bundled shirt against the wound and met her gaze. "Hate. Love. It is all the same. For it consumes every last ounce of the soul. Does it not?"

Jonathan shoved his way between them and froze. He stepped back toward Victoria, shielding her. "Christ." He jerked toward her and grabbed hold of her shoulders, his eyes wide as he frantically scanned her body. "Are you—"

"N-no." She choked. "Oh, God. I didn't—"

"Your wife has impeccable aim," the *marchese* drawled. "If I die, may it bring you both peace." He turned and staggered toward the man who guided him toward their horses in the distance.

All Victoria could do was stand there and gape after the man in complete disbelief. He had forced her hand into shooting him. Why? Did he feel remorse? Could such a man feel remorse? She supposed some men were too warped to ever understand.

Jonathan grabbed her and pressed her savagely against his body, his chest heaving. "I vow never to choose pride over our love again. That I vow. Forgive me. Dearest God, Victoria, say you forgive me."

She sagged against him and dug her fingers beneath the warmth of his morning coat. Never again would she allow anything to come between them. Never again. "I want to leave Venice," she whispered. "I want to go home. I want to be with my father."

He stiffened and after a long moment of silence whispered hoarsely, "Will you be leaving without me?"

Tears blurred her vision as she tore away from him.

She reached up and grabbed his face, yanking him down toward her lips. Kissing their softness repeatedly, she choked out, "Never. Wherever I go, you go. For you are my husband, Jonathan, and I am your wife."

SCANDAL EIGHTEEN

Every lady should read at least one poem by George Herbert. His words reveal a beautiful, yet simple understanding of life. 'Tis an understanding every lady requires, whilst facing a world that expects everything from her, yet callously dismisses her for being a woman. If ever in doubt, heed Herbert's own wise words and assessment: "The best mirror is an old friend."

How To Avoid a Scandal, Author Unknown

CORNELIA SNIFFED against tears and shoved the hatbox she was holding into Victoria's arms. "Take this. It is no longer mine and I have kept it long enough."

Victoria glanced over at Giovanni and Jonathan, who stood waiting by the entrance door. She eyed the hatbox in her gloved hands. "What is it?"

"Your letters to Jonathan. I apologize for reading them. But in many ways, I am glad I did. That is how I knew you were worthy of my brother." Cornelia leaned toward her and pressed a kiss to her cheek, bumping the side of Victoria's pleated bonnet. "Giovanni and I will visit you in England next year with the children. In the meantime, see to it Jonathan is well cared for and that he sleeps. He must sleep."

Tucking the hatbox beneath one arm, Victoria grabbed hold of Cornelia with the other and hugged her tightly. "I will see to that and more, but I cannot help but worry about leaving you and Giovanni behind. What if the *marchese*—"

Giovanni snorted and smugly hit his fist into an open palm as he made his way back toward them. "I expect no retaliation. He willingly shot himself. Now let us hope he bleeds to death."

Victoria released Cornelia, feeling as though she were leaving both a friend and a sister, and turned toward Giovanni. She smiled and held out her hand for him to kiss.

He tsked. "Do not insult me with your British ways." He grabbed hold of her shoulders and hugged her heartily, then soundly kissed each cheek. Twice. "*That* is how it is done."

Victoria grinned, shaking her head and stepped back. She would genuinely miss them both and wished she had had an opportunity to kiss and hug all of their beautiful children goodbye. But they'd all long been put to bed in the nursery.

"Victoria." Jonathan's voice cut through the silence and she knew her moment of farewells had passed.

She sighed and hurried with her hatbox toward her husband. As they floated toward the Grand Canal in the lulling silence of the night, all of the old stone and marble palaces around them seemed to glow brilliantly in the moonlight. The water glittered around them like a diamond-illuminated path.

Jonathan wrapped his arm around her and tugged her solidly against him. A sense of stillness overcame Victoria. One she thought she would never feel. It was happiness at long last.

"We have no further need for these." Victoria opened the hatbox and flung all of the letters inside of it out into the water.

Jonathan jumped, causing the gondola to sway momentarily as he tried to grab the fluttering parchments, but they all disappeared out of reach as the gondola drifted on. His arms dropped back around her. He huffed out an exasperated breath. "Now our children will never have proof. We have no ring and no letters. Christ."

Oh. She hadn't thought about that.

Victoria turned in the cushioned seat of the gondola and looked back at the moonlit water littered with her letters. "Should we collect them all?"

"They are ruined." He eyed her. "Why did you do that?"

She rolled her eyes in exasperation, set the hatbox at their feet and settled back against his arms. "I was tossing away the past. 'Twas supposed to be metaphorical. You know, like when you offered that plate to me in the garden."

Jonathan paused and let out a laugh. His arm tightened around her shoulders as he leaned in and kissed her soundly on the lips. He nuzzled his face against hers, crushing her bonnet. "You still remember that? What a damn sop I was."

She smirked. "You still are, Jonathan. Believe me. You still are."

Twenty-three days later
Evening
London, England

HER FATHER was dying.

It was something no one, and most certainly not her, had expected to return to. And even though her father was confined to his bed, barely breathing, unable to move, and his last rites had already been offered many hours before she and Jonathan had arrived in London, the earl with his iron will had somehow waited. For her.

Victoria stripped her traveling bonnet from her head, letting it tumble to the floor beside her father's bed. Flint whimpered as he weaved past her feet. She tearfully sat on the edge of the bed beside her father, whose chest raggedly rose and fell beneath his soaked nightshirt. His eyes were closed but his brow creased, as if he were struggling to find peace but simply could not.

She gently gathered his gauze-wrapped hand, leaned toward the side of his face and whispered into his ear, "I love you, Papa. And I promise that your grandchildren will know of you and will love you, too."

Her father's hand slowly tightened around her fingers, causing her to lean back so as to better look at his face. A face that was lesioned, tired and old. A face that had once belonged to one of the greatest men she had ever known.

He gasped, his eyes snapping open. He stared up at her for a moment, his expressionless green eyes ever so slowly sharpening.

She smiled through the tears blurring her vision, but said nothing. There was no need to. All that mattered was that she had been allowed to look into his eyes one last time. Be she Camille. Be she no one. She knew what had once been.

He blinked rapidly and his forehead creased. "Victoria?" he rasped. "Wherever have you been?"

Her eyes widened in a disbelief that was laced with a bittersweet joy she never thought she would feel in that moment. A half sob and half laugh escaped her, knowing he was speaking to her. *Her.* "I was in Venice, Papa. I was visiting with my husband's family."

"Husband?" he whispered. "You are finally married?"

"Yes. To the husband you chose for me. I am married. Like you wanted me to be. And I am so happy. So very, very happy."

A small smile puckered his lips. "Remington. You chose Remington."

She squeezed his hand more tightly, her lips trembling as she tried to smile for him. "Yes. I did."

"Is he here?" he whispered.

"Yes." Victoria glanced toward Jonathan, who quietly lingered by the bedpost.

Jonathan quickly approached. He leaned in against the side of the bed. "My lord."

The earl glanced up Jonathan and with his other hand pointed at him. "She is yours now. Yours. Care for her."

Jonathan nodded, his features tightening. "I will, my lord," he offered in a low, assured tone. "I will. Always. I vow."

"Good." The earl half nodded, his hand lowering back to his side. He closed his eyes, tightening his hold on Victoria's hand. "Good. I knew. All is as it should be. All is…" The earl stiffened, his face twisting in pain as his hand tightened savagely around Victoria's.

"Papa?" she whispered, trying to mask her panic. For his sake.

He gasped, his chest quaking, causing the loose lacing of his ruffled nightshirt to stretch. He gasped again, his jaw tightening, then completely stilled.

His creased brow softened, fading the deep lines in his aged face. His lips slightly parted as his long fingers loosened against hers. His large hand now weighed heavily within her own.

He was no more. He was with Mama and Victor now. Where he belonged and could suffer no more.

Victoria sobbed, lifted his limp, gauzed hand to her lips and kissed it. "Be happy, Papa," she choked out, tears tracing down her cheeks. "Be happy and know that I am, too. Thanks to you. Tell Mama and Victor that I love them and miss them very, very much. Tell them. Be sure to tell them."

A hand gently touched her shoulder. "Victoria." Jonathan's soft tone conveyed his deepest condolences.

She released her father's hand, turned and grabbed hold of her husband, pulling him down toward her. She wept against his broad shoulder. "He is gone. I cannot believe it. I thought surely he would live longer."

Jonathan's hand tucked her head against his chest as his other arm slid around her. "I am so sorry," he whispered against her hair. "A greater man I have never known."

They held each other in complete silence.

Though Victoria knew that the world had lost a

great man, a man who had been her father and her friend, the world still held so much meaning and so much hope. For this wasn't the end for her. No. Not at all.

This was only the beginning.

* * * * *

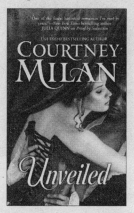

PRESENTING…THE SEVENTH ANNUAL
MORE THAN WORDS™ ANTHOLOGY

Five bestselling authors
Five real-life heroines

This year's Harlequin
More Than Words award
recipients have changed lives,
one good deed at a time. To
celebrate these real-life heroines,
some of Harlequin's most
acclaimed authors have honored
the winners by writing stories
inspired by these dedicated
women. Within the pages
of *More Than Words Volume 7*,
you will find novellas written
by Carly Phillips, Donna Hill
and Jill Shalvis—and online at
www.HarlequinMoreThanWords.com
you can also access stories by
Pamela Morsi and Meryl Sawyer.

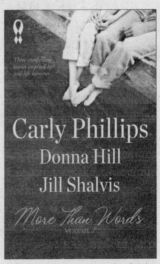

Coming soon in print and online!

Visit
www.HarlequinMoreThanWords.com
to access your FREE ebooks and to nominate
a real-life heroine in your community.

Proceeds from the sale of this book will be
reinvested in Harlequin's charitable initiatives.

MTWV7763CS

REQUEST YOUR FREE BOOKS!

2 FREE NOVELS
FROM THE ROMANCE COLLECTION
PLUS 2 FREE GIFTS!

YES! Please send me 2 FREE novels from the Romance Collection and my 2 FREE gifts (gifts are worth about $10). After receiving them, if I don't wish to receive any more books, I can return the shipping statement marked "cancel." If I don't cancel, I will receive 4 brand-new novels every month and be billed just $5.74 per book in the U.S. or $6.24 per book in Canada. That's a saving of at least 28% off the cover price. It's quite a bargain! Shipping and handling is just 50¢ per book in the U.S. and 75¢ per book in Canada.* I understand that accepting the 2 free books and gifts places me under no obligation to buy anything. I can always return a shipment and cancel at any time. Even if I never buy another book, the two free books and gifts are mine to keep forever.

194/394 MDN FDC5

Name	(PLEASE PRINT)	

Address		Apt. #

City	State/Prov.	Zip/Postal Code

Signature (if under 18, a parent or guardian must sign)

Mail to the **Reader Service:**
IN U.S.A.: P.O. Box 1867, Buffalo, NY 14240-1867
IN CANADA: P.O. Box 609, Fort Erie, Ontario L2A 5X3

Not valid for current subscribers to the Romance Collection
or the Romance/Suspense Collection.

**Want to try two free books from another line?
Call 1-800-873-8635 or visit www.ReaderService.com.**

* Terms and prices subject to change without notice. Prices do not include applicable taxes. Sales tax applicable in N.Y. Canadian residents will be charged applicable taxes. Offer not valid in Quebec. This offer is limited to one order per household. All orders subject to credit approval. Credit or debit balances in a customer's account(s) may be offset by any other outstanding balance owed by or to the customer. Please allow 4 to 6 weeks for delivery. Offer available while quantities last.

Your Privacy—The Reader Service is committed to protecting your privacy. Our Privacy Policy is available online at www.ReaderService.com or upon request from the Reader Service.

We make a portion of our mailing list available to reputable third parties that offer products we believe may interest you. If you prefer that we not exchange your name with third parties, or if you wish to clarify or modify your communication preferences, please visit us at www.ReaderService.com/consumerschoice or write to us at Reader Service Preference Service, P.O. Box 9062, Buffalo, NY 14269. Include your complete name and address.

MROM

#1 *NEW YORK TIMES* BESTSELLING AUTHOR
USA TODAY BESTSELLING AUTHOR

SUSAN WIGGS

Daisy Bellamy has struggled for years to choose
between two men—one honorable and steady, one
wild and untethered. And then, one fateful day,
the decision is made for her.

Now busy with a thriving business on Willow Lake,
Daisy knows she should be happy with the life
she's chosen for herself and her son. But she still
aches for the one thing she can't have.

Until the man once lost to her reappears, resurrected by
a promise of love. And now the choice Daisy thought
was behind her is the hardest one she'll ever face....

Marrying Daisy Bellamy

Available wherever books are sold.

DELILAH MARVELLE

77537 PRELUDE TO A SCANDAL   ___ $7.99 U.S.   ___ $9.99 CAN

(limited quantities available)

TOTAL AMOUNT	$ _____
POSTAGE & HANDLING	$ _____
($1.00 FOR 1 BOOK, 50¢ for each additional)	
APPLICABLE TAXES*	$ _____
TOTAL PAYABLE	$ _____

(check or money order—please do not send cash)

To order, complete this form and send it, along with a check or mone
order for the total above, payable to HQN Books, to: **In the U.S.**
3010 Walden Avenue, P.O. Box 9077, Buffalo, NY 14269-907.
In Canada: P.O. Box 636, Fort Erie, Ontario, L2A 5X3.

Name: _____

Address: _____ City: _____

State/Prov.: _____ Zip/Postal Code: _____

Account Number (if applicable): _____

075 CSAS

*New York residents remit applicable sales taxes.
*Canadian residents remit applicable GST and provincial taxes.

HQN™

We *are* romance™

www.HQNBooks.com